D1366617

THE
HOUSES OF
TIME

THE
HOUSES OF
TIME

JAMIL NASIR

A TOM DOHERTY ASSOCIATES BOOK
NEW YORK

THE HOUSES OF TIME

Book design by Spring Hoteling

A Tor Book
Published by Tom Doherty Associates, LLC
175 Fifth Avenue
New York, NY 10010

www.tor.com

Tor® is a registered trademark of Tom Doherty Associates, LLC.

Library of Congress Cataloging-in-Publication Data

Nasir, Jamil.
    The houses of time / Jamil Nasir.—1st ed.
      p.   cm.
    "A Tom Doherty Associates Book."
    ISBN-13: 978-0-7653-0610-4
    ISBN-10: 0-7653-0610-7
    1. Dreams—Fiction. 2. Virtual reality—Fiction. I. Title.
PS3613.A754H68   2008
813'.6—dc22

                          2007047753

First Edition: April 2008

Printed in the United States of America

0 9 8 7 6 5 4 3 2 1

For Mary

THE
HOUSES OF
TIME

ONE

DREAM GIRL

David Grant woke up in the basement den of his grandmother's
house, sitting at a table that hadn't been there for thirty years. It
was night and the lights were off, but he recognized at once the
smell of the varnished pine paneling, the floor tiles cool under his
bare feet, the dark outlines of red sling chairs. He knew he was
dreaming right away, without doing any of the checks from the
Trans-Humanist Institute's Lucid Dreaming lessons. One of his
exercises was to dream a scene from a specific time and place in
his life, and he had picked this: his grandmother's house on the
ocean, in the spring of his nineteenth year.

His heart beat with excitement, as it still did whenever he realized he was awake in a dream. He slowed and deepened his
breathing, relaxed his muscles so as not to wake himself; nevertheless, for a second he felt his body lying in bed, hands touching
the sheets, even as he was still sitting at the table in the dark basement. Then something in the dream caught his attention, pulling

him back in. His great-aunt Dee, who had inherited the house from Grandmother many years before, was moving around in the dark, stacking bottles of wine in a small cabinet. The wine glowed neon blue.

He wanted to say something to her because she had been dead these many years, but he was worried he would scare her in the dark. No sooner did he have that thought than all the lights in the basement were on, and he could see through the kitchen doorway and partway down the hall to the stairs and bathroom and pantry, and the basement was cozy and close against the darkness outside the windows just as it used to be when he had stayed here; but, as though erased by the light, Great-Aunt Dee was gone.

Grant's chair legs scraped the floor as he stood up, startled. Dream "reality laws"—as the THI Lucid Dreaming lessons called them—were far different from those of the waking world; some things happened if you barely thought about them, though others seemed untouchable by your intentions. A shiver of excitement went up his spine, and before he knew it, he was hanging in the air near the white ceiling tiles, which he had never seen up close before. They were rough-textured and dusty.

He knew something about dream flying from recent experience. He let his body go limp, consciously let the excited feeling drain out of his spine. He sank to the floor. The energy in the spine made you fly, and the more excited you got, the more you flew. But he didn't want to fly right now; he wanted to look around, visit this place, as the THI lesson had bid him do.

He walked into the kitchen on the cool floor tiles. It was just as he remembered: small and bright, paneled like the rest of the basement in beveled, varnished pine, open on one side to the den, on the other to the hall, with a small wall-mounted table you could fold down, the big, old-fashioned automatic dishwasher his grandmother had used as a dish rack. Everything was still and silent. He looked out the window over the double sink, into the back yard. Two birch trees stood there, their silvery-white trunks glowing faintly in the light from the window. He didn't remember any birches in the yard; the idea flickered through his mind that they were dream trees, like flat paste-ons over the real remembered scene.

The trees began to slowly rotate, showing him that they were three-dimensional.

He was up near the ceiling again with excitement. If he could make trees turn, what else could he do? He cast around wildly for an idea to try. How about women? Here he could invent the most perfect woman possible. . . .

Sure enough, he heard the outside door at the top of the basement stairs open and close, and light steps come down. He floated gleefully into the hall.

A girl was coming hesitantly down the stairs, holding the banister. She was blonde and small, maybe only five feet two. She was beautiful. So beautiful that he sagged back down to the floor with the seriousness of the situation.

"Hi," she said. "Are you David? Grant?"

The sun had bleached her chin-length hair to shining cornsilk and lightly freckled her fair skin. She had wide-set azure eyes, cheeks fresh as a child's, and she was magnificently casual in flip-flops, low-rise jeans, and a T-shirt that left a smooth, tanned inch of her stomach showing, her body beautiful and alert, with an unconscious poise that came from some physical skill like dancing or . . .

"Yeah. I'm Dave."

She seemed relieved. "I'm Jana." She put out a hand. He shook it. It was small but frank and strong. "This is the address you gave me," she said, to fill an awkward silence.

"I did? Well..., come in," he said, using his clumsy nineteen-year-old's manners. He backed up until they were in the living room, then found that he was staring at her again.

She looked even younger than him, though with that air of maturity girls get suddenly in their mid-teens, as if she were really ten years older. That in itself was intimidating, but on this girl it was barely a starter.

"Oh!" he said, a memory suddenly coming to him, as they do in dreams. "You're the surfer." He barely kept himself from saying "surfer girl."

She grinned at him. "The surfer girl," she said as if reading his mind. "Right."

He lay in his big bed in the suburbs, the streetlight at the end of his driveway making a pale rectangle on the wall, and it was decades later. He was a forty-nine-year-old lawyer, Aunt Dee, the last of his surviving relatives, had long since died, and a realtor hired by Grant had sold Grandmother's house years ago.

Too bad he had woken up just when the beautiful girl arrived. That had been one of his best dreams yet. Good; he would put it on his weekly report, and maybe they would advance him to the next level, and he could find out what THI taught besides lucid dreaming. Life Revision was the program he had signed up for, and the promises the Institute made for it were not modest. Vague, but not modest.

In the meantime, it wouldn't hurt to try for another surfer-girl dream. Grant rolled onto his side, pulled his covers straight, and snuggled into his pillow again.

He woke on a futon in a small bedroom, and it was morning.

He lay still for a minute, studying the ceiling. The smell of grass and dirt warmed by the sun came through an open window partly shaded by the big heart-shaped leaves of a philodendron.

He wondered suddenly if he was dreaming, a question the THI lessons had taught him to ask a hundred times a day, but especially whenever he woke up. He got up on an elbow and took his watch from a small night table, looked at the writing on its face just below the *12*. TIMBER, it said in tiny letters. He looked out the window, then back at the watch. ARCTIC, the tiny letters said now. He suppressed a thrill of excitement. He *was* dreaming. Text and numbers were notoriously unstable in dreams: they changed 75 percent of the time on two readings, 95 percent of the time on three, making a simple test. If you didn't check, you would often just go along illucidly rationalizing the most outrageous oddities, which was the way of "normal" dreaming. It was only when you could consciously say to yourself "I'm dreaming" that you became lucid.

He stood up stiffly and shuffled through his small book-lined living room to the kitchen to make coffee, and suddenly his heart jumped. Though grown up now, he was having dinner tonight with the beautiful surfer girl he had met at his grandmother's house.

The colors of the apartment began to fade; he could vaguely feel his body lying asleep. His excitement had begun to wake him.

He spun around in the middle of the kitchen like a child making himself dizzy. Spinning was one of the best ways to keep from losing a lucid dream: the whirling sensation and dizziness seemed to pull your attention back to the "dream body," blocking the sensory input from your sleeping physical body. Though often when you returned to the dream, the scene had changed.

He walked along a sandy gravel road in near pitch-dark, gusts shaking drops from the branches of trees, bushes and small stands of bamboo hissing and swaying in the rainy darkness like sentient beings. Over the wind he could hear the crashing of waves from the beach thirty yards away. At the end of the gravel road yellow light came from the windows of a cottage, where Jana lived with two roommates. It was surrounded by an overgrown garden and a rusty chain-link fence whose gate swung creaking in the wind. He followed a walk of flagstones half-covered with sand. He knocked, and Jana opened the door, shocking him anew with how beautiful she was, her face clear and intelligent, shapely eyes alert.

$$\boxed{\text{TWO}}$$

Dr. Thotmoses' Trans-Humanist Institute

On a Friday afternoon two weeks later, wearing his dark gray Brooks Brothers suit, Grant got out of a cab on a cracked, dirty sidewalk in a run-down part of town. Traffic roar came from a highway overpass two blocks away, and the air, barely warmed by weak autumn sunlight, smelled smoky. The building he now entered stood between a windowless telephone company switching station and a parking garage, five stories of pale 1950s brick with tarnished metal letters above a concrete awning that read AMANA MEDICAL BUILDING. The peg-board directory in the tiny, scuffed lobby showed a Painless Dentist or two among the travel agencies, mail-order businesses, and tax-exempt organizations, but it had been a long time since prosperous medical offices had operated in this part of town. Only one of the two elevators had light behind its floor indicator, and the car, when it finally came, was painted an industrial beige, and lacked the polished brass and mirrors of more pretentious buildings.

The suite he was looking for was on the fifth floor, near the end of a narrow hall that smelled of air freshener and sour, elderly wood. A plastic laminate sign on the door said:

TRANS-HUMANIST INSTITUTE
DR. P. THOTMOSES, D.D., PH.D., DIRECTOR
"THE FOOL WHO PERSISTS IN HIS FOLLY WILL BECOME WISE"

Grant paused to absorb the motto, which seemed odd for a New Age self-improvement institute. The name was unusual too: Thotmoses. No name had ever appeared on the Institute's e-mail lessons; nor, until the previous week, had an address. Grant had been surprised that the Institute was right here in town; he had assumed it was based in some exotic city like Taos or San Francisco, the kind of place you expected to find institutes teaching Life Revision.

The most recent e-mail hadn't explained why they wanted an office visit now, but he suspected it was the progress he had made since meeting the dream surfer girl Jana. Embarrassingly, he now had a well-developed dream life revolving around her, despite the fact that he also had a perfectly acceptable real daytime girlfriend. In his dream life he was a bestselling writer, and he and Jana lived together in a town a few miles from the ocean; she drove her beat-up station wagon to the beach and surfed every day while Grant sat on their screen porch writing. Enthusiasm for this alternate life caused Grant to become lucid nearly every night now, and he had refined his ability to act consciously in dreams, just as if he were awake in the places where they seemed to take place—their "sensoria," as the THI lessons called them.

The Institute had certainly chosen an appropriate setting for its offices, he mused as he opened the door: this hall and building would fit perfectly in the mysterious, run-down dream neighborhoods where he sometimes found himself on foggy nights, looking for an office behind a flimsy wooden door just like this one.

The reception room had the same atmosphere: elegant in a threadbare way, with antique, dark wood furniture, a worn Oriental carpet, real paintings on the walls, and tarnished brass lamps giving quiet, clubby light under the ceiling fluorescents. It was empty except for a receptionist who barely fit behind the small antique desk at the right, and who looked startled at Grant's appearance, as if the last thing he had expected was a customer.

He was an angular, broad-shouldered, and very handsome young man with long hair, an aquiline nose, chiseled chin, and intense dark eyes. His combination of youthful features and mature bearing put him anywhere between twenty and the mid-thirties. He opened a large appointment book as Grant approached and announced himself.

"Oh, yes. Four o'clock, I see you," he said in a deep, gentle voice. "If you'll have a seat, I'll let Dr. Thotmoses know you're here."

Envy moving in his gut, Grant picked a chair and watched the young man speak into a telephone and then go back to reading something. Women would fall all over a man like that, Grant knew; for one thing, he had the unfair advantage of youth, which women seemed to think was a more respectable thing to fall for than money or wit. He felt suddenly depressed.

Grant had been miserable in high school. He had started ninth grade short and chubby, and in eleventh had grown suddenly tall, skinny, and pimply. But the shame and futility that had hung over him as far back as he could remember went deeper than his lack of physical grace, as if the silent rage between his parents had infected him, so that he wasn't like other people, but ugly, dirty, and

defective. Soon after he started college, his parents were killed in
a car accident, as if finally incinerated by their hatred for each
other. Having so recently rejoiced at escaping from them, he had
been surprised by his grief and fear at having no one particular
to him, no one whose two voices on the phone were like ropes
securing him to the earth. Maybe that was why he had gone off
hitchhiking for the two years after they died: to prove to himself
that his own resources and company were enough. His parents
had left him enough money to finish college and go to law
school, so after his travels he had done that and, still too ashamed
to socialize or get a girlfriend, always scored near the top of his
class. After graduating he got a job at a blue-chip firm in a
medium-sized city, far away from the town where he had grown
up. He had never married. But in the end that turned out to be a
piece of luck.

Grant's revelation had come in his early thirties, on an
anonymous February day, snowflakes floating from a flat gray sky,
the still air sleepy with a kind of dreamy distraction, as if now that
the holidays were over no one was paying attention, so that this
unobtrusive day at the far reaches of the calendar would slip by
without anyone noticing. Sitting at a stoplight in the warmth of
his car, half-hypnotized by this emptiness, Grant had glanced idly
into the Mercedes next to him, where a young woman was on
the phone, eyes wide and lips parted. Her hair had not yet dried
from her morning shower, and the tresses lay carelessly on her
shoulders.

And suddenly the gray jewel-box of the day opened, and the
goal and purpose of life were laid bare. Though in ten seconds
the light changed and he never saw her again, the woman's loveliness had flashed through the stillness and emptiness of the day,
and Grant was like St. Paul struck with religion on the road to
Damascus. From that day forward he was changed, from a man

wandering through the years to a man with a mission. There was only one thing worth having on this earth, he had realized; all else was simply either a means to it or filler. You could either fight to get as much as you could, or you could resign yourself to a life whose small meanings always shriveled in your hands, so that you were left with an endless series of days in which you found yourself at the office or at home or at the grocery store, studiously ignoring where it all led in the end, hearing endlessly in your head your parents screaming at each other, little knowing they would soon be in the grave. And once Grant had finally faced that truth, only a life of discipline and self-realization would do.

It was terrifying at first. Men are born in two kinds, the strong and the weak, and high school separates them. High school girls, with their high breasts and newly made hips, lustrous hair and eyes like contemptuous jewelry—whom nature has made the arbiters of male fitness—pass over the weak and bind themselves to blockish football players and foxily smiling Eminem look-alikes who sell drugs; and so the species is kept stocked with the fearless and the strong. The panic of the weak man at approaching a woman can never be explained to the strong, nor the assurance of the strong be taken on by the weak except through the most arduous means. Grant—whose own weakness had begun in the womb, he was certain, in the mutual revulsion of the male and female parts that had combined to make him—adopted these means. Unsure how to begin, he read books with titles like *How to Pick Up Girls* and *How to Succeed with Women*. He joined a gym and got a personal trainer. He attended seminars on grooming, fashion, and what are called "accessories." He spent hundreds of hours in therapy convincing himself that he was not grotesquely unattractive. He caused himself to lounge at bookstores and art museums, go to bars and nightclubs. He forced himself to speak to women in public places: the grocery store, the elevator, cafés. He learned to read their reactions like a hunter learning to spoor, practiced maintaining tension, withholding approval, wordlessly implying excitements just in the offing. He collected rejections like any artist starting his career, brooded over them in solitude, but finally began to connect, and then to connect regularly, and finally after years of practice had become a virtuoso, with his own style and theories, so that he now knew which parts of the dating books he had studied so long ago were true and which parts myth. Now, at forty-nine, he could have written his own book. Recent years had proved over and over the value of hard work and persistence, together with a mature bachelorhood that allowed one to keep his equilibrium during the storms of romance. In the last year alone these proofs had included Nicola, Liz, and Michelle.

Before them there had been Maya, Jane, Lisa, Diane, and all the others—and so his youthful hurts had been repaid in full. Unmarried, in good health, not a drinker or addict, senior partner at a large, profitable law firm, so that he had time to spare and lots of money, with all the unattached women in the world spread out before him, a vast, fascinating mosaic of faces, bodies, and orgasms, of voices, vices, and stories.

How could a man be happier?

Well, for one thing, his hair was turning gray. Sometimes now when he saw in the mirror the tall gym-muscled figure with the immaculate suit and ironic Cary Grant face, he was shocked to recognize one of those "mature" men from the magazine whiskey ads, usually pictured wearing tuxedos, dashing half smiles, and statuesque beauties on their arms. Truth to tell, maybe what bothered him most about this was that the statuesque beauties were usually also women of full adult years—still unblemished, but who, one could imagine, in the natural course of things would soon take the path from the full, glorious ripeness of late summer to the dry, yellowing sunlight of autumn.

Looking back, maybe it was that annoyance, that oddly recurring image of himself as the hero of a *Modern Maturity* advertising campaign, that had brought on his disturbance. Sitting in his office one September Friday morning looking out the floor-to-ceiling windows at his river view, the warm, exciting feeling of the approaching weekend had come over him—doubly exciting because he had recently broken up with Michelle and was now on the prowl for something else, a new goddess to last until he changed his religion. It was just then, trying to decide what bookstore or museum to visit, that he had idly wondered how many more weekends he had left. One morning—perhaps a bright one like this—would be his last, after all, and then he would end up in a hospital somewhere, and then a small obituary in the newspaper, and then nothing more, no sign of him anywhere, he extinguished like a flame, perhaps quietly, perhaps in great agony and confusion, and then gone; the morning sunlight would fall on this world and he would be nowhere to be found. And on top of that, the weekends were always vaguely disappointing anyway, as if despite his best efforts he neglected to plan properly, let the time waste, the possibilities slip away. Yet somehow he had been hypnotized for years by this unending round of five days, then two days, then five, then two, always looking forward to something that never came.

A silly thing to dwell on, morbid, something for characters in books to babble about. But the thought had begun to recur at odd times, usually when he should have been relaxing: after sex with his new poetry-writing druggie girlfriend, or waiting for the curtain at a play, or when he got in his car after a satisfying day at work. It had begun to bother him, finally. Maybe that was why he had copied the phone number from the Trans-Humanist

Institute's small classified ad in the back of a tattered magazine he picked up idly in a dentist's waiting room—

"Mr. Grant," said a deep, hoarse voice, making him jump. He looked round. The man standing by an inner doorway was bony but very big—almost freakishly so—and stooped, perhaps so that he could look into normal people's faces. He was old, with white hair and loose pink jowls on a long, bony face, and his vast unfashionable suit was rumpled. The general impression was of a huge, kindly headmaster the students made fun of behind his back.

He was smiling with a touch of melancholy humor, as if he somehow knew what Grant was thinking about. "I am Dr. Thotmoses. Please come in." He extended a hand the size of a shovel toward the inner office.

With the door shut, the office was claustrophobic: tiny, windowless, dominated by a large antique desk, and crowded with two bookshelves and a visitor's chair, the air stuffy, as if it had been through the huge man's lungs too many times. Grant took the visitor's chair, and Thotmoses squeezed himself behind the desk, put some reading glasses on the end of his nose, and looked down at an open folder, his old head wavering slightly back and forth.

He read slowly in his deep, hoarse voice: "David Grant, forty-nine years old, occupation attorney, never married, only child, all relatives dead."

Grant nodded.

"A man who has everything," Thotmoses boasted, waving a hand away from his chest in an awkward gesture. "A good job, good health, a good social life. And a great deal of money."

Grant felt his depression deepen. "What is your interest in my money?" he snapped irritably.

"Oh, goodness, no!" said Thotmoses, his rheumy, oysterlike eyes getting a pained expression. "What I am wondering is, why would a man who has everything wish to become Trans-Human? Emerge into an entirely new life?" He studied Grant, blinking solemnly. "The changes we create in the Life Revision Program are effectively irreversible, as they take place at a physical level, in the brain."

That statement had been repeated in nearly every one of the Institute's lessons, as well as in the waiver-of-damages agreement he had signed. But there was no need to tell this giant buffoon about the whiskey advertisements and his uneasiness about the end of things. Or that learning dreaming tricks seemed neither very irreversible nor likely to lead to an entirely new life.

He had assumed Thotmoses' question was rhetorical, but the man was still looking at him as if expecting an answer. He roused himself. What *did* he want? Why had the Institute's promises attracted him? "I suppose," he said slowly, "I suppose it's because I want to—know the truth—about life and all that. What it really means, deep down."

He felt sheepish, as if he had been tricked into saying something silly, but the old man was watching him intently, and Grant thought he caught a hungry look in his eyes that made him seem for a second less foolish before he began shuffling through his folder again. He selected a stapled sheaf of paper and picked up a pencil, which looked comically miniature in his hand. He gave Grant a polite smile that pulled his face into a network of creases and wrinkles. "Very good. Then let's begin, shall we?"

Thotmoses took him through a long questionnaire, carefully marking Grant's answers to questions both inane and bizarre. Grant was by turns bored, impatient, and annoyed. Did they think he had nothing to do all afternoon but sit in this airless cubicle and answer questions like "What do you see as the difference between animate and inanimate objects?" and "Who have you been at different times in your life?"

Finally, though, they finished, and Thotmoses put down his pencil. "Excellent. My assistant Andrei will have to score this, of course, but my impression is that your progress has been first-rate." He smiled blandly at Grant, his face wrinkling. "That means you have learned to maintain the waking-level activation of the primary association regions of your dorsal postcentral cortex even when your pontine reticular column is putting out the electrochemical messages that make you sleep and dream. Though of course you haven't paid any attention to the underlying mechanism, any more than an athlete knows the biochemistry of muscle tissue." He gave another brief, practiced smile, as if to say, Don't worry that you're a layman—I can simplify it for you. "You are now on the cutting edge of modern science. As recently as the 1970s it was thought that waking and sleeping were incompatible, until researchers at Stanford confirmed what has been reported since time immemorial, that there is a state incorporating both. They wired lucid dreamers to EEG machines, and when they were sure by their brain waves that they were asleep and dreaming, used prearranged codes for communicating with them. The researchers would flash a light in the dreamer's face, for example, and the dreamer—who perceived the flashes as part of his dream—would respond by moving his eyes back and forth five times—the eyes are the only part of the body not paralyzed when you are in REM sleep. It was the first laboratory communication between the waking and dreaming worlds!

"Andrei will schedule you for another appointment in a week's time. Soon you will be able to take the next step in your lucid dreaming adventure." He beamed at Grant, as if expecting him to be excited by this marketing jingo.

THREE

A MYSTICAL ENCOUNTER AT MACY'S, AND A MYSTICAL DINNER

A week later on Saturday afternoon Grant was at Macy's with his girlfriend Stacy. Macy's was her favorite store, and Grant had often been on the point of making a joke about that, but had always stopped himself because the names didn't exactly rhyme, and anyway she had probably heard it before, and probably didn't like it. Stacy was a brunette with hot brown eyes and was from Missouri, though she looked Transylvanian. She was twenty-five and tended to wear biker jackets over tight denim, and wanted to be a poet—*was* a poet if you considered that she wrote poetry. Grant considered (to himself) that her best poetry was her own damaged, flaming body and soul, her hard hips, taunting voice, the way her hair got in her face, her sick eyes, and the raging way she had sex, as if trying to break through some invisible suffocating Missouri membrane. She didn't seem the type who would like Macy's, but she did: it excited her. Maybe it was the Missouri membrane, another part of which was the ample allowance her banker father sent her every month. In any case, almost every weekend, either before or after some often tiring but always interesting debauchery, Grant would end up at Macy's with her.

This Saturday was damp and cold, yellow leaves blowing from the guy-wired saplings in the parking lot under a lowering sky, and Grant felt restless almost as soon as they got into the store. Stacy was foraging in the women's leather department when he said, "I'm going to walk around."

Her face was flushed with non-bohemian pleasure as she looked up from a rack, dark hair hanging over one eye. "I'll be done in half an hour. Promise."

He nodded, stuck his hands in his pockets, and strolled, relaxed and contented with the unusual condition of having nothing to do. He went along between Intimate Wear and Women's Casuals, the bright overhead light thick with the store's sumptuous quiet. After that was Cosmetics, with glamorous, empty-eyed ladies practicing good posture behind gleaming display counters. He headed over to Men's Shoes and browsed, though he already had enough Men's Shoes to last him the rest of his life, probably.

It occurred to him suddenly to wonder if he was dreaming, and he checked his surroundings per THI. A small sign on a table of shoes said FOR YOUR ACTIVE LIFESTYLE. He looked away for a few seconds, then back. The sign still said FOR YOUR ACTIVE LIFESTYLE. He looked away and back again; the sign hadn't changed. He glanced around Men's Shoes without spotting any environmental anomalies. He was awake.

He went up the escalator, through Appliances and Bedding, and then through Kitchenware, admiring German-made skillets and knives. In an aisle with boxes showing seductive pictures of saucepans, a young woman was walking toward him. His eyes were drawn to her especially by her sun-bleached hair; just the kind of hair Jana had. And also, of course, there was something about dating a brunette that made one look wistfully at blondes, just as dating a blonde made brunettes look particularly tasty.

A shock went through him.

He stopped dead and gaped at the lightly freckled face, wide-set blue eyes, the taut, small body that could have been a commercial for her low-rise jeans and thin sweater. It was hard to tell how old she was; she was one of those ageless Scandinavian types that could be anywhere between sixteen and twice that.

She was close to him now, ignoring him, moving aside to pass him as he stood flat-footed and open-mouthed.

"Jana?" he said.

"Pardon?"

She turned and looked at him, eyebrows raised. From three feet away it was uncanny: it was exactly and precisely her, beautiful and poised and impatient, down to the direct, unaffected voice.

"Is your name—," he said, feeling foolish, but his heart pounding, "—Jana?"

"No."

If he hadn't had so much practice flirting, he would have retreated in confusion and embarrassment. As it was, he tried desperately through the whirl of his thoughts to find something to say to hold her while he got his bearings.

"Nice pans," he said, gesturing.

The girl smiled knowingly, with the teasing quirk of the lips Jana had. She turned to go, laughing to herself as if already thinking how she would tell her roommates about meeting a weirdo in Macy's.

"Actually, miss, you won't believe this—but I think—I *know* I've been dreaming about you almost every night for weeks."

She laughed over her shoulder. "Yeah. Nice try."

"I know that sounds weird," he said as she receded. "But I

swear to you. I've been taking a course in this thing called Lucid Dreaming, and I seem to have met you. And—gotten to know you. In my dreams. Lucid dreams."

At the end of the aisle she hesitated, putting her hand on the corner of a shelf. She half turned toward him, and he could see that her brow was slightly knitted. She studied him. "Lucid dreams?"

"Yes. And you've been in them, I swear. Lately." He stood hanging on to a shelf himself with one hand, looking at her entreatingly, as if the aisle were a tunnel he needed help getting out of.

She had turned full toward him now, but mutely, as if unsure what to say. He realized suddenly that he knew her body language, and the thought gave him a fleeting sense of relief, and then of amazement, as if the confirmation of what he was telling her was beyond belief. He took a timid step forward, leaning as he went on the shelf as if unconsciously emphasizing his harmlessness. He stopped just at the periphery of conversational distance.

"I'm Grant," he said, putting a hand to his chest as if talking to a primitive tribesman.

"Uh-huh." Her small nostrils flared. "Are you shitting me?"

"I swear," he raised his hand. "I swear."

"I've been lucid dreaming since I was a little girl," she said. "I don't recognize you, but there has been someone lately. . . ." She gave him her direct look again. "I'm Kat."

"Cat?"

"Katerina." He shook her familiar small, practical, and somehow fierce hand.

Senses was one of the swankiest restaurants in town and had a two-week waiting list, but Grant had cultivated the maître d', tipped profusely, and could get a table anytime. Aside from its girl-impressing lavishness, Senses had another advantage: Stacy would never be able to get past Eric at the entrance foyer in case she came looking for him. Grant had left her a vague phone message about a work emergency. Truthful, depending on how you defined "work," and "emergency."

He sat at the tiny but well-situated table Laurence had been able to find him, and waited for the girl named Kat, cursing himself for failing to get her phone number or e-mail address or *anything*— He caught himself imagining *Jana* coming down the three steps to the dining room, the surfer girl used to nothing but cut-offs and sweatshirts over a swimsuit, shy but poised in her small, magnificent body. She had been a maid at a big beach hotel before she met Grant, and had had to pull back her hair and wear a uniform eight hours a day, but since she had moved in with him—"Since she had moved in"—in his dreams! Anxiety churned his stomach. How could a living, breathing woman look and sound and move exactly like a dream woman? It had to be coincidence—he had to remember not to automatically treat her like Jana, assume she would react like Jana. But on the other hand, Kat obviously thought it was some kind of mystical dream thing. Which was good because it had gotten her to agree to have dinner with him.

He was telling himself for the tenth time that she wouldn't come when she appeared on the stairs, Laurence conducting her elegantly. Grant had expected her to be beautiful, but he was astonished all over again. She had brushed her hair so it was like gold silk, she wore a black dress, and people turned to watch her as she walked self-consciously and gracefully toward him. Moving just like Jana, he realized in a confusion of desire and amazement, standing to take her hand as Laurence pulled out her chair, his heart big and full in his chest. She gave him Jana's smile with the humorous quirk, as if she knew the effect she was having and thought it "queer," as the young people said.

"You look fabulous," he said when he had sat back down across from her. "Fabulous is faint praise for how you look."

She started to roll her eyes, but caught herself. "Thank you."

She probably got that too often. He tried another approach. "Can I ask you a personal question?"

She shrugged, her smile dimpling her cheeks.

"How old are you?"

She laughed. "Can I ask you one? How old are *you*?"

"Forty-nine. How old are *you*?"

She laughed again. "Older than you."

"Uh-huh. How old? I know it's rude to ask, but please tell me? Please?"

"A couple of hundred years," she said casually.

He laughed, warmth filling him. Her wide eyes were an ocean, a land of woods and gardens and mansions, paradise. "You're young for your age."

"Thank you. Are you married?"

He gaped at her, thrown off balance. Then he laughed. "No. You?"

"No. Okay, now it's time for personal questions, right?" She pretended to think. "Who's your closest living relative?"

He grinned at her, fascinated at how effortlessly she had taken control of the conversation. It made him realize how used he was to dominating the young girls he dated, and how boring that could be after a while. He tried to think through his fascination. "Um. Funny you should ask that. Um. I guess a third cousin, but I've never met him. Weird, huh? I'm all alone in the world. Neither of my parents had brothers or sisters, and they're dead now. How about you? Closest living relative, I mean, not are you dead."

"Oh yes, I see. My parents are alive."

"Ah-ha," he said shrewdly, as if he had elicited a key confession. "And where do you live?"

"Wait, it's my turn," she said. "Turn and turn about. Shh, don't shout, we're in a restaurant, remember?" She touched his hand and looked around with mock surreptitiousness. Her touch was cool and light, but it made him drunk, filled his body with sweetness, as if he had been injected with honey and hope. "Are you happy with your life?"

"Do you have a boyfriend?" he blurted.

She was startled for a second, then put her face down and laughed helplessly, and he laughed too, giddily.

"No," she said finally. "You?"

"No."

"Girlfriend?"

"No," he lied effortlessly. In fact it wasn't really a lie, because he wouldn't have one as soon as he got to a telephone. It was more like truth cleansed of the obscuring details of mere biography.

Just then they were interrupted by Trent, the headwaiter, who greeted Grant honorifically, suggested the porterhouse steak, and consulted with them about wine.

When he had gone away, satisfied that they had made the right choices, the conversation had rebooted itself, and Grant's momentary feeling of drunken intimacy had ebbed, leaving a thirst for more.

"So tell me about your dream," Kat said. "Where you saw me."

He hesitated, but she had said she was a lucid dreamer too, so she was probably prepared to believe that kind of thing. And hopefully many other things besides.

"Well, where I *first* saw you was at my great-aunt's—my grandmother's house at the ocean, in the half basement where they had a den and a kitchen—"

Her eyes widened, and he thought the pupils widened too. "Oh, my God. Is this house at the edge of a bluff overlooking a beach? I mean, the house, and then a lawn, and then a bluff with trees—?" Her hand blocked out three zones on her side of the tablecloth.

"Yes!" he said, sitting up straight with astonishment and exhilaration. "Yes! Have you—?"

"Shhh." She laughed, putting her head down and glancing at the people at the next table who had looked over.

"Sorry." They leaned over the table, giving each other up-from-under looks like two kids plotting together. Like best friends sleeping over and talking long after they should have been asleep, after midnight. Warmth and excitement filled him.

"The driveway is just a continuation of a dirt road, a sandy dirt road, that comes up along the side of the house and makes a circle around a huge tree," she went on quietly but excitedly, moving one hand on the tablecloth.

"Yes!" he hissed. "My God—!"

"We've been having the same lucid dream," she said wonderingly and triumphantly.

"But you didn't recognize me."

"I get un-lucid just before I go inside. I don't know why. So it's hazy after that—just like a regular dream, but I know there's someone—I go down some stairs, and then— What do we do?" she asked him suddenly, blushing as she saw his grin. "Oh, my God!" she said like a high school girl when he just kept on grinning. "Oh, my God! I don't believe this. Oh, shit."

They put their heads down and laughed, almost touching.

Their salad came, Trent smiling at them quizzically.

"When and where does this dream take place?" she asked, poised and beautiful, putting her napkin on her lap and holding her fork properly. Again like Jana, an odd combination of the savage and the aristocrat.

"My grandmother's house on the coast, thirty years ago."

"Date?"

"What?"

"When exactly, and what address?"

He looked at her curiously, chewing a forkful of salad, then patted his mouth with his napkin and said: "April 1974. I was on spring break and I went to visit. Two eighty-nine West Road, Wilmington, Maine."

"Early April? Late April?"

"Does it make a difference? It would have been—let's see. It must have been late April. The last week in April. Why do you want to know that?"

She looked suddenly shy. "Well, I'm trying to figure out whether—there really is some kind of unusual thing between us. I mean, obviously there is, but—I've kept a dream journal since I was twelve, ever since I realized that my lucid dreaming was special, that everyone didn't lucid dream, and I wanted to check and see what I dreamed that night. To see if there's any connection."

Grant got the warm feeling in his chest again.

Their steaks came, and the 1997 Sangiovese-Merlot Trent had recommended, and things got quiet as they started to eat.

"But wait a minute," Grant said suddenly, his mouth full, realizing something. He swallowed and continued. "You weren't even born in 1974, so how could you have been keeping a dream journal then? Ah-ha." He narrowed his eyes and pointed his knife at her.

For a second she looked flustered, as if he really had caught her out at something, but then she grinned. "I told you, I'm a couple of hundred years old. Now I have a question," she said, as if it were her first one. "When you were a kid—" She paused, as if trying to formulate the question. "Do you think you had a different way of looking at things than other people?"

Her face was serious. He made an effort to be serious. "I didn't lucid dream, if that's what you mean."

"But what about when you were awake? Did you have any kind of—times when you would fall into a trance or meditative state, or anything like that?"

"Well—yes. That's weird. Why do you ask? Especially on windy days. I noticed that. Why?"

"I have a theory that people who are really good lucid dreamers grow up with a certain kind of brain thing. Syndrome, condition, whatever you want to call it. Tell me what happened to you on windy days," she commanded him, taking a bite of steak.

"It was mystical. Like what I'm feeling now."

"I'll let you flirt with me later, I promise. Tell me about the mystical thing."

He leaned forward and said politely and with complete seriousness, "You're the most perfect woman I've ever met."

She flushed. "Hold that thought. Tell me about the mystical thing."

He leaned back, feeling drunk with her attention and the wine, trying to figure out how to describe it. The thought flashed through his mind that he had known this woman less than an hour and he was already telling her the most intimate thing about himself, the thing that he had always felt separated him from everyone else.

"It doesn't happen much anymore. Sometimes it can be just a mood change or a string of thoughts—weird thoughts, but nothing actually happens. But sometimes—well, nothing actually *happens*—but everything changes, if you know what I mean. I get this feeling that time has stopped; and it seems like every-thing, the air all around me, the whole world, is conscious, *listening,* like something important is going to happen. The weirdest part, though—you'll think this is weird—is that it's like a dimension seems to open up, made of *stories*— You can go ahead and eat that."

Kat's fork, with a piece of steak on it, had stopped halfway to her mouth as she listened.

She put it down on her plate instead.

"What about you?" he asked. "Do you have experiences like that?"

"A 'dimension made of stories,' " she said.

"Well, that's the thing, you see. I don't know exactly how to describe it. But it's like the world—the universe—grows a whole new direction you can move, and you're moving through *stories.* Like the fundamental organizing principle of the universe is a strange mystery novel. I don't know where this came from, but when I was a little kid I used to have this fantasy that there was a—something like a path that led—" He waved his hands, trying to explain. "—upward and downward—not in a physical sense, but along this story dimension, and that this path led in one di-rection to heaven and in the other direction to hell. Like there's space, and time, and then there's this other direction, that if you move along it you can go to worlds that are the same in space and time, but either higher or lower. The higher worlds are ce-lestial, and if you travel upward along them you would come to heaven eventually, and the lower worlds are foul, and if you travel that way, you would come to hell."

She leaned forward, face flushed with what he thought was controlled excitement. "Okay," she said breathlessly, "you can flirt with me now."

FOUR

A Mystical Evening at Home, with Variations

They sat on the sofa in the sunken living room of his big suburban house. He had turned the lights down to as romantic a level as one could get away with on a first date, and he sat as close to her as he dared. Now that he thought of it, the girl Kat even *smelled* like Jana, a sweet, musky smell that reminded him of a small, fierce, beautiful animal.

But she seemed to have gotten out of the flirting mood. "Tell me about yourself," she said, as if he hadn't been doing that all evening.

"What do you want to know?"

She considered, her hand absently caressing the foot of sofa leather between them. "Tell me about the most magical thing that ever happened to you."

"Aside from this?"

"Yes." She pushed his shoulder in a Jana-like gesture, grinning.

"You don't think this is magical? We've both been dreaming about each other and then we run into each other—?"

"Yes, yes, it's magical. It is, okay? Although it happens—I've read about it. The people it happens to usually have some special bond, like they're siblings separated at birth or a parent and a child he's never seen." She laughed at what he realized was his horrified expression. "Don't worry, I don't think you're my father. What I'm saying is that we must have something that ties us together that we don't know about."

He wasn't going to get a better cue than that. He slid toward her, lips parting passionately, his hand going into her hair.

She stuck her hands on his chest and pushed, laughing. "Whoa," she said. "Down, sir."

Looking into her face, he saw that this wasn't just coyness. He let go of her and slid back to his former position, embarrassed. "Sorry."

"I shouldn't have said that about a special bond," she laughed. "You looked like you were going to eat me."

"Sorry. You're right. It's just that you're so much like Jana— the girl I live with—in my dreams, I mean—that I—"

"It's okay," she said, cheeks dimpling in a smile. "I understand." And after a pause: "Are you going to tell me about the most magical thing that ever happened to you?"

Glad for the change of subject, he tried to ponder, cool himself off. Finally, he said: "Well, something comes to mind. It wasn't magic. But it felt like it to me. You weren't in it, though. I mean, Jana wasn't."

"Tell me."

"When I was twelve we moved to a small city in the Midwest. Whenever I think of it, I get this picture of a town in the middle of a countryside of—tempestuous forests, trees waving back and forth in a rainstorm. Don't ask me why. Anyway, something happened to me there, though it was really nothing. I mean—I was riding a city bus one morning during summer vacation to go visit my best friend, who lived partway across town. My parents used to let me do that as long as I didn't get off anywhere else. Anyway, it was windy, sort of stormy, with patches of sun and rain.

"The bus was going through a business district, which was almost deserted on a Saturday morning. The wind was gusting, I remember, shaking the trees planted along the street. You could see the city skyline out the window, framed by dark clouds. Then at a stop a man got on. An older man—I don't know how old, but he seemed old to me.

"There was nothing strange about the way he looked, really, but suddenly he seemed—*familiar.* As soon as he got on the bus, I was sure I knew him really well, like he was my father or something. I'm afraid this isn't going to be very magical," he said apologetically. "I guess it really isn't magical at all."

"I want to hear it."

"There isn't much to hear. He got off before my stop. I wasn't supposed to, but I got off after him. It was like I was—I was going to say hypnotized by him, but it wasn't really that. I couldn't shake the feeling that I knew him, and that he was someone important to me, like part of my destiny. Anyway, I followed him off the bus. But he was walking fast, and by the time I reached the street corner he had turned down, he was gone. The street went up a hill between buildings and old houses. I just stood there, looking up it. The trees rustled and waved in the wind, and the wind had the smell of the wet sky. See, I told you," he said lamely, smiling in embarrassment, "it wasn't really anything. Not magic."

But she was looking at him hungrily, as if the story had wound her up somehow. "Do you remember the exact day it was?"

"Saturday. It was a Saturday, because that was when—"

"I mean do you remember the date, month, year."

"Oh, you mean, for your dream-journal thingy. Your dream journal that you kept before you were born. No. I could probably figure out what year it was, but probably not the month. When you're a kid, everything seems to run together, you know?"

She seemed to relax. She smiled. "You can kiss me now," she said. She held up a finger. "Just once."

He leaned forward eagerly, but just then there was a honk outside.

"My cab," she said. And a minute later he was waving to her as the cab backed out of his driveway.

As soon as they got into the house and Grant shut the door and took her coat, Kat asked where the bathroom was. Grant pointed to it, concealing a thrill of excitement: a beeline for the bathroom usually meant that some anti-pregnancy device had to be inserted. But when she came back out and joined him on the sofa in the big sunken living room, he saw that she had changed; the teasing, vivacious girl from the restaurant was suddenly subdued and docile, cuddling submissively in his arms and opening her mouth softly to his kisses. He knew that public persona and bedroom temperament often diverged; but when she absently rubbed her left arm for the second time he became curious, and made sure that his next embrace covertly pulled up the sleeve of her dress. Sure enough, there was a red patch in the hollow of her elbow, with a tiny purplish hole over the vein. With a shock he realized that she had just shot something up in his bathroom. There was more to the sunny, witty, teasing girl with whom he had just had dinner than met the eye. It excited him, in part because his experience with women who used hard drugs—Stacy, for example—was that they tended to be wild in bed.

In this, however, he was disappointed. Instead, Kat simply surrendered to him. He undressed her in the silent moonlight and laid her on his bed. She was Jana, her small, pale body muscular and beautiful, her mouth sweet and clingy. She lay like a trapped, sweating animal as he possessed her, her chest and stomach rising and falling desperately.

Afterward he lay next to her, happy the way a man can only be when he has laid claim to the woman of his dreams by making love to her. Kat lay torpid, half-covered by a blanket, face composed, eyes black in the darkness. He fumbled on his nightstand for his watch and glanced at it. 1:02 A.M. Out of habit he checked the tiny letters just below the *12*. They said THOUGHT. He looked away from the letters and then back. MOSES, they said now.

"Oh, shit," he said, sitting up.

"What?"

"We're dreaming. Or I'm dreaming." His heart sank. "I should have known better than to think that you—that this was actually real."

"What do you mean? Let me look."

He handed her the watch. She concentrated on the face, looked away for a second and then back.

"Well, that doesn't mean I'm not here. I bet when you wake up I will be."

"Yeah," he said ashenly. It was amazing how fast his mood had changed; and based on what? he asked himself. Just an idea. Nothing had changed in his actual experience, his "sensorium." But that didn't make him feel better. "Okay." He lay back down on the pillow and closed his eyes. "I'll see."

The THI lessons included half a dozen ways to wake up from lucid dreams, but falling asleep in them was the one that worked best for him, like a return through the mirror to the real world. Sure enough, a few minutes after he had closed his eyes, blocking out the dream's faux-sensory input, he felt himself lying in a different position in bed. As his sleep paralysis wore off he stirred an arm, then a leg. Then he opened his eyes.

To his excitement and relief, a beautiful girl with tousled blonde hair was opening her own sleepy eyes, rubbing them in the early morning gray through his bedroom windows.

"You see?" she murmured. "I told you." He slid over and held her, and she stretched; he felt the delicious catlike flex of muscle and bone, the push of her breasts on his chest.

But then anxiety flooded him. How could she know what her dream character had told him? The falling-asleep-in-your-dream trick usually woke him, but he had false awakenings sometimes, too. He picked up his watch again. On his first read the tiny letters spelled CAREFUL. On his second they spelled THOUGHT.

She sat up next to him, holding her knees under the covers, leaning over to look at the watch with him.

He smiled at her. He remembered now: she had left in a cab just as he had been about to kiss her for the first time. So all was not lost; it only meant that there was work to do; she wasn't easy prey. "False awakening. You're not real," he announced, putting the watch back on the night table.

She was smiling at him. "You're silly."

"I'll prove it to you," he said, lying down again, closing his eyes. "This time you'll be gone."

He waited for the floating sensation that was the dawning perception of sleep paralysis, the muscle atonia that gripped your physical body in REM sleep.

"This is weird," he said to her, or to himself. "I want to wake up."

"Are you sure?"

He opened his eyes and looked into her beautiful, cool young face.

"Aren't you enjoying yourself?" she asked.

The dream began to dissipate even as she spoke, as if in response to his intention, colors fading, the heaviness of his body lying on its side intruding on the feeling that he was looking into Kat's face, the cool morning air on his chest and arms—

He opened his eyes blearily, rolled onto his back, and focused on the ceiling of his bedroom in the gray early morning light that came through the windows.

He turned his head. Kat lay next to him fast asleep, a little spittle on the pillow by the corner of her mouth.

"Shit," he said, and grabbed his watch. His heart started to beat fearfully. He had never been completely unable to wake up from a dream, had never had more than two false awakenings in a row. He looked at the tiny letters under the *12*. They said KENNETH COLE and below that, NEW YORK. That was what they were supposed to say, he realized. He studied the ceiling for a few seconds, then looked quickly back. KENNETH COLE—NEW YORK. He tried again, and then a fourth time to be sure, and the relief that flooded him made him so buoyant that for a second he thought he had lifted off the bed and into the air. But you could do that only in dreams, not real life.

FIVE

KATERINA AND HER MOTHER

"How did you sleep?" Kat asked as Grant poured her tea from his fancy English teapot. He had set the breakfast table with a white cloth and his best china and silver, so that it gleamed like something out of a 1930s movie about rich people. Kat was wrapped tightly in a white terrycloth bathrobe many sizes too big for her, and sat framed by the breakfast nook's bay windows, outside which gray early morning mist softened the lawn. Ever since she had gotten out of the shower, Grant had felt her observing him. Her eyes were on him now as she nonchalantly ate toast and marmalade. He had covertly checked his watch several times, but the result was always KENNETH COLE—NEW YORK. Also, all the appliances in his kitchen worked perfectly, and he had been able to switch the lights on and off normally. Machines—especially lights and telephones—usually didn't work as expected in dreams.

"I could have sworn—or I guess I dreamed that you left last night instead of staying over. And then I kept seeing you in my bed and thinking I was dreaming, and I did my checks and I *was* dreaming. I kept thinking I would wake up and you would be gone, and you kept betting me you wouldn't." He laughed, embarrassed that he was still a little shaken by the dream. "I had three or four false awakenings like that, until I finally woke up for real, and there you were." He pondered, sitting in front of his own toast and marmalade. "The weird thing is . . ."

"What?"

"Well, the memory of you leaving last night is just as strong as the memory of you staying and us making love. Not that it wasn't fantastic," he added hurriedly. "But that's just how vivid the dream was. Like it was really real, not just lucid, if you get what I mean."

When she didn't answer, he looked up at her and saw to his surprise that a tear had leaked out of her eye, and that she seemed to be struggling to control herself. "Are you all right?"

She smiled brilliantly at him. "Yes, I'm fine. Very fine. Can you take the day off? I want to take you somewhere."

"Where?"

"To meet my mother."

He stared at her, and he must have been goggle-eyed, because she flushed.

"It's not what you think, okay? My mother is—just a very unusual person, let's say. I want her to have a look at you." She looked up at him defiantly, reminding him more than ever of Jana. "Do you want to come or not?"

"I'd love to," he said, and realized with surprise that he meant it. A warm feeling had come into his chest, a feeling he got sometimes when he realized suddenly how much he liked a woman, or when he suddenly felt game for some particularly crazy adventure. "I'm just not used to— Is she a lucid dreamer too? How far away is it? I need to take a shower first."

"Okay, you take a shower and I'll make the reservations. Don't worry, you'll be back by Monday morning. You asshole. You're making me feel really stupid."

Grant traveled so much on business that airports had long ago lost their excitement for him, but today he felt it again as he and Kat hurried among the crowds toward their departure gate, flight announcements echoing in the concourse: a kind of mystical anonymity, as if it were possible to leave your sadness and mistakes behind simply by flying away from them, moving to a different place, finding a clean slate on which to write.

Kat bought some jeans and a white cotton shirt at an airport store, changed clothes in a women's bathroom, and soon they were on a commuter jet bound for St. Clair, a town a hundred miles away across the state. It struck Grant, gazing out the window past Kat, that he felt no panic about getting entangled with her. In fact, the thought filled him with warmth. She was what he had been looking for all his life.

The St. Clair Regional Airport was small, low-ceilinged, and bucolic after the crowds and hurry of the city. A gentle-looking smiling man with thinning hair, wearing khaki pants, a blue turtleneck, and a sports jacket, was waiting for them at the security gate. Kat hugged and kissed him, and he offered to carry Grant's overnight bag.

"Alex works for my mother," said Kat as they headed across the miniature terminal, Grant carrying his own bag. She sounded excited and happy, and asked Alex a lot of questions about people and pets, which he answered in a quiet, cultured voice, crow's-feet crinkling at the corners of his eyes. Grant decided that he liked Alex.

Outside, the sky was overcast, and there was a vast fresh feeling in the air, as if they were near the ocean. Alex led them across

damp pavement to an SUV in a VIP parking space. The airport
road crossed railroad tracks and ran through an area of drab industrial buildings, and then they turned onto a four-lane street
between neighborhoods of big old trees and stately Victorian
houses. They crossed a gray-brown river on a WPA-era bridge,
then merged onto a state highway, seams in the pavement making
a rhythmic sound as Alex drove rapidly but without stress. Kat,
slouched on the back seat next to Grant, murmured in his ear: "I
hope you like her."

"What if I don't?"

She smiled. "You'll be part of a significant majority." She
asked Alex out loud: "Is Mother ready for us?"

"She seems ready for anything," he said, smiling at her in the
rearview mirror.

After half an hour they left the highway for a county route
that ran through a hilly rural landscape, the overcast making the
green of the woods, meadows, and fields deep and rich. At intervals the speed limit diminished and they rolled through villages
that were just a few old houses, a gas station, and a traffic light.
Finally one of these was bigger than the rest, and immaculate, as
if someone had built a six-block Hollywood set of a quaint small
town. The rustic storefronts seemed mostly expensive antique
shops, art galleries, and colonial-era restaurants, with a few spe-
cialty jewelers and gourmet grocers thrown in. Most of the people on the tree-shaded brick sidewalks looked like sightseers
come for the shopping on the train that stopped at the tiny Amtrak station. Alex turned right at the single traffic light. A few
miles on, he slowed and turned left on a narrow unmarked track
into some woods. After a minute, and out of sight of the road,
the track widened, and new white gravel crackled under their
tires.

A quarter mile on, the woods began to be interrupted by

trimmed hedgerows, immaculate rustic stone walls, and long split-rail fences enclosing pastures where sleek horses grazed. Alex cracked his window, and the smell of the woods came in along with a cold, clean smell that again suggested the ocean.

At intervals, gravel tracks with PRIVATE PROPERTY signs curved away between hedges or among trees. Occasionally the peak of a house could be glimpsed, and once the land fell away on the left so that over a low stone border they saw a valley of woods and meadows, two streams glinting dark green in the gray light, a few enormous, beautiful houses visible in the distant prospect. Then the trees closed in again, and Alex turned right at a stop sign onto another gravel road that ran uphill along a wide park separated from the road by split-rail fencing and a screen of sycamores. There was a metal post with standard green street signs at the corner too, as if this were the middle of some suburb instead of a gravel track off a secondary country road in the middle of nowhere—a gravel track meant to discourage the lost or curious from cruising around what Grant could only assume was a hidden rich people's neighborhood.

A vehicle came toward them, raising dust, and Alex and a black Hummer with a private security company logo edged past each other, Alex exchanging a wave with the uniformed men inside.

The road turned steep. Near the top of it Alex swung left, and the swish and rattle of branches against the sides of the SUV joined the rumbling of gravel as they climbed a driveway pressed on both sides by trees and undergrowth, the smell of greenery strong and close through the window.

When at last they emerged from the tunnel-like driveway, a very big brick house with gables and half a dozen chimneys loomed up the slope behind a four-car garage.

"Whoa," said Grant.

"Isn't it nice?" Kat asked happily.

She pulled him by the hand out of the SUV and along a flagstone walk, and they emerged from a stand of trees looking across a big lawn and flower beds at the front of the house. Despite its size, it was beautiful and somehow unassuming, fitting into its surroundings as if it had grown there, as if it had been built to live in, not to show off. To the left, where the land fell away from the hilltop, stone steps descended into what looked like wild gardens with exotic trees and shrubs. Beyond the tops of the garden trees was a view of the valley they had seen from the road. Grant again felt that he was near the ocean, as if it were an ambience that the very rich could buy and install wherever they lived.

Another unaccustomed feeling had come over him too: nervousness. As a high-caste corporate lawyer, he had a lot to do with rich people, of course—CEOs, Chairmen, big shareholders—but one always met them at the office, where a uniform style of business luxury prevailed—and Grant doubted whether many of even his very rich clients lived in places like this, where the refinement of very old money produced just the right balance of expense and ease. Who could have guessed you would find a neighborhood like this in the middle of the scruffy countryside along US 109? He had read about the "out-of-sight rich": fabulously wealthy old-money families who had found ways to live discreetly in a country where conspicuous consumption in the Gilded Age had drawn an angry reaction from the masses during the Depression. He glanced sideways at Kat. He should have known she came from wealth; his dreams of her penniless surfer-girl look-alike had thrown him off. Her physical perfection, the clarity of her features—the result of pure bloodlines, healthful leisure, and expensive cosmetics—should have tipped him off, reminded him of the infrequent receptions and dinners where he had met the wives and daughters of his most patrician clients, their graceful manners that made you feel completely at ease while you were with them, suspecting only later that they had been patronizing you.

"It's beautiful," Grant said, trying not to sound intimidated. Kat was worth even more than he had thought. What if he made a bad impression on her mother? He glanced down at his clothes and was momentarily reassured. The best of casual clothes worn jauntily, almost carelessly, as if he didn't know or care that they had cost many hundreds of dollars. He might be poor compared to these people, but he still had taste.

The front door of the house opened, and Alex strolled across the grass toward them, smiling his kind, almost beatific smile. "She's ready to see you."

Kat took Grant's hand again and they followed Alex to the door, the smell of cool grass mingling with Grant's nervousness. They climbed a half-dozen steps to a stone portico. Inside was a high, quietly lit hallway with a curving marble staircase near the back. Just inside the door were an umbrella stand, mirror, and a little ornate table with a telephone next to an affably shabby antique armchair and some large potted plants. Age-darkened paintings hung on the walls. It was somehow both opulent and homey, as if the people who lived here had bought the best of everything and then adjusted it for their comfort. Alex led them along the hall with the same relaxed, jaunty step he had used on the lawn, and three-quarters of the way down turned and opened glassed double doors.

Within was what Grant believed was called a drawing room. It was big and airy, with cozy nooks and bookshelves covering the walls and two broad, square pillars whose lower parts were four-sided leather seats. The far wall was a lattice of glass panes nearly to the high ceiling, with sets of French doors that opened onto a view of the wild gardens down the hill. A sideboard near the door was set with white linen, silver, china, and plates of pastries. Grant smelled coffee.

Near the French doors, armchairs, lamps, and a couch were arranged around a worn but precious-looking Oriental rug. Three men in suits were efficiently rolling up architectural plans and stowing papers in briefcases, as if they had just finished a business presentation. They nodded to Grant and Kat, and hurried from the room.

On the couch a woman sat holding a toy-sized spaniel. She was small like Kat, her features perfect and clear—though her purplish-blue eyes were darker—and as with Kat, it was hard to tell how old she was. She wore a flowing ivory-colored outfit, and her silvery hair was tied behind her head with a ribbon, but nothing about her was cutesy. Her face was nervous and intelligent. She scratched the lapdog's neck absently.

"Hello, Mother," said Kat, hurrying over and plopping down next to her on the sofa, leaning forward for a kiss and to scratch the dog too. It lifted its head and snuffed her hand excitedly, its small golden tail thumping.

"Hello, darling," said the woman, and looked up at Grant. "Is this the gentleman you told me about? How do you do," she said as Grant stepped forward and shook the hand she offered. It was small and strong like Kat's. "Tatiana Hatshep."

"David Grant. Nice to meet you."

She was studying him with her sharp, shapely eyes. "Thank you for coming to see me. Please sit down. No, over here next to me, so I can get a good look at you." Grant changed course and sat on the sofa where she indicated. "You dragged him all the way out here to meet me, darling?" She turned to Grant. "Isn't she impulsive?"

"She's fabulous."

"Yes," said Mrs. Hatshep seriously, turning to study her, and Kat smiled shyly like a little girl being discussed by adults. At arm's length from Mrs. Hatshep, Grant could feel her presence, the kind of force field that surrounds movie stars and politicians. "How did the two of you meet?"

"At a—at Macy's," Grant said, glancing at Kat to see if she wanted him to tell Mrs. Hatshep the details. Kat smiled helplessly and shrugged. "I saw her, and—well—talked to her."

"When?"

"Oh, um, well—let's see—" He glanced at Kat, who was grinning now as if to say "you're on your own," and looked into the air. "Yesterday," he said finally, surprised.

"Ah!" said Mrs. Hatshep. "Impulsive." Her gaze was polite but penetrating. "And what do you do, Mr. Grant?"

"I practice law, ma'am. I'm senior partner in the corporate practice group at Alder, Swinton."

"Ah. Then perhaps you're not after her money."

"I didn't know she had any," he said. "But if she does, I certainly wouldn't object to helping her with it."

"Have you slept with her?"

"Mother!"

"I—um—yes," said Grant, watching Kat like mad for cues, but feeling reluctant to lie to the older woman.

Mrs. Hatshep nodded a little absently. "Young, beautiful, rich, and sexually accessible," she mused. "What a dream."

"Thank you," said Grant modestly.

The two women looked at him in surprise, and then burst out laughing.

"He focuses well," Mrs. Hatshep said to her daughter. "How did he travel?"

"Completely on his own," said Kat.

"What?" asked Grant.

Mrs. Hatshep was watching him curiously. "Everything about us is quite sudden, I'm afraid, Mr. Grant. I hope you will humor us. Particularly when I cut through a lot of preliminaries and ask you a question. Do I have your permission?"

"Of course."

"What is it that you want out of life?"

"Um—okay, give me a second." He was taken aback, but tried to think. No use risking his reputation as a wit by trying another wisecrack. What was it he really did want out of life, without being too sappy? Sensing that his thinking time was up, he said what he had half-formulated before when the enormous Dr. Thotmoses asked the same question: "I guess, to know the truth about things. What life means, and all that. Why we're here, and what happens when we leave here, and all." He looked at Mrs. Hatshep, surprised and a little embarrassed at his own earnestness.

"What would you be willing to give to achieve that? To know the truth?"

"I'm not exactly sure," he said truthfully.

"He'll do," said Mrs. Hatshep over her shoulder to Kat, her eyes still on Grant. "As long as everything else goes well."

SIX

A Mystical Video Game

Grant took Kat to fine restaurants, the theater, the symphony. Now that he knew she was rich, he couldn't help spending money on her. She seemed to go along with this good-naturedly. He was falling for her head over heels, he knew. Of course, he was used to falling head over heels. One of the secrets of Grant's success with women was his sincerity. He told each one he fell in love with: "You're what I've been looking for all my life," and he always meant it. He would lie awake at night imagining her eyes, seeing in them a land of forests and mansions; or else his imagination would set her in a scene from a novel: a graveyard at the top of an ocean cliff, or a country road in autumn; and often, focusing on her in the scene, he seemed able to draw a taste of his "story dimensions" into himself, a little of their vast, quiet consciousness and almost-grasped meanings leaking into this world, making it for a while mysterious, beautiful, and alive.

Because now, in his middle age, the episodes seemed to have

almost dried up; they came only at long intervals, and according to no pattern he could make out, arriving out of the blue when he was driving, raking leaves, or looking out a window, then fading after only a few minutes. So loving women was a means as well as an end, a way of peeking through a crack in the material scheme of this world. Female beauty was a supernatural thing, a bounty without any earthly reason or material cause. Perpetuation of the species had nothing to do with it: mammalian sex drive guaranteed ample reproduction even when all females were as plain as plates. Fitness had nothing to do with it: most of the women who fascinated Grant were unfit for reproduction—or even survival—under any reasonable definition. Beauty was outside biology and causation: a beautiful woman was a flaw in that scheme, a chink in the wall between this dark world and somewhere else, which allowed you to see, or imagine you saw, celestial light. A beautiful woman was the image of a goddess who bestowed visions.

At least she was for a while; and that was the part that didn't fit, the one shadow over his beautiful method. It was Grant's sad experience that after a few months even the most exquisite goddess lost her radiance and became a being of decaying flesh like everyone else. You began to smell it on her breath in the morning, began to see wrinkles and sags where before there had been only perfection, began to sense a sadness—the sadness of mortality, which was the property of the human race. And then she was no longer a goddess, but just one more burdensome person you had to take out, make small talk with, even let sleep in your bed, to *deal* with, as you had to deal with clients and the people at work. At the same time, the process of goddess deterioration always made him feel vaguely guilty, as if it were his fault, as if his demands, his needs and appetites, had sucked away her life force, gorged on her perfection and so aged her, wrinkled her, made her sad and a little pathetic.

That was the part that didn't fit. Because if every door to the other world turned out to be imaginary, didn't that mean the other world was imaginary too?

But with Kat, everything seemed to be different. For one thing, the mental critic who started cataloging a woman's faults almost as soon as he had conquered her had precious little purchase on this one, who was young and beautiful but also cultured and smart. There was also the fact, he had to admit, that she hadn't slept with him since that first night; now whenever their kissing went beyond the chastely affectionate, she would disengage herself smilingly, saying she should call a taxi. It was probably a low manipulation, but it had made him crazier about her than ever. He had come to think now that he had been mistaken about the mark on her arm that night: there was no sign she was a drug addict or anything remotely like it.

Instead, she was the perfect girlfriend. Jana—of whom he had stopped dreaming once he had met the real thing—had been a girl barely out of her teens, but he didn't remember her looking much younger than Kat, who was nevertheless fully adult. In fact, he sometimes felt like a young stud to whom an older woman has taken a liking, an unaccustomed but entirely agreeable feeling. One example of her grit was that he couldn't get her to tell him what had been behind the trip to her mother's the second day of their acquaintance; she would just give him a delighted, dimpled smile and change the subject.

This was what he had been waiting for, he told himself exultantly; he had been right to hold out all those years when the self-help books and his friends had told him he ought to be "realistic." Most people didn't have the courage or the patience to wait for the perfect one, but he had gambled and won, had found the one who fit him exactly, his dream girl. He guessed now that their shared lucid dreams had not been some kind of freak ESP episode but a natural concordance, a sympathetic vibration of nervous systems or some other phenomenon unobserved by science simply because it was so rare that two people so perfectly compatible met among the billions in the world. He telephoned Stacy and told her that some personal issues had come up and that he needed to be alone for a while, that he knew he couldn't ask her to wait for him, though he would call her as soon as he felt better. He hardly heard what she said in reply; the memory of his parents' fights made escape his only thought on the frequent occasions when such conversations were necessary with a soon-to-be ex-girlfriend.

There were a couple of slightly weird things, though.

The first was that Grant wasn't even sure now that he and Kat *had* had sex that first night. They had drunk quite a bit of wine at the restaurant, he recalled. But instead of the normal haze over memory you expected from that, he actually seemed to have two *alternate* memories. In one, he slept with Kat; in the other, they kissed on his sofa and she called a taxi around midnight. It was very odd; he couldn't remember ever having had a similar experience. Maybe the sex had been part of a lucid dream, the one from which he had had several false awakenings. He was embarrassed to ask her what had really happened lest she think him a psycho so early in their relationship; and anyway it didn't matter: they were quickly falling in love, and his mind was on the future, and he was as happy as he could ever remember.

The only other small thing was that he never picked her up at home; she always insisted on meeting him at his house or somewhere downtown after work, and after their date she would always call a cab. He guessed she lived somewhere palatial and didn't want to intimidate him; but he had to concede that there were other possibilities too. Maybe she didn't want different boyfriends running into each other, or maybe she wanted to make sure he didn't stalk her after she dumped him. These thoughts gave him a twinge of romantic anxiety, something he felt so rarely that he sometimes found himself purposely stoking it up as if for a thrill; it was like a horror movie: scary enough to be interesting, but remote enough to seem delicious, sharpening his interest in her even more.

One Saturday night she was early for their date.

"I brought you something," she said when he opened the front door, knotting his tie.

They sat on the leather sofa in his living room. He was used to getting presents from women, but not like the bundle of wires and plastic she pulled out of a paper bag. He turned it over in his hands. It was a Nintendo GameCube console with some impressive-looking rewiring. Duct tape held a circuit board in the memory card slot, a dozen wires running from it to a transparent plastic box taped onto the top of the console, inside which was another board with a CPU chip. The total effect was as if someone had turned a small computer inside out.

"I love it," he said emotionally. "Did you pick it out yourself?"

She laughed. "Where's your TV?"

"Sweetie, we don't have time. We're going to be late for *La Traviata*. By Verdi."

"I'm *tired* of high culture."

"Tired of high culture?" he asked anxiously. "Have I been boring you? Have you just been playing me along, a vital, vivacious young girl with a dumpy, tired old—?"

"I'll tell you if you tell me where your TV is."

He pointed at a lacquered Chinese cabinet.

She opened it, revealing a large screen, knelt lithely in her tastefully sexy black gown and plugged in some jacks from the

GameCube, then snaked the electric plug to a wall outlet. The console lay on the rug in front of the TV like some tentacled creature.

"Okay." Kat took a game controller from the bag and jacked it in. Then she turned on the TV, pressed a button on the controller, and looked up at him with her intoxicating, wide blue eyes, her feline body crouching in the black dress.

"Okay," she said. "Play."

He squatted down and started to fondle her breasts. She pushed him off so that he rocked back on his heels, catching himself with his hands.

"With the video game," she explained.

"Is this something to do with lucid dreaming again?"

She nodded.

"What's it supposed to do?"

"If you play it you'll see." She pushed the controller into his hands.

"I *have* been boring you," he said sadly. "An old, dreary man with a young, vital, sexy—"

"You haven't been boring me. Stop fishing for compliments and play the game. We can see *La Traviata* anytime. I'm curious about something."

"What?"

"If I tell you, it'll prejudice the results. You wouldn't want that, would you? Come on. Play. Please?"

He sat cross-legged in his suit pants and wingtips, his crisp white shirt and tie. *"La Traviata,"* he said sadly. "By Verdi."

He pushed the START button, and the TV screen started to flash painfully, like a strobe. He turned his head away, squinting. "Ow. It's broken,"

Kat was turning off the lamp by the sofa. "No it's not. You just have to get used to it."

"I don't want to get used to it."

She came and knelt by him again, ran her hand through his hair. "Come on, don't be a wimp," she said. "I'll put eau de cologne on your temples afterward."

He squinted at the screen.

"It's a phase space whose regions are different colors, amplitudes, and flash frequencies," she said. "I want you to learn to navigate it."

"Why?" His eyes were watering madly; he had to shut them every few seconds against the strobing.

"You'll see."

"There's something you're not telling me," he complained. "You're not just some chick. You're a spy or a—a graduate student. I should have my lawyer present. How did you learn how to build something like this? What are you trying to find out?"

Through the pain in his eyes, nausea, and dizziness, he thumbed the toggles that normally moved you through game worlds, and he saw what Kat meant about different "regions." The colors, brightness, and flash frequency varied as he moved, merging into one another like parts of a real, abstract landscape. He soon found several "places" he had to avoid: as soon as he got near them, the dizziness and nausea got worse until he felt very bad indeed.

Kat, watching intently next to him, seemed to home in on these areas. "Go there," she said, pointing. "No, left and up."

"No way. I'll barf."

"Up and left," she said. "Come on, Grant, be a sport."

"I'm going to barf."

"You won't barf. Come on. That's it. More. More."

"Oh, Lord. Ack!" The room spun crazily as he went through the area, but he just barely didn't barf.

"Awesome! Super!" she said. Excited, she pulled up her gown

so she could sit cross-legged. He glimpsed the dark edges of the panty part of her nylons, and found himself encouraged.

She directed him through several other barf-inducing regions. She must have played this herself, he realized through headache and eyestrain. Finally he approached a region where green wisps undulated like seaweed, making his stomach turn over.

"No, straight in—what are you doing?" He felt Kat's hands over his on the controller. "Straight in, like that."

"Aaaa! Owww!"

The undulation got slightly quicker, and seemed to sway across the screen, and smaller, faster undulations started on the ends of the larger ones, igniting a fire in his brain. The room spun downward like a drill bit into darkness, at the center of which was a stillness that he wanted very much to reach. He let himself fall into it, and at the last moment he saw a plant or weed, perhaps two feet tall, waving and fluttering in the wind, and there was sunlight, and the weed stood by a chain-link fence.

The last thing he heard was Kat's fading voice crying: "Keep going!"

Her voice saying "What did you see?" was the first thing he heard when he came back.

He looked up into her beautiful blonde face, her hair tucked behind one ear. He was lying on his back in the living room.

"What happened?" He found he could move his arm, but then realized when he did that he had a splitting headache and felt like throwing up.

"What did you see?" she asked again. "You need to tell me before the memory dissipates."

"See when?" he asked, lying still and closing his eyes. His head stopped just short of bursting, and his stomach just short of surging.

"When you passed out. What did you see?"

"When I passed out?"

"Yes, when you passed out. I just said that."

He thought about it gingerly. "A plant."

There was no rest for him, however, until he described it to her in detail, the wind, and where the plant had been, and whether it had been day or night. It had been a windy summer early afternoon, Grant knew, somewhere he had lived when he was a baby, but which he didn't remember now.

"Good," she said finally, and he thought she was suppressing some excitement. He opened one eye slightly, but chisels bit into his skull, so he closed it again. Then she was all apologies and concern, caressing his head, getting him four Advils and a cool washcloth, and kissing him lightly on his face and head, which made him feel better.

SEVEN

A Nasty Surprise

Grant's next appointment at THI was Friday. No one was in the waiting room or at the receptionist's desk when he came in, but then a door opened and a woman came out. She was small and blonde, and wore a business suit.

She was Kat.

"Hello," she said with her dimpled smile. "Do you have an appointment?"

He stared open-mouthed as she grinned.

"Kat. Jesus. Are you—? Do you come here too?"

"I work here."

"Did you know I was—?"

She nodded. "I was assigned to evaluate you." She said it just a tad too enthusiastically.

"So—" He stood looking at her sadly.

She lowered her voice as if she didn't want anyone else in the empty reception room to hear her suddenly emphatic tone. "I know what you're thinking, but it's not true. What's happening with us has nothing to do with my job." She led him to an antique sofa, pulled him down next to her. The sofa had an elderly, musty smell, as if it hadn't been used in a long time.

"Getting involved like this is totally against the rules, aside from being stupid." She looked up at him timidly. "Do you forgive me? I knew you'd be upset, but what was I supposed to do?"

Her repentance and anxiety were encouraging, but he was suddenly curious. "Who are you, really? Will you explain what those—tests were you made me do? With the GameCube and asking me about my childhood and all that?"

"Yes," she said eagerly, as if relieved at being let off so easily.

"And tell me if you have any other hidden agendas or lies?"

"I promise." She held up her hand prettily.

"And let me strip you and tie you up and punish you for deceiving me?"

Given the breezy irony they had cultivated, he expected her to laugh or repel him with a cynical snub, but instead he got a shock. A sudden snarl came into her face, a panic and rage so intense that it made him rear back. For that second she looked like nothing so much as a wild animal in a trap. Then she was human again. She licked her lips and began to smile, and he could see her processing his suggestion in her humorously cynical way.

But now he realized that he himself was very angry, furious. His heart pounding made him dizzy; his head spun, and he could feel his limbs spring into rigidity.

"Then the answer is no," he snarled into her face. "Go to hell. Go fuck some more of your *test subjects.*"

He stood up and walked out of there.

Work was busy that week, as it often was in October, as if autumn's bracing air and clear sunlight awoke in large corporations the courage to sue each other. Grant was at the office early and late, which had the advantage of keeping his mind off Kat. It also gave him an excuse to cancel his Friday-afternoon appointment at THI, but for some reason he didn't, even though she might think he was coming because he wanted to see her—which, he finally admitted to himself, he was. After so many years of starting and suddenly abandoning intense romances, he was wretched and confused. Gazing out the window as his cab navigated the downtown streets, he tried to settle on a plan of action. Should he apologize? Wait for her to apologize? Propose a date as if nothing had happened? Act cool and unconcerned?

But he didn't need a plan, as it turned out. Kat wasn't there. Grant sat dejectedly on the antique sofa, reproaching himself for having half-believed her reassurances—the very kind of fiction he himself had used on more than one occasion when stumbling across a recently jilted lover: a small fantasia to keep things from getting too unpleasant for the few minutes until you could escape, one of the simpler tricks in the sordid little bag of the seducer. He was deep in these gloomy thoughts when the inner door opened and Dr. Thotmoses' deep, raspy voice said his name.

Grant was so preoccupied that it was hard to pay attention to Thotmoses' drone in the stuffy, overwarm room until the giant head of the Institute squeezed himself alarmingly onto Grant's side of the desk and leaned over him. But he wanted to do nothing more than carefully check Grant's eyes, ears, nose, and throat with a doctor's tools and gentle facility, take his blood pressure and pulse, and palpate his neck and around his jaw with dry, giant hands, now and then giving distracted bursts of monologue.

"Have you ever asked yourself why you need sleep? The brain is not a muscle, and even if it were, much of it is more active in sleep than in waking. So the 'resting' hypothesis has been rejected."

He hit Grant's knees with a rubber-headed stainless steel hammer.

"Some theorize that sleep permits daytime experiences to be processed, or long-term memories to be laid down, or chemical balances to be reestablished. But even if one of these theories is correct, none of them explains why *unconsciousness* is necessary. From an evolutionary point of view, wouldn't it be more adaptive for animals to remain conscious while these processes are going on, to monitor threats, or continue food-gathering or mating?"

He had Grant touch his fingers together in front of his face, then turn his head as far as he could in each direction.

"A convincing theory of sleep must account for the need for a loss of consciousness, the actual process of disengaging from the waking sensorium. What could that be?"

Finally he went back to his own side of the desk, made some notations, and then said, "Congratulations, Mr. Grant. Your results have been excellent, and I believe you are ready to go on to the next step of your Life Revision training. No more self-hypnosis exercises before bed for you. You need something more powerful now."

"Why didn't you tell me about Kat?"

Thotmoses looked at him gravely, hands folded on the desk. "It's our standard procedure. Not the romantic aspect—that was an unfortunate mistake, a serious lapse of judgment for which she has been reprimanded. But in the normal course we need to make sure, very sure, that we are not moving you along too fast, and do so in a way that you are unaware you're being monitored. I'm sorry about the subterfuge. You should blame me if you blame anyone."

"I do," Grant said tightly. "What do you mean something 'more powerful'?"

"Your experiences are still insubstantial, aren't they? Very much like dreams."

Well, of course they were like dreams, Grant was on the point of saying when Thotmoses stood up and opened a door that Grant had thought was a closet, and switched on a light. In the center of a small windowless room Grant could see a dentist-type chair amid a welter of wires and electronic boxes stacked on wheeled shelves. The chair had arm- and leg-straps, and bundles of wires ran to a boom whose metal arms held electronic medical-type devices. Grant stood up too, in some alarm.

"Don't worry," said Thotmoses with his skin-deep professional smile. "The procedure is very gentle. Your brain gets more of a workout at your average real estate seminar." He squeezed into the room and pressed buttons on two laptops that lay open on a wheeled cart. Their screens flickered on, and instrumentation lights on a tall stack of black boxes flickered on in response.

"How many people have—done this?" Grant's palms were wet.

"Not many," said Thotmoses. "Not many people are interested in knowing what you want to know. Even fewer get as far as you have with the exercises. It takes a certain—hunger."

"But—what are your qualifications to do this?" Grant stuttered. "What are you a doctor of, I'd like to know?"

"It's completely painless." Thotmoses regarded Grant innocently. "Of course, your fee for the treatment is completely refundable if you decide not to continue."

Grant's mind went involuntarily to the silver-haired *Modern Maturity* whiskey ad man. "Well, what is it—what is it you're going to do?" His voice shook slightly.

"Ah, I should explain, of course. In order to correctly customize the next phase of your program, I need to know a few things about your neurological makeup, to learn how you are 'wired' in a couple of important respects. Not in detail, you understand, but enough to have a general idea. That's what these machines are for." He waved a hand at them.

"If you do anything I don't like, I'm out of here."

"Of course. Absolutely."

Sitting in the dentist chair, Grant was relieved that Thotmoses made no move to fasten the arm or leg buckles. Instead, after fiddling for a long time with something behind Grant's head and tapping clumsily at the laptops, Thotmoses sat on a high stool to his right, opened a drawer in a wheeled cart, and took out a couple of flat paper and plastic packets of the kind sterile medical instruments come in. He tore one open and took about five minutes pulling a pair of surgical gloves onto his huge hands, where they looked stretched to the breaking point. Then he tore open the other packet and, with rising concern, Grant saw that it contained what looked like an IV needle. His concern turned to near panic when Thotmoses took a sterile swab and wiped the side of his neck, the cold of the evaporating alcohol seeming to chill his whole body.

"Whoa," he said, lifting his arm against Thotmoses' huge one. "What are you doing?"

"I'm sorry, I should have explained: I'm going to put a very small intravenous feed into your carotid artery and dispense tiny doses of a naturally occurring chemical. Then I will ask you questions about what you experience. Based on your answers, I will be able to make the measurements I need."

"I don't want a feed in my carotid artery."

"Ah. Well, then, we can't proceed." Thotmoses sat back,

holding the swab between thumb and forefinger. "In any event, you have gained a lot from the introductory portion of the Program, have you not? The ability"—he waved the swab poetically—"to do anything you want. In lucid dreams, of course. If you do not wish to proceed to the next step of the Program, your lessons have still been well worth your time." He added casually: "Kat was planning to take you home afterward, to make sure you were comfortable. She was eager to see you."

"What I mean is," said Grant, his voice cracking, "are you sure this can't hurt me? Do you guarantee that? I get to ask that, don't I?" He was crazy to let this weird old man do anything to him, he knew; but the alternative was *Modern Maturity*—and maybe no Kat, it occurred to him suddenly.

"Of course, of course. Yes, I can assure you that it's harmless. The maximum dose I am going to give you will be in the tenth of a milligram range; by comparison, tens of milligrams regularly circulate in the brain. In fact, the main risk is that the effect will be too mild for you to perceive. That is why I will ask you to relax completely and close your eyes while we conduct the procedure."

Grant could do neither. His heart pounded, and he realized that his wet palms were squeezing the arms of the chair. He would see Kat afterward, he told himself; in the end it was probably only that thought that kept him in the chair. Thotmoses was explaining something in his deep monotonous voice; Grant tried to pay attention, though it sounded like gobbledygook.

". . . neurochemical pulses when you fall asleep bring on the brain's disengagement from the waking sensorium. If we can mimic these pulses and focus them on the centers responsible for what we call 'metaphysical proprioception'—the 'memory' of how to reconnect with the sensorium—effectively interrupting the brain's default back to it . . ."

Thotmoses leaned close. His monologue had faded to a low humming. Grant, nearly fainting, felt the needle slide into a sensitive part of his neck, and then huge fingers taping it there. Then the fingers attached a very thin transparent tube to the needle and taped that lower down. Finally Thotmoses clapped his hands and rubbed them together, the surgical gloves making an odd splat and squeak. "All right. We're ready to start."

He loomed over Grant, breathing heavily through his nose and carefully adjusting something Grant couldn't see. Finally he said quietly: "Tell me if you experience anything, and describe it as best you can."

At first Grant felt nothing, but then it was extraordinary. Nothing changed in the room or his body or his head, but suddenly and quite clearly he heard an orchestra playing. He jumped in the chair.

"Hold still," Thotmoses ordered. "You have to hold very still to make sure you don't damage your artery. What are you experiencing?"

"Music," said Grant too loudly, trying to talk over the sound. "Just like I'm hearing it."

But that wasn't quite right, he realized; something was missing, something he had never noticed about music until it was absent, a subtle vibration and faint pressure on his ears: the tactile sensation of sound. The hauntingly beautiful but unrecognizable music had an uncanny feel in the absence of that vibration and pressure, as if the orchestra were in another dimension: an orchestra of the other world, or for the dead.

He sensed Thotmoses adjusting something again. "And now?"

The music deepened, and then the audible part of it disappeared. But what he realized suddenly and with surprise was that the audible part of music was just its surface; the essence of it was pure *feeling,* and that was what remained of it now: a powerful inner manifestation of beauty, full and rich. Tears were flowing down his cheeks. But then the perception rarefied even more, and he was left only with the precursor even of the feeling of music, the spring of absolute creativity and light from which it came, a lively silence that was its very soul.

And now he felt dreamy, sitting in a stroller long ago near a low chain-link fence on a hazy summer day, and from almost under the fence a tall weed grew, whose leaves fluttered in a wind that played over the grass, stirred his hair, and kept the hazy sunlight from being too warm. Back and forth the weed bobbed, and the space around it was a place one could rest and look out at space, time, causation, history, infinity, so that even this cozy place was bound up with a vast mystery; as he stared, fascinated, that sunlight, the grass by the fence, the trees behind it, the smell of a summer day became the origin point of the story dimension.

"A weed. Waving in the wind," Grant felt rather than heard himself murmur thickly.

Then he lost consciousness.

EIGHT

BAD MUSSELS

Grant woke up in his own bed, tangled in a sheet soaked with sweat. His head felt pierced with knives, and his vision was badly blurred.

Someone came to the edge of the bed, and he felt hands on his arms. "Are you all right? Lie down. No, lie down." It was Kat's voice.

"My head—," he gritted through the pain.

The hands went away. "Take these. Open your mouth." He opened it an inch, as far as he could without splitting his head apart. "Here's some water. Swallow." He felt the pills go down his swollen throat and the hands help him lie back down. He felt something soothing, and realized that it was a cool washcloth on his forehead. After what seemed like a long time, the pain got less and he fell asleep.

———

He didn't know how long it was before he woke up again, this time dragging himself out of sleep by slow degrees, resting along the way. Finally he could feel his body, his head throbbing dully, but without the piercing pain he had had before. He forced his sticky eyes open. He could see, more or less. Someone was sitting cross-legged next to him on the big bed. After a minute of blinking and focusing, he recognized Kat. She seemed to be wearing his gray pajamas, the arms rolled up so they didn't flop over her hands.

"Hi," she said softly.

He turned his head gingerly. It was twilight outside. "What time is it?" His voice was thick and croaking.

"Almost seven. P.M."

"What happened?"

"You got sick after dinner. Food poisoning, probably from the mussels."

"Dinner?"

"Don't you remember? After your treatment you took me to that seafood place, and then we came here. Then you started to vomit, and lost consciousness. You scared the shit out of me. You don't remember," she concluded, studying him.

"No." He searched his memory, but he couldn't remember anything after sitting in Thotmoses' treatment chair. "Could it have been something Thotmoses did to me, that treatment?" He shakily touched the side of his neck.

"The doctor said it was definitely food poisoning."

"The doctor?"

"At the hospital. Don't you remember? We came back from the emergency room in a cab. You've been asleep almost twenty-four hours since then."

She leaned over and kissed him tenderly on the forehead. "I was worried about you," she said softly.

He realized that he actually didn't feel so bad. He eased himself into a half-sitting position. "So you've been taking care of me."

"I told you I wanted to. Forever."

He grunted with what he hoped was weary cynicism.

"Grant, come on; I told you the truth about everything except one thing, and yes, that was a big one, but it doesn't wipe out everything else. Do you think I sleep with all my clients and take them to meet my mother?"

A warm feeling crept into his chest.

"Do you feel like talking?" she asked gently after a minute. "Or do you want to sleep?"

"I'm tired of sleeping."

"Okay." She pretended to think. "Then tell me about the most magical place you ever went."

"Are you starting again? 'I've been lucid dreaming since I was a little girl, and I wrote a diary—,'" he lisped irritably, mocking an innocent little girl's voice. "You answer some of *my* questions for a change."

"Okay," she said meekly.

He didn't have any prepared, so he threw out the first one that came to him. "Tell me about the THI Institute."

"It's volunteer work."

"A woman of leisure, you help out the weird giant geezer," he said, pleased that it rhymed.

"Be careful what you say about the weird giant geezer. The weird giant geezer is my father."

He stared at her in astonishment. "So your name is Katerina Thotmoses?"

"No, I have my mother's name. Why are you so surprised?" she asked defensively. "He retired from teaching and decided to start the Institute, to put his research into practice. I help him out sometimes."

Grant's astonishment had sapped his strength; he sank back on his pillows and closed his eyes. "What other amazing secrets do you have? Might as well get them all out now so they don't fester."

"I don't understand what's so amazing. Why shouldn't he be my father? Is it so—?"

He opened his eyes. "It's just that there's no real family resemblance."

"Well, why should there be? There are plenty of people who don't look like their—"

"I'm *sorry*. Look, shh, you're disturbing the sick. You want to hear about the most magical place I ever went?"

That stopped her. "Okay."

He relaxed against his pillows and closed his eyes again, resting in preparation for thinking.

"Are you asleep?" she asked after a minute.

"For heaven's sake. Just wait a minute." He was silent for a while, thinking. "Well, there was this town I came across in Canada, in Ontario, a few hundred miles west of Toronto, in the middle of nowhere. My friend Sam and I had hitchhiked out to Vancouver on the Trans-Canada Highway, but we got separated on the way back because we were desperate for a ride out of Thunder Bay, and someone stopped who only had room for one. So I let Sam go on ahead, and I had to wait another six hours."

"When was this?"

"Summer of 1974. July. The town was called Reginald. I remember because when I saw the sign it made me think of Regina, which is a town in Alberta that they pronounce to rhyme with 'vagina.'" He was searching for images from his nineteenth year, trying to reconstruct that world in his mind. "It was overcast. Quiet, very calm. No wind."

"So July 1974. When in July?"

"The last week. I remember we left Vancouver on the twenty-third."

"How many days out were you from Vancouver when you got there?"

"Why do you keep asking that? The exact dates of things?"

"I might want to meet you there."

He looked at her curiously.

"If we ever get separated. It could be a rendezvous where we could meet in our dreams if we ever get separated." She seemed perfectly serious.

Despite the craziness of that, another warm feeling came into his chest. He closed his eyes, remembering. It had been one of his biggest youth adventures, so he had kept it alive in his memory over the years. He held up a finger for each day he remembered. One day to Banf; another to Medicine Hat; another in which they got a ride all the way to Thunder Bay; then the thirty-six-hour wait and finally the ride in the morning to Reginald, in the flat middle of Ontario. He opened his eyes again. "It would have been five days out of Vancouver."

"So the twenty-eighth? When you reached Reginald?"

"The twenty-eighth around noon," he confirmed finally after turning it over in his mind.

"If we ever get separated, I'll meet you there. July twenty-eight, 1974, in Reginald, Ontario, around noon." She seemed perfectly serious.

After a while he began to feel sleepy again.

"Take these," Kat said, holding out two pills and a glass of water. "The doctor said they would help."

He took the pills and gulped the water thirstily, then snuggled into his pillows.

When he opened his eyes it was dawn, and Kat was asleep under the covers next to him in his oversize gray pajamas. His head still hurt dully, but it was better. It took him a little while to wake up enough to wonder if he was dreaming. He fumbled on the nightstand for his watch, did a triple-read.

Feeling him move, Kat opened her eyes and stretched. "How do you feel?" she murmured.

"I'm dreaming," he said, and smiled at her. "Are you here or not?"

"That's a weird question."

The doorbell rang.

It was a dream doorbell, but after a moment's hesitation he got out of bed. Asleep or awake, a person's doorbell has a certain claim on his attention. "I'll get it."

"No, you're sick," Kat said, sitting up. "I'll get it."

"I'm fine. And this is a dream, so it won't hurt me to get up, because I'll still be lying down. And anyway, I'm tired of lying down."

He put on his bathrobe. The doorbell rang again, and then a third time as he stiffly descended the stairs to the foyer. Kat leaned on the railing at the top of the stairs and looked down.

Grant opened the door. Dr. Thotmoses stood on the flagstones in a wrinkled gray raincoat and a scarf. It was dawn, and Grant's large suburban lawn was hazed with blue-tinted mist, the quiet residential street beyond only faintly visible, the chilly air smelling of wet dirt.

Grant stepped back, unnerved. Of course, the Institute had his home address, but—

"Ah, Mr. Grant," said Thotmoses. "I apologize for coming so early, but I'm going away, and I wanted to be sure I caught you."

"Oh. Well—" He had been about to say "come in," but he stopped himself. He was unsure what Thotmoses would think if he saw his daughter wearing pajamas at a man's house at six o'clock in the morning. "So you're going away."

"Yes. I will take just a moment of your time." Thotmoses had on enormous black galoshes that looked slightly comical. "You may be thinking that things are turning out rather strangely. I just came to give you a few words of encouragement."

Grant glanced up at Kat leaning over the railing, listening. She seemed intent but not surprised.

"This is a dream," Grant said to Thotmoses.

"My dear Mr. Grant." Thotmoses put a huge hand on Grant's shoulder. "It is now time for you to give up that way of thinking.

"Look around, Mr. Grant. Look, for instance, at me. I walk, talk, breathe, do everything a real person does. In 'real life' how do you know I'm real? The answer is that I walk, talk, breathe, and so on. You have no more reason here to believe that I'm not real than you do in real life. As far as you're concerned, this dream is just as real as real life, isn't it?"

"I know what's real and what's not," said Grant. "I just triple-read my watch."

"Ah," said Thotmoses, untidy eyebrows rising. "So you can identify absolute reality based on some tiny letters on your watch? Hm.

"A few words of advice," he went on, his breath steaming in the chilly, damp air. "Dreams are not the goal of Life Revision. They are an educational device only. Sleeping is the only experience most people have of disengagement from their default sensorium, and dreams are the only experience most people have of alternate sensoria, so we use sleep and dreaming to familiarize our subjects with disengagement from the default sensorium and engagement with alternate sensoria. You will go beyond sleep and dreaming now—far beyond. There is often some initial confusion as the brain reequilibrates. However, no matter how strange things may seem, remember that you will soon get them sorted out, so that they will seem as normal as your normal life did before. The main thing is not to lose your nerve. Avoid calling attention to yourself, because doctors, psychiatrists, priests, police, all the arbiters of everyday reality, can only hold you back now."

"What do you mean?" Grant asked anxiously. "Am I going to go crazy?"

"Absolutely not, and that is what I want you to keep in mind. In fact, I am delighted to find you looking so well. And you have enough money to carry you forward until you get your feet on the ground. Thus my previous interest in your financial condition," he finished with a slight bow.

"What do you mean?" asked Grant again, and then angrily: "Tell me what is going to happen."

Instead of answering, Thotmoses pulled a folded sheet of paper from his pocket and handed it to Grant. Then he waved fondly. He had begun to fade. As Grant watched, he became nearly transparent, like a figure formed from the mist.

"What is going to happen?" Grant demanded again in alarm.

"Good-bye," said Thotmoses merrily, beginning to curl away at the edges. "Remember to think carefully about any strange experiences. Congratulations! The Fool Who Persists in His Folly Will Become Wise!"

And with that he smudged completely and floated upward, swirling like smoke. Grant stepped out into the chill air and watched it rise and get lost in the mist. Then he came back in and shut the door, climbed the stairs. Kat was watching him.

"I want to wake up," he said.

She followed him back to the bedroom and sat on the edge of the bed as he lay down.

"I'll see you in a minute," he said, patting her hand, then closing his eyes to fall asleep in his dream and wake up to reality.

Soon he felt his body lying in a position different from what it had just been. He forced his eyes open. Bright early morning sunlight filled the room. He sat up, blinking. Kat's side of the bed was rumpled, but the smell of her was now faint and cold.

"Kat?" Silence. His gray pajamas were draped over a chair. He put on his bathrobe and went stiffly downstairs to the kitchen. "Kat?" The house was quiet, and he knew, somehow, that she was gone.

He put his hands into the pockets of his robe.

His right hand closed over something. He drew it out: a crumpled piece of paper. He uncrumpled it and smoothed it to read the print. His heart beat harder: a note from Kat?

It said:

Dear Mr. Grant:

    Forgive me for addressing you through this letter, but experience has taught me to withdraw when my students are first dysinhibited, as their initial incomprehension can cause various forms of unpleasantness—

Grant's eyes skipped down the page. It was signed with an enormous flourish, worthy of the enormous hand that had written it.

It was the paper Thotmoses had given him in his dream last night.

He had to concentrate to read the rest of it; even so, he barely understood it.

You will be tempted, of course, to consider yourself the victim of unscrupulous medical practice.

A sick dizziness came over Grant, and he put his hand to the side of his neck.

Please be assured that this treatment was administered with meticulous precision, hygienically, and for good reasons. There are crucial differences between your condition and the neurological pathologies it may resemble. For one thing, you can take advantage of more than a year's practice processing alternate sensoria, gained in your lucid dreaming practice.

By focusing Homo sapiens' *brain on only one world, evolution equipped him with a powerful adaptive tool, but in the process deprived him of a profound view into reality. A person like you, who no longer needs the tool, may yet benefit from the view. I sincerely wish you great joy in it.*

P. Thotmoses, D.D., Ph.D.

NINE

THE OLD BRAIN

It was Tuesday, Grant figured out with some difficulty. He didn't recall Monday. He called the office and told Pam he wouldn't be in. He felt odd: disoriented and deeply tired. He fumbled with the telephone book, figured out a neurologist's number, and told the receptionist it was urgent. Even so, the doctor couldn't see him until the afternoon.

Downtown, the wind was chill and fresh under scudding clouds, as if it blew from a seacoast that Grant had not known of before. The smell and feel of it seemed almost to wipe the city from existence—as if its reality had been founded on a smell that was blown away now, leaving only an image on the eyes—or seemed to change it into a sea town, where huge oceangoing ships were moored in the surging, cold blue water that fell to unmeasured depths half a mile out, as if the town verged on the edge of infinity itself. As he got out of his car a couple of blocks from the Amana Building, an urge came to him to look at a map to see if there really was a coastline nearby; he reminded himself angrily that he knew very well there wasn't. His ears were nipped by the chill as he hurried along the sidewalk, the earth seeming to rock slightly in the rush of wind, sunlight, and cloud, and his mind disobediently wandered to the cry of seabirds, the tourists in summer, the lazy hush of the waves, or their roaring on a day like this one.

He turned a corner onto a narrower, more sheltered street, and the buildings loomed over him decrepitly. A gust around a corner brought a chill of tiny raindrops. The gray front of the Amana Building was like a blank, aging face staring at the thickening clouds.

After the rush of wind outside, the Amana's small, stuffy lobby seemed still and watchful, echoing the sound of his breathing back to him. The fifth-floor hall was silent except for an ancient radiator across from the elevator ticking out heat, and the floorboards creaking as he went along the worn runner.

He almost didn't recognize the door: the sign had been removed, leaving it bare and fragile-looking. It was unlocked. But the Trans-Humanist Institute was gone.

Emptied of the shabbily genteel furniture, the waiting room looked big and worn out, like a vacant welfare office. Grant switched on the ceiling fluorescents, and in their pale glare walked through the inner rooms, the worn floorboards, now uncovered, giving off the faintly sour smell of age. There were signs of hurried moving: electric outlets with their covers off, fresh scratches on the walls, an inner door taken off its hinges, strips of discarded tape, wadded newspaper, a few empty cardboard boxes.

They had gone. The thought filled him with fear and confusion. He leaned weakly against the wall by a dirty window that was beginning to streak with rain. The narrow street below was gray. Over gray roofs and through the mist of rain he could see the dark green of a small park, a flashing red light on a radio transmission tower, the neon of some stores half a dozen blocks away. What had they done to him? What had Thotmoses really done? He remembered no restaurant, vomiting, or hospital; just waking up with his head bursting after Dr. Thotmoses' brain procedure. Kat had been lying all along, about everything, he guessed, just to play him along so Thotmoses could do whatever he had done. Had they given him brain damage that caused hallucinations? He had hallucinated this morning, he was sure. The letter in his robe pocket proved that it hadn't been a dream, but he couldn't have seen what he had seen. Maybe the vaporizing Thotmoses was some kind of REM overlay on reality, he thought hopefully, produced by sleepwalking and lucid dreaming at the same time when Thotmoses came to the door.

The neurologist, Dr. Taggart, was a large, handsome young man with a reddish complexion, curly hair, and muscular shoulders, which, together with his self-confident manner, suggested varsity football. But Grant noticed with satisfaction a thick gold ring on his left hand: his masculine goods had been withdrawn from circulation, or, if they were still available, were offered only on the black market at a steep discount. As long as young men made mistakes like that, Grant thought, the way was clear for older men who didn't.

His thoughts were running in their usual pattern, he noticed with relief, sitting on Taggart's examining table in a blue paper gown, the doctor washing his large hands at a sink. They were soft and professional when he touched the sore spot on Grant's neck. "Does it hurt when I press?"

"Not really. A little right there."

"Headache? Fever?"

"Not now. At first."

More palpating. "How did it happen?"

"Someone gave me an IV of something."

"Ecstasy? Cocaine?"

"What? No, nothing like that. It was supposed to be some kind of treatment. For depression, kind of. Part of a—a self-help program."

"Treatment by a doctor?"

"I'm not sure. I think so. But he didn't have what looked like a medical office." Mortification broke through Grant's other feelings. How could he have been so *stupid*? He was supposed to be a lawyer, canny and skeptical, and he had let himself be tricked into "treatments" by a man whose charlatanism should have been obvious. And by his beautiful daughter: fleeced like one of those octogenarian millionaires who marry twenty-year-old strippers. The thought made him feel old and ashamed.

Dr. Taggart said, "I want to send you for some tests."

Two days later, his thumb riffling the corners of the CAT negatives that had been fastened into Grant's brand-new chart, Dr. Taggart asked him: "Have you ever had epilepsy, seizures, anything like that?"

Epilepsy. A choking coldness came into Grant's chest. "No."

"Your scans show what looks like a lesion on your right temporal lobe. Do you ever hear music at odd times, that doesn't seem to have a source? Or have sudden feelings that aren't connected to what's going on right then?"

"Music coming out of nowhere?" Grant stared at him. "How would that—how would—?"

"The lesion is close to the tertiary association cortex for music. Sometimes people who have them there hear music when they're having a seizure."

"So I would hear music if this—this thing was stirred up?"

"Maybe, yes."

Grant moved his lips stiffly. "He—this doctor or whatever he was, who gave me the IV, I heard music while he was doing it. Music from nowhere."

"Did he tell you what was in the IV?"

"No."

Taggart sat down on his stool, turned away from Grant, and made notes in his chart on a counter against the wall.

Grant blurted out: "How bad off am I?"

Taggart turned back to him. "I'm not sure, but I think not so bad. You may have what we call 'complex partial seizures.' "

Hearing his problem described this way, a small relief went through Grant. These were medical problems, he realized. Something doctors were trained to cure.

"What happens in a seizure is that, instead of taking part in the brain's normally modulated synaptic communication, damaged cells start all firing together—kind of like a dozen people chanting in a crowded football stadium. Think of the normal functioning of the brain like everyone in the stadium talking to their neighbors, holding separate conversations, conveying information to each other. But then a dozen people start chanting a fight song, and then the people around them pick it up, and the fight song spreads through the crowd until a big enough group of people is chanting so that you can hear the song emerging from the general background hum of voices. If enough of the brain gets involved in this neural 'chant' you get a grand mal seizure; if a smaller part is involved, you may get a sudden feeling or smell something or hear or see something—that's called an epileptic 'aura.' "

"So I have epilepsy?"

"You may have. My only concern is, there are drugs that are what we call 'epileptogenic,' or epilepsy-causing, which can make an existing epileptic condition worse by causing damage to the cells around an existing lesion. There's no way to tell if the IV this doctor gave you contained one of those drugs, but you say you heard music and then lost consciousness. So on the off chance there's new tissue damage, I want you to stay on the look-out for strange feelings or sounds, smells, unusual fatigue or dizzy spells, anything like that."

TEN

UNUSUAL FATIGUE, DIZZY SPELLS, AND OTHER THINGS

At first Grant took a week off work, then another, and then a third, but finally, realizing that he was in worse shape than he had thought, he filled out the paperwork, had Taggart make the required certifications, and got an indefinite medical leave of absence, which under the general partnership agreement entitled him to 80 percent of his full salary until he either returned to work or became permanently disabled. Much of the time he felt like himself, but other times things became strange. To his dismay, he began to have spells where he was uncertain what had really happened in the past hour or two. Once he saw his teapot on the kitchen table with steam coming from the spout; his triple-read told him he was awake, but he couldn't remember making tea. He poured himself a cup and drank it; it was real enough; but later he came into the kitchen and saw no dirty cup or teapot, yet he couldn't remember washing up. In the end, he was unsure whether he had made tea and drunk it and cleaned up or whether none of those things had happened. Sometimes these dual memories gave him the disturbing feeling that he was living a double-exposure, two lives that ran on parallel paths but were not the same. He couldn't tell whether he was having actual hallucinations or just disorders of memory; but this just made them all the more frightening. Even more frightening, sometimes he was flooded with memories of things he had *never* seen or done, and once or twice he even seemed to forget who he was, imagining himself a superhuman who could travel through time or across worlds, before snapping out of it and remembering that he was just a disturbed middle-aged man with an increasingly tenuous hold on reality. He stopped telling Dr. Taggart about these episodes when Taggart suggested hospitalizing him for observation. Grant had visited state mental hospitals and nursing homes with his freshman psychology class and had never forgotten them: he had sworn to himself then that he would never end up in a place like that.

In the end, that was why he didn't contact the police, the state medical board, or anyone else about Thotmoses, as Dr. Taggart urged. Better not to call attention to himself, not to get on the radar screens of the authorities, civil, criminal, or medical. He was uncomfortably aware that Thotmoses' letter had recommended just such a course of action.

Yet his decision to lie low came at a price. After Pam packed up his office and the moving company stowed the boxes in his basement, he had no one to talk to and nothing to do. He was afraid to go to the gym or out to eat because of the possibility that he would have one of his "partial complex seizures," or whatever they were, away from the safety of home. Instead, he began to use the exercise equipment in his basement and order his meals delivered. He subscribed to all the newspapers he could and read them cover to cover, spent hours surfing the Net, more hours jogging around his long suburban block. He resisted the temptation to call someone, anyone at all, just to have someone to talk to. His jilted girlfriends would probably love to hang up in his face; his ex-colleagues would simply be puzzled; and worse, someone might get the idea that he needed help and report him to the authorities.

He could have programmed lucid dreams and had all the company he wanted—at least for a few hours a night—but with waking reality already so confused, the idea of lucid dreaming terrified him. As it was, his sleep was disturbed. He would start up in bed half a dozen times a night; sometimes he would find he was dreaming, sometimes awake. Sometimes he would lie all night tense with regret and murderous rage, imagining again and again killing Dr. Thotmoses and especially Kat. He had briefly wondered whether they were a couple of half-crazy people whose lives he had inadvertently ruined doing some corporate merger or real estate deal—but that was too much like a movie. More likely they were some fully crazy people who actually believed they were doing something important and good by pithing him, who actually believed in their Trans-Humanist Institute.

Fertilized by idleness and loneliness, his desire to punish Thotmoses and Kat grew until it was nearly an obsession; but perhaps even more important was simply his need to have something to do. Finding them would be the perfect project. After all, if he shut himself up with only his delusions for company, he really would go insane. Hunting—by phone, through the Internet, through brief forays from home—would break him out of solitary confinement, give him enough social contact to keep him sane, but not so much that anyone could figure out that he was crazy. It would be a reason to get up in the morning, a reason to keep trying to get better.

His first try at playing detective was gratifying. He called the management company that handled office rentals for the Amana Building; he was Thotmoses' office moving company with an unpaid bill. A sympathetic rental agent regretted that their policies prevented them from disclosing information about tenants, then gave him Thotmoses' home address and telephone number.

The number was disconnected, but now that he had made his plans, his fear of leaving the house diminished. He found West Elm Street easily enough, a residential street tucked away in one of the older suburbs close to town, berries from untrimmed trees staining the sidewalk purple. The houses were all on one side of the street, their small lawns patchy from tree shade; on the other side, nearly hidden behind more trees and a dense tangle of prickly undergrowth, a corrugated metal barrier blocked out the sight—but not the sound—of Interstate 66. Driving slowly along West Elm in the pale fall sunlight, Grant wondered idly what the neighborhood had been like before the highway came, before the constant hiss and whine of tires and the faint smell of exhaust had, like nerve gas, driven the yuppies away and turned the houses into low-cost rentals.

A dozen blocks on, West Elm climbed steeply and widened, the sky opening above it, and the houses became better kept. Number 4242 was a small stone rambler with a dry lawn and stunted-looking pines. More pines grew across the street, and beyond them was a steep slope, undergrowth hiding the highway barrier starting a few yards down it. Grant drove past the house slowly, as he had seen done in detective movies. It looked empty:

there were no cars in the gravel driveway or curtains in the windows. He wasn't surprised; moving out of the Amana Building practically overnight had showed how serious Thotmoses and Kat were about disappearing. He parked a few blocks up and walked back, glancing casually up and down the deserted street.

High, filmy clouds had been gathering since midmorning, and now, a little after lunchtime, the filtered sunlight was pale and cool. The air was filled with the faint but constant hiss/hum of the highway, a dumb, patient presence pervading the empty neighborhood, surrounding houses, mailboxes, and trees, swingsets on the worn grass of back yards, hovering over 4242's lawn. In Grant's ears the sound became waterfalls of a river invisible beyond the undergrowth, an unmanifest wind in the still pines, a smudged erasure of the lives in this street, as if this was not an abode of people at all but only a place where they came to sleep, their presence canceled when they went away to work, the surfaces of the houses scoured clean of human association by the pervading sound, leaving a landscape that seemed utterly deserted, a perfect place for people who wanted to hide, like a TV channel full of static.

In 4242's small front yard, a tang of dry pine overlay the exhaust smell from the highway. Grant knocked at the front door without result. He squeezed himself behind a bush and cupped his hands against a front window. Inside was a living room with a small stone fireplace and drab yellowish-tan carpeting that disappeared through arches to the left and rear. The house was bare of furniture and everything else.

He walked around to the weed-grown back yard. A couple of rusty garbage cans contained nothing but a bad smell. He was about to look in the back windows when he heard the hum of a car engine and the crunch of tires on the gravel driveway.

In unhesitating panic he jumped the low fence that separated the rambler's back yard from the yard behind and ran, the thought blaring in him that some neighbor had seen him nosing around and called the police. When he reached the sidewalk in the next block, he forced himself to slow to a casual stroll. He strolled several blocks until he was convinced no one was coming after him, and then retraced his steps to the corner of West Elm and looked nervously down the street. His car was there; hopefully whoever had seen him at the house hadn't connected him to it—burglars rarely drove Mercedes. He walked to it casually, climbed into the reassuring smell of warm leather, and drove away.

That night, rain falling outside his windows, by turns restlessly sleeping, waking, and dreaming, Grant's mind ran over and over his visit to the West Elm Street house. He shouldn't have panicked when he heard the car in the driveway, he knew. If it *had* been the police, he could have told them any number of things, even a version of the truth: that he was trying to track down the former tenants, whose bogus Institute had cheated him. And probably it hadn't been the police at all, just a real estate agent or prospective tenant, or even just someone turning their car around. Or even—his heart pounded at the thought—Thotmoses or Kat coming back to take care of some detail. He should have stayed, he told himself angrily; had he deteriorated so much that he doubted his ability to bluff his way through even such minor difficulties? He had been living too much with fear. It mustn't be allowed to take over his life.

Gray clouds moved over the city, wide and dull with its smokestacks and storage tanks, train tracks and expressways, glass and brick buildings rising in terrace after terrace up the hill from the river crossed with bridges, a tour boat gliding on its gray water, and in glass and steel canyons horns honked and people streamed in waves across wide streets, and the fresh wind blew down dumpster alleys behind crowded restaurants.

Grant took a shortcut to the suburb he had visited yesterday and negotiated hilly streets wet from overnight rain, yellow and orange leaves plastered on the pavement and parked cars, gray gusts bringing down drops from the trees. Warm yellow light showed in a few windows, but no one was on the sidewalks and only a few cars passed slowly, sleepily, as if the drivers wished they were home in bed. The lawns and hedges were a deep, vivid green, almost fluorescent. Grant shook his head to clear it of the hallucination-like impression. His pupils were dilated because of the dim light, he knew, causing colors to look brighter. He couldn't let the line between reality and delusion blur; he had to maintain objectivity.

Concentrating on keeping his perceptions under control against the seductive sleepiness of the day, he missed West Elm. He doubled back, but again couldn't find it. He drove slowly up and down Hamilton Street within a mile of 66, still without luck. It was one of those streets that weren't where you pictured them, he realized, the twists and turns of the suburbs distorting the right angles you unconsciously assigned to corners, taking things far away from where your mental grid said they should be. He would have to skip the Hamilton shortcut and approach West Elm as he had last time, when he had followed his map. He had come over a steep, shady street called Lebanon, where the sidewalks were cracked and tipped from the roots of old trees. He looked at his map to confirm that Lebanon was where he remembered, then wended his way through residential streets made narrow by parked cars.

Lebanon was even dimmer than the other streets, though it was midmorning by now, branches of oaks that still had half their leaves nearly meeting overhead. Grant eased his car down a steep hill. West Elm Street wasn't near the bottom, where he thought he remembered it. He continued along Lebanon, up and down more hills that looked a lot like the first one, but still no West Elm, until Lebanon finally ended at a street called Avery, big houses with manicured gardens slumbering in the overcast morning, now thickening even more, as if rain were trembling in the air.

Grant drove back over the entire length of Lebanon, reading the street signs. At the other end, where it met Wilson Boulevard, he pulled over, turned on his map light, and found Lebanon on his map. He followed it the few inches from Wilson to Avery with his finger, looking at the side-street names. Birch, Spring, Lowell, Chadwick, Oak, Linley, Lilac, but no West Elm.

Anxiety filled him, like a coldness seeping out from under his ribs. He checked the street index, then double-checked it, then looked over the whole map to see if there wasn't another index.

There was no West Elm Street on the map or the index.

Grant laboriously went over all the streets the map showed near 66, running his finger up the tiny lines to their names. He did this twice, taking about twenty minutes, but there was no West Elm Street. The map was out of date, he realized with momentary relief—but no!—it was the same map he had used yesterday, and anyway, this area of the suburbs long predated the map. Massaging his eyes, he noticed that his hands were shaking. Then, with another lifting feeling, he realized that everything could be explained if he had merely confused the *name* of the street. There was an *Elm* Street on the map, though remote from this suburb; perhaps he had merely mixed that name up with some other street that had so many elm trees on it that he had unconsciously assigned it the name West Elm, or something like that. His brain was not in the best shape right now, after all.

He drove the entire length of Lebanon, turning onto each side street, but never coming to the neighborhood at the top of the hill with the rambler. After a while he realized that he could also be mistaken that Lebanon was the street that led to the street he had thought was West Elm. It wasn't until late afternoon that he decided to give up driving all the streets within a mile of US 66.

He pulled over and turned off the engine, closed his eyes and tried to relax shoulders and arms tense from clutching the steering wheel too hard. Had the house been a hallucination, an extended REM episode indistinguishable from reality? And West Elm Street too, the entire neighborhood, which his map didn't show, and which he couldn't find? He realized with grinding fear that if the house had been a hallucination, so had his discussion with the Amana Building rental agent about the address, his notes with the address on them, his finding the house on the map, a whole series of events strung out over several days, all adding up to a firm belief that there was a real street and a real house.

Or maybe he was dreaming now. That would make more sense than an extended hallucination. He quickly triple-read, quadruple-read, quintuple-read his watch. It said KENNETH COLE—NEW YORK every time. His heart sank. Either he wasn't dreaming or else it wasn't possible to identify dreaming by triple-reading anymore. Either way, he was in trouble. He closed his eyes and felt his heart beating rapidly and smoothly, his hands sweating.

Maybe when he opened his eyes he would be somewhere else entirely—back at his house or back at the West Elm neighborhood—or perhaps even somewhere abstract, unrecognizable, where he would wander and stumble locked in an internal void until someone on the outside found him and they put him away. He opened his eyes hastily, but he was still in his Mercedes by the curb of a narrow residential street under a deep gray sky, large drops of rain beginning to spatter on the windshield and thump on the roof.

ELEVEN

EXIT

It was strange. The waking world still acted from moment to moment as it always had—there were none of the sudden shifts, physical impossibilities, or surreal landscapes that Grant had learned to recognize in lucid dreams. He could drive his car home over the familiar and continuous streets and highways that led there, park in the garage, go inside and make a sandwich and a cup of tea, and have nothing suggest anything out of the ordinary. It was the long-term coherence of things that seemed to be disrupted, so that a house, a street, an entire neighborhood had become somehow disconnected from the world Grant saw around him today, where there was no such house and no such neighborhood. He couldn't even find the telephone notes he had made talking to the Amana rental agent.

He had assumed that insanity would be just the opposite: strange, frightening things happening before your eyes against the backdrop of a normal world. But why should he ever have

believed that? Such an insanity would be a mere inconvenience
after you learned to parse the real from the delusory, instead of a
crippling condition that undermined your ability to decide what
was real at the most basic level.

That night Grant lay in bed exhausted, his mind running over
the same terrain again and again like a rat trying to find its way
out of a maze. He had no idea how many hours he had lain there
when he thought he heard a sound downstairs, and felt the slightest shift in the air, a nearly imperceptible change in pressure, as if
someone had silently opened and closed the front door. He lay
perfectly still, listening. His doors were locked, but a kind of
sixth sense told him there was someone in the house.

Kat.

He had given her a key, he realized, heart pounding. Maybe
she had planned to slip back in once he had reached a certain
point of desperation. Or maybe she had forgotten something, or
had come back to steal something, or kill him—

He crept along the hall and down the stairs, cool air tingling
on his skin. The darkness was silent but pregnant with a presence, as if she were sitting in the living room, or standing in the
foyer in her jacket—

The foyer held the subtlest suggestion of fresh air. He crept
to the living room, peered between two potted plants. At one
end of the leather couch a pale figure sat. Grant's heart pounded
harder, but his body relaxed as the need for stealth was gone.

"You," he said, the warmth of his voice filling the darkness
like black velvet.

She was silent, motionless. He came forward, fumbled with a
lamp, switched it on.

She flew at him with inhuman speed.

He jumped backward with a yell. When he could focus again

she was gone, the shadows of furniture and potted plants that had leaped out to make the flying shape unmoving now, her pale form resolved into a cream-colored cushion and part of a painting hanging above it. Grant stood staring in the silence of the living room. He could still feel a presence, still smell the fresh air.

He walked through the house, turning on lights. It was empty. When he opened a window and looked out, he saw only streetlight shining dimly on the dark green leaves of climbing ivy in the still, humid air, a curl of mist floating in the street at the bottom of his driveway.

He tried staying home for a couple of days after the West Elm Street debacle to clear his head, plan his next move, but he soon found it unbearable. A hallucination stalked him. At odd hours would come the faint pressure change of a door opening and closing, and then Grant would imagine he smelled a hint of outdoors, as if Kat had just come in with a waft of bracing fall air and was quietly unbuttoning her coat in the foyer, eyes sparkling and cheeks rosy. If he tried to ignore it, the impression would grow stronger, the smell more unmistakable, or he would hear small sounds, a breath or a coat sliding off, or a step in the hall, or water running in the kitchen, as if she were making tea. But whenever he finally jumped up to look, heart hammering, sure that this was finally the real thing, the house was always empty and still.

There was only one place left to search for Kat and Thotmoses, and his fear that he was getting worse drove him to take the trip while he still could. He bought a ticket on the commuter plane to St. Clair—the same flight he and Kat had taken—rented a car at the small airport, and drove through the industrial district until he came to the broad avenue that led to US 109. He cudgeled his brain for the name of the exit they had taken; he couldn't remember it, but he took an exit that looked familiar after about the same amount of time he thought they had stayed on the highway. At first this seemed hopeful: the two-lane county road passed through a rolling countryside that looked right, but when he failed to find the little immaculate town after an hour he realized it was wrong after all. He retraced his route and tried a few other exits, but without success.

Next afternoon as he sat in his kitchen with a cup of tea he remembered something and stood up abruptly, knocking his chair over. It was something he should have remembered long before, but which his troubles had somehow driven from his mind. He didn't remember Kat ever taking away the video game console she had brought him.

He hadn't opened the cabinet under his TV since that night. He opened it now. The GameCube bristling with wires and circuit boards was stuffed into the shelf next to some old VHS tapes. Grant took it out carefully. It might be his only connection to Thotmoses and Kat, the only physical object that could be traced to them, though he didn't have any idea how that might help. He stood holding it indecisively. Finally he turned on the TV, jacked in the controller, and sat cross-legged on the rug.

As it had the first time he played it, the TV screen started flashing black and white, making his eyes water. He closed them, then gingerly opened them in stages, forcing himself to look. When he pushed the miniature joystick, the flashing bent and whirled as if blown by a wind, and when it settled back down it was gray and green, blinking slightly faster.

He "played" until his head felt like it was about to split, and the light through the glass doors to his patio was the orange and purple of sunset. Then he gulped four Advil with the rest of his cold cup of tea, put a cold washcloth on his forehead, and lay on the sofa with his eyes closed. The modified console showed a "phase space," he recalled Kat telling him, where different co-ordinates showed different colors, shapes, and types of movements. What else had she told him? Very little about anything, he realized: most of their talk had been about him, which at the time had seemed natural. She certainly hadn't said anything that might give him a clue how to find her.

Except that she had told him where to meet her in lucid dreams if they ever got separated.

Of course, meeting her in a dream wouldn't really be meeting her. On top of that, he didn't dare lucid dream or do anything else that might further weaken his hold on reality. Though he wanted to, he knew as he drifted off to sleep on the couch.

Far out in Ontario, on some undefined boundary between the prairie and the settled lands, he had been let off on a little-used two-lane stretch of the TransCanada Highway, and Reginald was down a road that crossed the highway and ran off into the flat lands. Though it was midday, the sky was a misty whitish gray that made it seem no particular time at all. The air was still, and the temperature was neither warm nor cool, so that it seemed the weather had stopped, all the winds and pressures and temperatures canceling out to this still, neutral equilibrium.

Under normal circumstances, in the middle of the day and several hundred miles from his destination, Grant would have kept hitching, stood by the road next to his backpack with his thumb out to the occasional car or pickup that rattled past over the patched road with a blast of air and dust. But the utter repose of the light and weather seemed to make him dreamy and absent-minded, the muscles of worry and haste in his shoulders relaxing, as if time wasn't moving anyway, so why should he? The village under its huge old trees drew him, and he sauntered toward it.

There was a bridge over an irrigation canal sunk deep in its banks, whose still, greenish-brown water reflected his wondering face with only a small ripple, and behind him in still and greenish light that made it look vastly deep and sleepy, the world: clouds and rusty bridge beams, the branch of a tree. Pulling himself away, he turned toward the village, which, now that he had looked in the water, retained the sleepy, still look of its reflection. There was no one on the street beyond the bridge, where small houses and a few parked cars nestled under the trees.

A thought came to him.

A sign on the village side of the bridge said Bump. He looked away, then back. The letters said Kat.

A thrill of excitement went through him, and then he remembered everything in a cascade of shock, dread, and anger: the Trans-Humanist Institute, Kat, the brain damage, his search, the video game—

He felt himself simultaneously standing on the bridge and lying on the leather couch in his living room. Then he was awake, sitting up, breathing hard, the now-warm washcloth falling from his forehead.

It was dark now. He switched on a lamp and triple-read his watch to make sure he was really awake. It was midnight. He stood up and stretched, went over and turned on the TV, sat down on the rug and took up the controller. The dream had reenergized him. Though he wasn't sure what playing the game would do, it had apparently been part of Kat's and Thotmoses' program, presumably intended to produce some specific neurological effect, another of their "interventions." For that reason it was probably dangerous. But what was his alternative? Stay this way forever, crazy, alone, puzzled? Navigating the curling, flashing, stinging patterns at least he felt he was doing something, moving in some direction, instead of just sitting and waiting for something that would probably turn out to be nothing.

As he thought that, he swooped into an "area" where expanding emerald suns wavered, making his stomach turn over. His thumb rammed the joystick to get out of there, but then he stopped. Kat had urged him toward such nausea- and vertigo-inducing places. He reversed the stick, squinting against the stinging of his eyes and pounding of his head. The emerald suns elongated and undulated lazily on the screen, with little ripples on the ends, like plants waving in a breeze.

A fire ignited in his brain. The room flipped over and dived down into blackness.

But not before, with the utmost clarity, he saw a tall weed next to a chain-link fence waving and fluttering in a summer wind on a warm, sunny afternoon—

TWELVE

ON-RAMP

Grant woke up cold and stiff, head propped on his backpack, a rock digging into his back. Rows of dry yellow cornstalks stood around him, hiding everything but the cheerful early-morning sky directly above. He sat up. He could hear a high far whine of distance and speed, and the damp dirt-smelling air held a hint of exhaust: a highway was nearby.

He automatically glanced down to do a triple-read, but his thick brown wrist was bare. Of course; he hadn't worn a watch in his teens. There had been no need for it; hitchhiking got you where you were going in the time it took to get there; you flowed with the highway. So of course a lucid dream of his hitchhiking years wouldn't include a five-hundred-dollar Kenneth Cole watch.

He stood up, brushing dry dirt off his jeans and denim jacket, stamped his feet to get blood flowing. His breath steamed in the chilly air, but it would warm up as the sun got higher; it was summer, and even in these northern regions the days were warm. He was in Ontario, coming back from Vancouver; he and Sam had gotten separated in Thunder Bay when a car could take only one rider—

And he was on his way to the little town where Kat had promised to meet him, he realized with sudden excitement. But for once his excitement didn't start to wake him—there was no intrusion of the feeling of lying down, or any diminution in the clarity of the dream. He should wake himself up anyway, was his first thought; but the idea of going back to the claustrophobia of his house made him nauseous. He wouldn't wake up just yet, he decided, but smell the air of youth and freedom a bit more first. What harm could it do, since he was already here?

He had breakfast: a few tablespoons from his jar of peanut butter and a long drink of water from his plastic bottle. Then he pissed a small hollow of wet in the dirt, shouldered his backpack, and trudged between the head-high stalks toward the highway sound.

Twenty yards away, the cornfield ended, without fence or hedge, at a border of grass along the curve of a deserted on-ramp. He walked up the ramp, his worn boots scuffing the asphalt. A blinding yellow slice of sun on a horizon of pine trees shot rays through the fresh morning mist. This lucid dream was the kind that you couldn't distinguish from reality in the absence of a watch or similar tool, he saw, and then another thought struck him. He hadn't gone to sleep normally: he had lost consciousness while playing Kat's video game. Anxiety blossomed in his stomach, but he kept walking, to the top of the ramp, from where the four-lane highway faded into misty green landscape in both directions, a semi-truck barreling down the opposite lanes, its tires singing on the damp asphalt.

The rest of the morning was occupied with the business of

hitchhiking: deciding how far down the ramps to walk to maxi-mize your visibility yet leave a wide enough swath for cars to pull over, trying to decipher in the available seconds whether the drivers who did stop looked dangerous or drunk, making con-versation, watching for patrol cars in case the local police had the quaint habit of enforcing the anti-hitchhiking laws. He got a hundred-mile ride with a salesman, a two-hundred-mile ride with a trucker, and a thirty-mile ride with a middle-aged lady whose own son hitchhiked, and by evening he had made good progress. It wasn't until he was picked up by a college student who had been driving for twenty-four hours and needed to sleep, and until he was driving the kid's old Barracuda fast along the headlight-illuminated midnight highway, that he focused on the fact that his dream had gone on too long. By his reckoning it had been eighteen hours since he had woken up in the cornfield. REM time usually tracked waking time. There were exceptions, but now he started to wonder whether it had something to do with the video game, or his fainting rather than falling asleep.

There was something else strange too, now that he thought of it. He actually had *two* sets of memories. One tracked his progress at the Trans-Humanist Institute and included Kat, his big house in the suburbs, the turmoil over his condition, playing the video game, passing out; the other tracked his aimless teenage life, setting off from Vancouver, the dust and alertness of hitch-hiking, the changing scenery, highway raveling away beneath the wheels of cars and trucks, the people whose lives he entered for a few hours. The two sets of memories seemed to merge at the moment he had woken up in the cornfield—a lucid dream in re-lation to one set, a natural continuation in relation to the other. Had past lucid dreams been like this? he wondered anxiously. They must have been; probably he had just never noticed. The effect was subtle, because you were used to carrying so many stories in your mind even when awake. And the memories that led directly to the cornfield were from the hitchhiking adventures of his youth, and therefore not strange to him, but part of the normal furniture of his middle-aged mind, though pushed into the background by more recent things.

He should just close his eyes and go to sleep, which would wake him up again in the real world. He tried this momentarily a couple of times, but he couldn't bring himself to do it in a speeding car. When it was his turn to sleep in the back seat, he would wake up. He could always program a dream later to return and meet Kat if that was what he wanted to do.

He drove six hours, and then pulled over at a truck stop and woke the kid. They got breakfast and the kid drank four cups of coffee and took the wheel, Grant curling up in the back. The kid drove fast but steadily, and the rocking of the car soon lulled Grant to sleep.

It was stillness that woke him, an intrusive stillness that interrupted the humming and rocking. Grant opened his eyes. It was daytime, but he couldn't tell what hour; pale gray light came through the open driver's door along with a fresh, damp smell. He remembered right away where he was, his long body curled in the back seat of the Barracuda. He sat up, stretching his cramped legs out across the seat.

"End of the line, man," said a voice. The kid who had given him the ride was standing by the open door and stretching. "This is where I get off. Sorry."

Grant heard and felt the wind of a car rushing by. They were pulled over onto the shoulder a few yards from a faded stop sign where a side road met the highway.

"No problem, dude," he said, part of him wondering at the effortlessness with which he made this barbaric locution. He opened the door and got out stiffly, pulling his backpack after him. It felt good to stand up. He stretched so hard that joints in his arms and back cracked. Then he shook the kid's hand Black Power style. "I appreciate it," he said.

The kid got in the driver's seat and pulled away with a wave, the Barracuda's wheels spinning slightly in the crumbled asphalt and dirt of the shoulder, engine roaring. The car surged across the empty highway—which this far out in the country was two patched lanes—and accelerated down the side road, the sound of its engine fading slowly into silence after it disappeared over a rise.

Grant's expert eye identified this place at once as poor for hitchhiking: the shoulder was narrow and soft, and while the crossroad made it look like a legitimate stopping place, the highway came around a stand of trees barely fifty feet away, not giving folks time to slow down before they were long past and thinking it was a pity they hadn't seen him sooner.

Fifty yards down the side road on his side of the highway a rusty bridge crossed an irrigation canal. He had arrived at the village—Reginald—and the air was perfectly still and neutral, overhung by a flat, pale overcast.

It occurred to him suddenly that falling asleep in the back of the Barracuda hadn't woken him.

His heart started to beat rapidly. He stood by the stop sign as a car rushed rattling by, trying to ignore the wind and rush of tiny particles that stung his face, to feel his body lying in bed—or on the rug in front of his TV, rather—to help his pounding heart wake him. He stood that way for long minutes. But he didn't wake up.

He tried to calm himself. You always woke up sooner or later, and as dreams went, this wasn't an unpleasant one. He could go looking for a dream Kat in the dream town where she had promised to meet him. In fact, maybe that was why he couldn't wake up: maybe he had unconsciously programmed the dream to be a rendezvous with her, and his brain wouldn't let him go until that happened.

That was all the reason he needed for shouldering his pack and walking toward the bridge, the crunch and scuff of his boots loud in the stillness. His body felt strong, limber, and balanced, breathing the clean, humid air of long ago, sounds of the occasional car rushing along the highway receding behind him.

His boots clunked on the bridge, then stopped, leaving only the sound of a few birds singing their tranquil midday songs as he looked down into his face in the still, greenish-brown water of the canal. Those decades ago he had walked only a few blocks into the town and then turned back, eager to get a ride to Toronto before sunset, but a memory had lain uneasy in him long afterward. To what had he been in such a hurry to return? What might he have found if he had stayed?

He crossed the bridge and followed the short stretch of road to the first of the neighborhood streets. Someone long ago had planted oaks, and now they grew above the small houses in the quiet neighborhoods like low clouds. Far down the block a pale fat man in shorts and a T-shirt came out of his house to get his newspaper. A car passed slowly, an old man driving. After a few more blocks, Grant looked up and for a split second caught a face watching him from a window.

The house was small and white, with a little moss growing on its brick chimney from the tree dampness. His boots clunked up the steps to the porch just as Kat banged open the door and threw herself into his arms.

"You made it! Oh my God! You made it!"

She was wearing bell-bottom jeans and a belly shirt, and looked younger even than she had at his grandmother's house, barely pubescent.

Grant had imagined a hundred times what he would do to her if they ever met again, but her youth and enthusiasm disoriented him. He allowed her to pull him into the house. There were no lights on, and the small living room was dim, daylight through the windows and open front door gray with the deepening overcast. The heavy stillness of the air outside filled the house. There was a cold fireplace, a rug on the floor, a small upright piano against one wall, a sofa, a couple of end tables with framed pictures on them.

"God damn you," he gritted at her.

She looked up at him with a child's wild alarm.

"You fucked me up," he said, trying to tap the rage and fear from his vengeful fantasies. "You fucked me up and left me behind."

He could see her calming herself with an effort, like a grown-up calming a child. There was no doubt in his mind that she knew what he was talking about, that this thirteen-year-old dream girl remembered and was responsible for the sins of the twenty-five-year-old real-life version of herself. Her voice wavered a little as she said, "If you're so fucked up, how did you make it here?"

"Here where?"

"Here. This world."

"This is some kind of fucked-up lucid dream."

"Have you done your dream-tests? Triple-reads, spinning?"

"No. I don't have to."

"Do them."

She picked up a book from the sofa end table and handed it to him. Worn gold letters on the cloth binding said THE INNO-

CENTS ABROAD. He looked away, up at the ceiling, then squinted back at them; they still said THE INNOCENTS ABROAD. He looked past the plants in the window, out at the deepening gray light, the deep green of pines and hedges around the house. He looked at Kat watching him. Then he looked back at the book. THE INNOCENTS ABROAD. He tried again and a fourth time, and a fifth, with the same result.

"Try spinning," she said.

She stepped back to stand against the wall. He stared at her for a second, then turned himself quickly around and around in the middle of the room, on the rug. Faster and faster, until he felt dizzy, and things around him were a blur, and his attention was drawn inside, into his stomach and arms and legs, the tingling, whirling, unsteady sensation, and trying to keep his balance. When he stopped he was still in the living room, several copies of which seemed to be circling around him. He managed to pitch down onto the sofa. Spinning, which was the most effective way to stay in a dream when you were waking up, was also the most effective way to change dream scenes, and nearly always worked if you gave it a couple of tries. As soon as he could, he stood up and spun again, closing his eyes this time to facilitate disengagement from the current sensorium, until he fell over something and banged his head on the fireplace, almost knocking himself unconscious.

Hands were holding his head, and as soon as he could focus he saw Kat crouched over him giggling uncontrollably.

He dragged himself up to sit against the wall. She caressed his head, cooing and laughing by turns. Then he pushed her aside and stood up and spun again, drunkenly, ignoring her protests. This time after only a few turns he sprawled on the rug, arms flailing to keep himself from hitting anything, and Kat collapsed again into her teenage giggles.

"Try machines and lights," she suggested, trying to be serious, not very successfully.

He got up unsteadily and turned on a lamp on the end table. It threw a circle of yellow light on the floor and ceiling. He tried the floor lamp, turned it on and off a few times. It worked perfectly, like a real light instead of a dream light. He went through a doorway into a small kitchen whose windows looked out on a backyard with foot-high crabgrass and an ancient, leaning shed. There was an electric can-opener on the counter, and canned food in one of the cupboards. Kat leaned in the doorway to the living room, watching him.

He opened a can of tuna. The can-opener blade even slipped off once in the middle and he had to stop and put the can back in properly, just like with a real can-opener. He put the open can down on the counter.

"Are you hungry?" she asked, coming forward. "Do you want a tuna sandwich?"

"You did something to make me dream like this," he mumbled. "You and Thotmoses. Why? What did you do to me? What did you do?" His voice rose to a shrill sob, and he faced her, fists clenched, the muscles in his arms knotted.

She stepped back, trying not to be scared. "We freed you," she said. "That's what you wanted."

"What I wanted?" he screamed. "I didn't want to go crazy! I didn't want to lose my mind! You fucking bitch," he snarled, and grabbed her small wrist.

She kicked him in the crotch.

When he could see again, he was down on his knees, both hands holding his testicles, and he noticed the toes of her small work boots and the pattern in the linoleum. He looked at her through watering eyes, crouching next to him, her face pale.

"This is the weird part," she said. "But you're smart. Think about it. What's the difference between reality and a dream that goes on and on? And what if there are only dreams like that, every one just as real as the others?"

"I need to lie down."

She helped him hobble to the sofa, and put a pillow under his head. He was tall enough so that he had to rest his feet on the opposite armrest. He worried vaguely that his boots would get it dirty.

He had a bad dream. He had been having a good dream, but when he woke, he couldn't get up, and found, after a few tries, that his wrists and ankles were held somehow. He lifted his head and looked at himself. He had on blue pajamas, and wide black straps held him to a bed with rails along both sides. There was a horrible smell, like a mixture of excrement and cleaning fluid.

A scream next to him made him shout with fear. As soon as the fear cleared out of his eyes, he saw that he was in a long room with half a dozen hospital beds along each side. People were lying in them. The man in the bed next to him had screamed. He was also strapped down, but he was writhing. If the writhing had been desperate, if the man had been desperately trying to get out of his straps, it wouldn't have been so bad. But instead the writhing was rhythmic, purposeful, as if the man was doing some kind of bizarre religious ritual, his body bulging and arching grotesquely, like a human-shaped bag of snakes. His bulged-out eyes circled endlessly, and his tongue was a pink, wet, trembling worm circling in his wide-open mouth, as if being born from some squamous nest.

He screamed again, his tongue sticking far out and vibrating, as if it were the worm that screamed that purposeful, mindless scream, as if it were part of a task the worm had set for itself, but a task utterly insane, unconscious, like the twitch of a dead frog's leg. Then the man started writing again, a temple of snakes.

They had found him, Grant realized. He had gone insane from the brain damage. Maybe Dr. Taggart had reported him, or maybe they had found him wandering in those neighborhoods where he had thought he was looking for Kat's house—or maybe he had never even gotten that far, but had come out of Thotmoses' "treatment room" a raving lunatic, and all the rest had been delusion, hallucination, dream. But however it had happened, he had been put away. Sick despair filled him. Maybe this was St. Elizabeth's State Psychiatric Hospital, which everyone knew stood huge and soot-stained in the slums on the old side of the city, but which no one talked about, and from which people rarely emerged. He looked up at the stained ceiling tiles and started to cry. Then he closed his eyes again, desperately, to block out the sight of his new life, and lost consciousness.

He woke up on the sofa, soaked in sweat and gasping with animal relief. It was night, and the mutter of thunder and the sound and smell of rain came through the open front door, but no lights were on. He was cold, he realized, despite the sweat. He lay waiting for his heart to slow down, but as his brain gradually began to engage, a terrible thought came to him. He sat up, feeling sick. "Kat?"

Her voice from the armchair a few feet away made him jump. "I'm here." In the faint glow from the window he could see her shadowed face, the gleam of her hair.

"Jesus," he said, putting his face into his hands. "Jesus." He didn't know whether it was a prayer or an expression of despair. A gust of wind brought a few tiny chill drops through the window screen, and thunder muttered again. It all seemed so real. He tried to keep his voice steady. "Kat, what is happening? What did you and your father do to me? And"—he choked on the words—"where am I really?"

"You're here," she said, her child's voice sweet in the dark. "In a house. At night. In the town where we agreed to meet."

"No." His voice was trembling now. "There is no 'here.' Look at me." He looked down at his body in the dark. "I haven't been like this since I was twenty. I'm forty-nine years old. And this isn't a dream; dreams don't last for days, and it's failed all the tests."

"It's no more a dream than your other life."

"What did you do to me?"

"We changed your brain to change your life. Like we said we would."

"But not by—by fucking it up. You didn't tell me you would do that."

"You wouldn't have gone through with it if we had. And it's only a little tiny bit fucked up. It's like breaking a lock so you can open a door."

"What did you do?"

"Ask my dad. He decided your seizures weren't strong enough; all they did was put you into a kind of trance. He gave you something to make them a little stronger. The game I made you play helped us figure out exactly what you see when you have the seizures. That helped him know when the drug was working, because it made you see that. It's from a kind of sea sponge. The drug, I mean."

"But for Christ's sake, why?"

She was silent for a minute, and then her soft, light voice said, "Imagine there are other worlds just like the one you used to live in. Billions and trillions of them. Imagine you can go from one to another just like you can in dreams."

But an overwhelming nausea and despair had come over Grant.

"I have a different story," he said, his voice trembling, shrill. "Not quite as nice or mystical, but it has the virtue of being true. You and your father—I shouldn't even say 'you,' because you're just a hallucination now, or some kind of dream figure—the person you are modeled on and her father are some kind of murderous schizos. You poisoned my brain so I would go crazy, and I've been completely dissociated from reality for who knows how long, and hallucinating about searching for you and finding myself in another world—I can't even put my finger on exactly when I lost it—but anyway, right now I'm in a ward in a mental hospital, strapped to a bed and hallucinating that I've found another world where I'm young again, and where I've found you—"

"That's a house you can visit if you want," said Kat levelly from the darkness. "It's just as real as any of them. And you're setting up a visit to it by what you're saying, explaining it to yourself, picturing it, believing in it. But why do you want—?"

"Liar!" Grant screamed, leaping to his feet. "God damn you!" In two steps he had her in the large, strong hands of his young body. "God damn you, I should kill you. I should kill you," he slavered, teeth grinding in rage. He yanked her out of the chair and twisted her backward, her body fragile like a birdcage of bone and flesh, back arched and shoulders twisted painfully backward, pale, delicate throat taut, her hands on his arms clawed in pain. Her face close to his in the dark was the face of a tortured, terrified child.

He let go of her, and she fell back in the chair. She lay sprawled, eyes half-open, head lolling back, as if she had fainted.

"You're only a fucking dream, anyway," he muttered.

He went back and lay down on the couch.

"What are you doing?" Her voice was a sobbing whisper.

"I have to wake up. If I choose to stop hallucinating, maybe that's a first step. Maybe I can get better, go back. . . ."

THIRTEEN

St. Elizabeth

St. Elizabeth's Psychiatric Hospital was more like purgatory than hell: with enough effort you could move from the lower circles to the higher; you could even get out if you played your cards right. By the time Grant had become coherent enough to understand this he had also learned that he had been involuntarily committed, the police having found him wandering somewhere ranting and shrieking. This meant that any release decision was in the hands of the doctors. As Grant remembered from a couple of pro bono commitment cases he had handled, the doctors in turn relied heavily on reports from the staff to make their decisions, so it was the staff—the overworked, gray-faced nurses and high school–dropout orderlies—with whom you had to ingratiate yourself.

Acting sane was not the key to doing this, he soon discovered—if you could even reconstruct what "sane" meant after being at St. Elizabeth's for a week. If you acted like a sane person would if strapped hand and foot in a stinking ward full of psychos, they would come and give you a shot and check your bindings. No, you couldn't act sane. The key was to be *docile*. Docility was what got you rewarded at St. Elizabeth's; in fact, docility seemed to be the institution's entire agenda. All the treatments were focused on it, from what they called physical restraints to electroshock, drugs, cognitive psychotherapy, and withholding rewards like sitting in the TV lounge.

Once Grant figured this out, his progress from the "restraints ward" to the TV lounge was swift. He stopped struggling against his straps. He never argued. He was always quiet. He was always grateful. He always abased himself before staff, and was polite to his psychiatry resident.

She was a thin, tired-looking young woman named Dr. Gani. She sent Grant for workups, scans, and tests, and a week later sat with him in a small consulting room that had posters of soothing outdoor scenes on the windowless walls. She studied him in his street clothes, neatly shaved for the occasion. He tried to relax and look as though the outcome of this interview wasn't life or death. He wasn't even tempted to flirt with her, though this might have been partly his medication regimen.

"How are you feeling?"

"Pretty good."

"Any voices, strange smells, anything like that?" He couldn't remember the exact name of his diagnosis, but he knew it had the word "delusional" in it.

"No. Not in a while." He could have been a rodeo cowboy talking to his doctor about injuries from a fall—patient, indifferent to the pain, eager to get back on the horses.

"Bad dreams?"

"No. They've been hazy—I can barely remember them."

She made a note in his chart. "That's the Xanax. Any side effects from your medication? Dullness, sleepiness, flat emotions?"

"A bit of dullness," said Grant, hoping he sounded casual. He fought back the urge to add that it didn't bother him, in case that sounded forced. Just let me the fuck out of here, he thought.

Dr. Gani nodded as if he had given a right answer, making a mark somewhere on the chart.

"All right," she said finally. "Your tests came back, and you seem to be coping well with your condition. I'm going to recommend that you be treated on an outpatient basis."

"Hooray," Grant said, grinning with casual excitement, like someone who had been told that his home baseball team had won a game.

The next day, after two weeks in St. Elizabeth's, half of which he didn't remember, he opened the hospital's street door unsupervised and stepped out into the cold, fresh air.

Under a low overcast, the squalid street of run-down brownstones seemed dazzlingly beautiful. A couple of ramshackle taxis were parked at the curb, apparently to catch the occasional recovered psycho. It was an hour's jouncing, squeaking drive to Grant's upscale suburb, throughout which the pock-faced driver maintained a neutral silence. Grant guessed that his experience on the nut shift had taught him not to fraternize.

The sight of his own neighborhood, the gentle hills, wide lawns, big houses powdered with snow among the dripping trees—then his own street, yellow leaves plastered on the smooth black asphalt under an iron-gray sky—and finally his *own house*— filled his chest with warmth and his eyes with tears, and he gave the driver a big tip, which still failed to move him to speech.

A few birds sang their soft snow songs, and water spanged in a downspout from snow melting on the roof. Two weeks' worth of newspapers lay on the driveway. Grant gathered them up, holding them by the ends of their plastic bags like a brace of pheasants. He could smell the wet mulch under his bushes, and then he was unlocking the front door—his own front door!—and stepping into the house over the heap of envelopes under the mail slot. A feeling of quietude and seclusion and blessed repose came over him as he shut the door. The house smelled faintly of firewood and leather furniture. He could feel tension draining away, his shoulders and neck relaxing. After two weeks in purgatory, earth seemed like heaven.

He dropped the newspapers on the slate tiles, wiped his feet, gathered up his mail, and went into the kitchen, sorting through it reflexively. Electric bill, phone bill, cable bill, junk mail from a supermarket, a health club, a lawn care company: the greetings of blessed uneventfulness, letters from the serene paradise of the mundane. He stood in the kitchen just looking around, at the clean counter, dishes all put away in the white cabinets, the window above the sink showing a broad swatch of snow-spotted lawn that ended in a screen of trees: beyond their nearly denuded branches he could make out the house next door, smoke rising from its chimney.

He tossed his mail on the counter and walked into the dining room, the living room, then upstairs to the bedrooms and his big master bathroom. It was all empty, as he had known it would be. Nevertheless, without the drugs Dr. Gani had prescribed—Xanax for his dreams, carbamazepine for the seizures, clozapine for the hallucinations—he supposed he would have been afraid to return here by himself, afraid of the noises he thought he had heard, the things he thought he had seen.

Thinking about those things, a dull blare arose in his stomach, a feeling that, stripped of layers of drug-numbness, would probably have been fear, but which in this form felt merely like some distant physical sensation—hunger, perhaps. He quieted his breathing and listened. The only sounds were the barely audible hush of the central-air system and a faint pattering at the window that told him it had started to sleet.

After a month going twice a week to a downtown psychiatrist, Grant felt good enough to go back to work, and his return was touching to him even in his quasi-drugged state. Everyone seemed glad to see him, and happy that he had recovered from what most seemed to think had been a bout of alcoholism or drug addiction. He sat torpid in his large, handsome office, at his big oak desk, and watched the river through his floor-to-ceiling windows, the wind occasionally blowing a crest of white on its iron-gray surface. In his office all was bright and still and quiet.

He roused himself and looked through his mail. Nothing important: a few pleadings he would farm out to some associates, a bill for his business credit card, some early Christmas catalogs. These last reminded him that he would need a girlfriend for Christmas: someone to snuggle on the cold evenings before the big day, to buy and wrap presents for, and look forward to presents from, to buy a tree with, get drunk with on Christmas Eve, and then sit cross-legged with in a welter of torn wrappings the next morning, excited as children, drinking hot coffee. The challenge, as he had discovered, was that women old enough to afford good presents were rarely young enough to be exciting snugglers, and vice versa. He would have to start his shopping early, he reflected, to find as good a product as possible.

What worried him, though, was that his desire for a girlfriend didn't seem nearly as strong as it should; his medications seemed to have calmed that hunger along with everything else. Sometimes he felt swaddled in a kind of invisible cotton wool, as if his perceptions of things came a second late and muted with distance, so that the sensation of delay and remoteness distracted him from the things themselves. Then his look became glazed and there was a pause before he answered people, so that he fit the stereotype of a drugged mental case—not an auspicious state for a seducer. In honest moments he even wondered whether he wouldn't rather just spend a relaxed Christmas alone this year. Except what was the point of a man's life if he lost interest in women? Who was he then?

He had tried to work around the drugs with coffee, exercise, and "reconnecting" to his old activities, as Dr. York, his outpatient psychiatrist, called it; but he hadn't felt up to tackling any really challenging cases yet. He knew that if this went on he could always join the ranks of Senior Counsel, mostly older partners who had lost the fire in their bellies, who worked light hours supervising routine matters without too much sweat or excitement, and whose salaries—though still tremendous by most standards—reflected their reposeful status. But what would be left of him if he lost his edge, his lust to win, which had given him a reputation as a top-flight lawyer? Who would he be then?

Some rest and relaxation in a land where nothing was very important was what he had needed, he knew. But he wasn't ready yet to let go of the struggles around which he had built his life, and without which he would be no different from an old man. In this state of mind, his uncertainty about whether he even wanted a Christmas girlfriend was the straw that vaguely affected the camel's back. He began asking Dr. York when he could get off his drugs. Dr. York looked upon the question with approval. Antipsychotics and anticonvulsants weren't something you wanted to stay on permanently if you didn't have to, and Grant's attitude signaled returning health.

Tapering the drugs was like coming awake very slowly. He got up in the morning and opened his window, and the damp smell of earth and dead leaves brought a feeling from long ago, when he had walked in the countryside around his grandmother's house in autumn rain for hours, humming to himself under an umbrella. Or a face on a crowded sidewalk brought a jolt of nostalgia for an old girlfriend, the smiling eyes and dimples, the long, pale hands haunting him for just a moment, to be lost again in the crowd. One night he had a dream—not a lucid dream, but a memory from when he was a very small boy, when he and his friend had walked to a candy store in a town where the sidewalks rose and fell over impossibly steep hills, at the tops of which fairytale clouds floated through a blue sky, and the air was hushed, like the air at the tops of mountains, with nothing around but unechoing sky, the sunlight bright and serene. The candy store was elderly and small, but sunlight and quiet made it exquisite. A bell on the door jingled dryly as they entered. Inside, a display case showed little balls in pastel colors piled on trays. The shop man was very tall and gray. Davey took a long time, moving back and forth along the glass from one small pyramid of colored spheres to another. Finally the old shop man laughed and went into the back of the store, and came back holding a small blue sphere in a pair of tongs. He held it out, and looking closely, Davey saw that it was a tiny replica of outer space: a billion tiny sparks spinning in luminous blackness. When he woke from this dream he had such a keen desire to see that street and town again that he was afraid and almost called Dr. York. But the feeling faded quickly, leaving him back in his quiet, clean, Euclidean house, things taking their proper dimensions again.

Finally, after an anxious couple of weeks, his fear of dreams gradually subsided, and he was able to wholeheartedly welcome the feeling that he was gradually emerging from a kind of trance.

Yet reputation lags behind reality, and at work he was still the unfortunate senior partner whose recent bout with alcoholism had left him distracted and fragile. That was probably why Stan Laskey came to him with the Willows case and private investigator Allan Norris. The Willows assignment was important but simple, requiring lawyer work but not exhausting lawyer work. Laskey, a thin, humorless Midwesterner with iron-gray hair and suspenders, was busy, and Grant wasn't, so it was a perfect match.

As Laskey described the case in his twanging monotone, the sky above the river was a deep gray green that muttered with thunder, and wind whipped the tops of the nearly bare trees. A few large raindrops hit Grant's windows, but it hadn't begun to pour yet. Where Grant, Laskey, and Norris sat, on the other side of the glass, it was still and bright, tranquil and warm. Like the architectural equivalent of clozapine, Grant thought idly, keeping everything sleepy and bright inside.

Indifferent to the metaphors around him, Laskey told Grant that a man named Lanscomb had written some memos to his boss complaining about certain accounting practices at the Willows Corporation. These practices had eventually led to the collapse of the company, leaving behind several hundred million dollars of worthless stock and a seemingly equal number of furious stockholders. Lanscomb had been interviewed off the record by some of Laskey's associates, and had told them things that were music to their ears, but when they came back with a deposition notice and a court reporter, Lanscomb had departed for parts unknown. Laskey wanted Lanscomb to come back and bear witness on behalf of his clients, and he wanted Grant, supervising the inquiring Norris, to make that happen.

After Laskey had left, Grant and Norris leaned over a map that Norris spread out on the conference table. It showed every village and country road east of the city to the state line, the region where Lanscomb had been born and grown up. Norris's professional view was that someone fleeing a "situation" would go to ground in such territory.

"Parents' home," said Norris, putting a blunt brown finger on a crooked line leading to a dot at the confluence of some other crooked lines in a wide, green part of the map. Small letters next to the dot said "Mumford." "He might even be there," said Norris. "I mean, he's not in trouble or anything. He just doesn't want to rat out his buddies."

"How do we find him?"

"We go out there and start asking questions, and leave the impression on people's minds that this man is going to be in a lot of trouble if he doesn't show himself. Sooner or later the word will get to him, and he'll show himself. Then you'll be there to persuade him to come back."

After Norris left, Grant pored over the map idly, looking at the wide green spaces with the crooked lines and vaguely imagining the cornfields and country roads, the country gas stations and Mini-Marts, rain falling far and wide over hills, woods, and fields—

He caught himself with a start. He wasn't supposed to daydream, indulge his penchant for floating off into fantasy. He and Dr. York had agreed that sometimes he allowed fantasies to seduce him, and that he had to exercise control, interrupt them as soon as he became aware he was having one. He looked around the office, trying to ground himself. He was working on Laskey's Willows Corporation case, and he had a small pile of documents to read so he would know what to say to the fugitive Lanscomb when they found him. He shifted his weight in the chair, put his feet on the desk, and picked up the first document on the pile with a contented sigh.

FOURTEEN

THE OCEAN

Mumford was a village with no accommodations suitable for a senior lawyer and his investigator, so Grant and Norris stayed in St. Clair. Grant, having prepared with Dr. York, stayed calm at the airport and studiously ignored familiar-looking landmarks as Norris drove their rented car through town. He would rather have stayed somewhere else, but St. Clair was only ten miles from Mumford and had a Holiday Inn. The bed in Grant's fourth-floor room was too soft, but he fell asleep anyway around midnight after watching a pay movie on the TV.

It must have been toward morning when he had a dream. In the first part of it he was looking at a map—not the kind he and Norris had pored over, but the folding kind gas stations sell. It was the map he had carried so many years ago as a hitchhiker: he recognized its creases and stains, the thick red and thinner blue lines that had been so important to him. Studying it, he was suddenly filled with a yearning, as if the map were a talisman that could transport him back to his youth if he could only travel its roads. One of the lines, a blue one, ran to a town marked "St. Clair" on the seacoast a hundred miles from the city. As he could see clearly from the map, St. Clair, with its gulls and sea breezes, its lazy summer afternoons full of the cool green smell of the sea, its weathered wooden porches and towering clouds, existed across a vast divide from the city, not only geographical, but across a gulf of *stories*. Once he moved there, he would never be able to return. The people he knew, the places and things, his qualifications, degrees, money, everything would be gone, irretrievable; he would start over as a teenager, sleeping in a room over someone's garage and mowing lawns or cleaning swimming pools for a living. But the yearning was too strong to resist. He could smell that air, hear the seagulls' cries, feel the vast calmness of the ocean, the strength and eternity of youth.

The dream changed, and he was standing just outside a low chain-link fence that surrounded a public garden. The world was sunny and windy around him. Growing just by the fence, as if missed by the mowers, was a tall weed. His attention was drawn to it. Perhaps it was the way it moved when the wind blew over it, but he had a momentary fancy that it was a sentient thing, which the wind, like a spirit, made intelligent. He stood perfectly still, watching the weed wave back and forth, seduced by its sleepy, unhurried motion, the wind playing over his face, vaguely aware that he was sinking but too absorbed in the exquisiteness of it to break away.

And then he remembered: he had seen this weed before, he had been here before, exactly here, watching it move in the wind. He remembered: the little path and the fence, the garden, the wind, and the tall weed stirring, stirring . . . He fell, it seemed, into unconsciousness.

Then he was in his room at the St. Clair Holiday Inn, and he was filled with exultation. He had done it! He had given up everything and made the move, come to find the new life!—and at that moment he became lucid and realized he was dreaming.

An icicle of fear went through him, and he willed himself to wake up. He felt his body lying among the rumpled hotel sheets and blankets, and as he did, memory returned. He was in the small town of St. Clair on work; there was no coastline a hundred miles from the city. In fact, there was no coastline for several states over: the maps showed a vast green landlocked state with only a few lakes. There was no new life waiting for him: the cries of seagulls and lazy summer days were remote, unreachable; not only because he didn't have time for beach holidays, but because the yearning he had felt was a yearning for things as a young man would see and feel them, as he couldn't do anymore. There was no divide you could cross to find a new life, to leave behind all the necessities and compromises of this one and start again. That was the greatest delusion of all, he thought sadly as he opened his eyes to the gray light coming through the crack between the curtains.

He switched on the bedside lamp, turned off the alarm before it beeped, and stumped into the bathroom. He studied himself in the pitiless fluorescent light over the mirror, bleary-eyed, hair disordered, skin pouchy with sleep—and realized that he was seeing himself old, the way he would look in a few years. Children were rosy and fresh when they woke from sleep; people his age were under a different influence, drawn to the cold outer planets. In a few years this would be all that was left of his good looks and charm, this spoiled-looking lump of meat, shoulders hunched, belly sticking out, and there would be no more chance of seducing young women, and almost worse than that, he wouldn't even care.

After a shower he felt and looked better. He dried his hair, shaved, and put on his starched shirt and dark suit while half-watching the TV news. He was supposed to meet Norris in the hotel restaurant at eight, and then they would start their bush-beating.

Done knotting his tie, Grant pulled open the heavy floor-to-ceiling curtains that blocked out morning light for the business traveler. The sunlight on his small balcony was misty; looking farther out, his eyes fell on a scene that he did not at first recognize.

It took him a few seconds to realize that this was because he was looking at something much farther away than he had expected. Half a mile away, the far bank of a river stood green and hazy in the morning mist. A rusty-looking railroad bridge ran across it, and beyond that the river's brownish-green water flowed into the calm gray-green water of the ocean, leaving a brownish track as it trailed away up the coast with the current.

With trembling hands, Grant pushed open the sliding glass door and went out on the balcony. Yes, there was no mistaking it, stretching gray green, calm, and vast into the mist without a hint of ending, far past the hazy end of a long pier, seabirds crying and wheeling tiny above the river mouth, the smell of water tanged with seaweed and silt.

His mind whirling, Grant went back into the room and opened the faux-leather binder with the room service menu. At the top of the first page was the name ST. CLAIR HOLIDAY INN and the address. He went back out onto the balcony and stared around, heart pounding, waiting for an answer to come to him. And then one did, and he grabbed the balcony railing, afraid of falling. He stumbled back into the room and tried to use the telephone, but his hands trembled too much, and a dizzy nausea rose in him. Finally he crawled into the bed.

And an hour later, having gotten an assistant manager with a passkey, that was where Norris found him, curled up under the covers in his suit and tie, trembling and mumbling to himself.

"So seeing the ocean disturbed you," said Dr. Gani, encouraging him with a nod to talk about that.

Grant was in his hospital pajamas and robe, sitting in the residents' office at St. Elizabeth's. He was back on clozapine and all the other things he had been on the first time, and the sticky web of neurochemistry that held back his hallucinations and fear also made it difficult to organize his thoughts. He focused on Dr. Gani's lips, which had just gotten done speaking. He was sleepy, his mind dry as dust.

"Yes," he said, the word coming out of him with an effortlessness that surprised him.

"Why?"

He concentrated. "Upset me seeing it *there*."

"Why was that?"

"Because"—he became cautious, not wanting to seem crazy—"I didn't think the ocean should be there."

"You didn't think the ocean should be there."

"The maps—," he said before he could stop himself. He didn't want her to think he still thought the maps showed a land-locked state with the city in the middle of it. Though that was what he remembered. Didn't he?

"The maps—what?"

"I thought I—remembered them showing St. Clair in the middle of the state. In the middle of the country."

"So St. Clair being on the coast upset you, is that what you're saying? You saw the ocean and thought you were hallucinating?"

"I guess so. Yes."

"What do you think now?"

There was only one right answer to that. "St. Clair is on the coast."

"And you said you were having a dream just before you woke up that the state was landlocked and that St. Clair was in the middle of this landlocked state."

"Yes. Well, first I thought it was on the coast, and then I seemed to remember that it wasn't."

Dr. Gani opened her desk drawer and rummaged in it, pulled out a map, unfolded it clumsily, and smoothed it down with her small, vulnerable doctor's hand. The part she had exposed showed a long uneven coastline verging on the blue that maps use to show water. The city was about a hundred miles inland, on a winding blue line that reached the ocean at a tiny white circle with the words "St. Clair" next to it. The state wasn't landlocked; it was a coastal state, about two-thirds the size Grant thought he remembered. He couldn't remember it that way, he corrected himself. It was some kind of delusion.

"Yes," said Grant after pretending to study the map.

"Do you think it's possible," suggested Dr. Gani, "that the dream temporarily confused you about where St. Clair was, and when you woke up and looked out your hotel window, the sight of the ocean made you think you were hallucinating, and you panicked?"

"I think that's what happened." Except for the fact that he thought he remembered maps showing St. Clair as landlocked, and visiting St. Clair when it was a country town in the middle of a vast farmland, and a whole life in which the state was landlocked. But he couldn't remember those things, he knew. And even as he told himself this, he realized that along with the landlocked memory he also remembered the state being on the coast, spending a week at a St. Clair beach house every summer with his parents, taking weekend trips to the beach with girlfriends, hearing the shipping weather on the local news—

"I do too," said Dr. Gani. "I think that's just what happened. I think your previous experiences have understandably put you on a hair trigger. I would have been shocked too if I woke up in a place I thought was landlocked and looked out the window and saw the ocean. There are two differences, though. First, you have more of a tendency than most people to believe that your dreams are real, to confuse dreams with reality. We see that kind of thing a lot in people with narcolepsy—sleeping sickness. Their brains have trouble separating waking and sleep, and sometimes they go directly from REM sleep to waking without a transition. When that happens, their dreams can continue into waking in the form of hypnagogic hallucinations, which they may experience as real. They might think their house is on fire, or the telephone is ringing, or that they can fly through the air—these events are so seamlessly merged with their waking perceptions that they experience them as completely real. So if someone else had woken up after dreaming the town was landlocked and then looked out the window, they might have had a greater ability to say 'Oh, I was dreaming it was landlocked.' A person with hypnagogic hallucinations might really believe the town was landlocked. The problem can be addressed with some new drugs that have recently come out, and by you continuing your cognitive therapy, to maintain your clarity about what is real and what isn't.

"Second, though, is the element of panic. All I can say about that is, when you think you're starting to have a hallucination, take it easy. Don't panic. Call me or your psychiatrist, or a friend if you need help driving or something like that. If you panic like you did at the hotel, people are going to *think* you're crazy, and then you may end up back here." She gave him a quick smile, seeing that he was with her on this. "If you feel out of control, just sit down for a while and think. Have you had a dream you're confusing with reality? Have you forgotten something and just been reminded of it? Or are you actually hallucinating, in which case all that will happen is that we'll increase your medication and maybe have you come to outpatient more often. Right?"

"Right," said Grant, still not all the way through her speech. She waited for him to catch up. "So you mean I have narcolepsy?"

"No, I don't think so. Your polysomnograph doesn't show the wave forms, though it is somewhat abnormal. And you haven't had any tendency to suddenly get muscle weakness or abruptly fall asleep during the day, have you?"

"No."

"Good. Something about the brain damage you suffered mimics some of the symptoms of narcolepsy, so I'm going to prescribe modafinil, which is the new drug I mentioned, and keep you in here for a couple of days for observation, but you can have your own clothes and you'll have a pass for the TV room. Okay?"

FIFTEEN

LECTURES

Grant's second return to work a week later was different from the first. People were just as friendly, but somehow Grant resented it now. Maybe it was his new medication, which made him feel wide awake, even a bit hopped-up—or perhaps the elite strike force camaraderie of the law firm had been subtly replaced as to him. People glanced at him out of the corners of their eyes as he passed in the halls. He was now considered a liability, he realized, even by the lowest workroom assistant. He was the lawyer who had gone crazy while out on a simple assignment; a delicious story, but one with a predictable trajectory. He was a drag on the firm now, and so ultimately would have to be dealt with, because this was not a charitable institution. While officially still a senior partner, in reality he was no longer a power, which meant that people had little incentive to piety toward him. They relaxed where he was concerned: they were friendly out of the kindness of their hearts, which meant sympathetic. At some half-conscious level, he registered with surprise how much he had come to take for granted the friendliness of people who had financial motives to be friendly.

He sat in his office studying the map Allan Norris had brought him before their trip to St. Clair. It clearly showed St. Clair on the coast. And he remembered it being on the coast his whole life. Yet he also remembered—in a kind of memory double-exposure—a broad landlocked state colored green, covered with the squiggly lines of roads, highways, and rivers, and St. Clair near the middle, not so much as a lake nearby. But he *couldn't* remember that, of course; the hypnagogic hallucinations had implanted the "memory" in his mind, in the space of a few seconds had suggested the traces of a history going back his whole life.

He sat brooding for a few more minutes, but that wouldn't do. The new drug Dr. Gani had prescribed for him was a modern kind of amphetamine, also used to keep air force pilots awake during long missions. It didn't blow your mind like the obsolete stimulants, being designed to tuck into just the right neuronal receptors, but at the same time it didn't allow you to sit around half-asleep all day. He had to find out exactly what was happening to him, he told himself. Without denying that he had been crazy as a bedbug, he needed another perspective. He put on his coat, told Pam he was leaving for the day, and went down to the parking garage for his car.

The State University's Psychology Department was housed in a monumental neoclassical building that future archeologists might mistake for an enormous funerary shrine, set back from the sidewalk up dozens of shallow stone steps. Inside, the ceilings were lofty and hung with massive metal chandeliers, but the floors were worn faux-marble and the halls were lined with narrow lockers, showing that someone had realized after all that students were going to swarm over the place. Up two flights of stairs and around several corners, in a quiet, out-of-the-way part of the building, were faculty offices behind wide wooden doors with old-fashioned pebbled glass panels. Grant searched until he found one marked RICHARD DARLING, PH.D., and knocked gently.

There was no response. He knocked again with the same result, but he thought he heard a movement within. He opened the door and poked his head in.

A small man looked up from a desk, which was turned endways to the wall so that he could see both the door and the view out a large window. The desk was clear; and the man, his eyes sleepy and calm, had apparently been just sitting with his hands clasped on top of it.

"Professor Darling?"

"Yes?" Professor Darling gave him a wide beatific smile, for all the world as if he had been waiting for Grant instead of ignoring his knocks. He was small and slight, with a thick shock of gray hair, jet black eyes, and a deeply lined face, but his smile was young and almost giggly, as if Grant were looking at a sixty-year-old little boy.

"Sorry to bother you," said Grant, opening the door wider. "I'm not a student or anything."

"I can see that," said Darling approvingly.

"I—you're Richard Darling the psychologist, right? The one who writes books about how the human mind decides what's real?"

"Ah-ha!" said the man, as if he had suspected this. Then he giggled, apparently pleased with himself, and asked: "What can I do for you?"

"I—I'm having a problem deciding what's real."

"Mm. Then you need a psychiatrist. I just write books. I wouldn't know what to do with a real live person."

"Well, could I ask you a couple of questions? I already have a psychiatrist and I'm on medication, so you don't have to worry about that. What I'm wondering about is more in the realm of— well, the realm of what is possible and what is impossible. Theoretically."

"Theoretically, everything is possible and nothing is impossible," said Darling, gesturing to a chair in front of the desk. "There, does that answer your question?" He laughed delightedly.

The chair was the welded metal kind with vinyl upholstery that all universities seemed to have bought wholesale in the 1950s. The office was large but plain, the desk of the same gray metal provenance as the chair, and there were bookshelves and a coat stand. The only hint of luxury was the view: a vast lawned quadrangle with mature trees, a few students walking along sidewalks in the weak March sunlight.

"Yes, I agree," said Grant politely, smiling also and sitting down. "But descending to a slightly less theoretical level, can I ask you—I guess my question is really how much you can trust your senses and memory—more really, I guess, how much you can trust your feelings, your instinct that something—a place or a situation, for example—is real. That wasn't very clear, I guess, but—"

"Close one eye," said Darling. He closed one of his own to demonstrate.

Relieved to be rescued from his question, Grant closed one eye.

"What do you see?" Darling asked, his open eye looking at the desk, the window, and Grant.

"Your office," said Grant, looking around too. "You. The window."

"Do you see a hole near the center of your vision? A blank spot?"

"No."

"Funny, isn't it? I can't see one either. But it's there. Where your optic nerve is attached to your cornea there are no light-sensitive cells, so you have a blind spot in the field of vision in both your eyes. When you have them both open, the blind spots are overlapped by vision from the other eye, but when you only have one open, there's a significant area in your field of vision where you simply can't see." Darling looked around some more with his one eye, as if trying to flush out the blind spot, then opened both eyes and looked at Grant, smiling. Grant opened his eye too. "Know why you don't see a blank spot? Even though it's there?"

"No."

"Because your brain is seeing not what comes into your eyes, but a model it has built based on what comes into your eyes. Now close both your eyes."

Grant did that.

"Do you remember what my office looks like? What is to your left?"

"A window."

"And outside the window?"

"A quad. Lawns, trees, classroom buildings."

"And to your right?"

"The door. Your coatrack."

"Very good. But you didn't see any of those things."

Grant opened his eyes and looked at Darling's smiling face.

"The sweeps of the room your eyes made when you came in here, if we could have recorded them and could play them back, wouldn't show anything like that. They would show just a blur of shapes at different angles. The reason you see a room is that you have a model of a room in your head, and a model of an office, and a model of a university office, and your brain takes the scraps of visual information your eyes took in and constructs a university office to fit them. If you were a baby coming into an office for the first time, you would have to crawl all over, touch everything, look at everything from different angles, taste everything, smell everything, then do it all again before you could have the vaguest notion of what the place was like. If you didn't have a model already set up in your brain, you would have to do that whole process every time you came into a room. Did you know that when the Spanish explorers landed on populated coasts in South America in the fifteenth and sixteenth centuries, the Indians saw them stepping up out of the waves of the ocean?"

"No."

"That's what they saw. Because they had no mental model for ships, they didn't see them. Didn't see these huge wooden things moored a couple of hundred yards out on the water. So they thought Cortez and all those folks just walked up out of the ocean, and that's why they thought they were gods at first. They had a model for gods, but not for ships.

"And then there's what's called the 'eyewitness effect,' which has been studied in great detail. Eyewitnesses to crimes and other events are notoriously inaccurate, because they tend to see what they expect to see instead of what is actually there. What people see is famously wrong. What you see is all wrong.

"But the problems don't end there, because on top of all that we have to take into account problems with memory. Memory is usually memory of perceptions, and because perceptions are built around mental models instead of facts, memory has a strike against it to begin with. But after that there are a lot of other things. It used to be thought, for example, that memories were stored all of a piece somewhere in the brain; that is, if you went to a football game ten years ago, the memory of the football game would be stored somewhere in your brain, and when you remembered it you got that memory out and played it back. But it appears that's not how it happens. When you lay down a memory, different pieces of it go to different places in the brain: memories of the colors you saw to one area, memories of the movements you saw to another area, memories of sounds to a third, memories of words to a fourth, memories of the score to a fifth, and so on and so forth, so that the 'retrieval' of a memory isn't retrieval at all: it's more like reconstruction, with the brain putting the pieces back together to form the memory. But this 'putting back together' isn't a cut-and-dried process like getting the pieces of a jigsaw puzzle from different parts of a warehouse. The stimulus—to use a word I hate—that causes you to retrieve the memory can make the memory itself come out differently. For example, if it's cold when you remember the football game, you may remember that it was cold on the day of the game; on a warm day, you may remember that it was warm. In turn, this difference can cause you to remember differently what people were wearing. And the memories can be affected by what you've come to believe since the event happened. So if you now believe that your team was weak in those years, you may remember it losing; whereas, if you believe that your team was strong, you may remember it winning.

"Now you'll ask, isn't that why we have science? To study things systematically and describe what they're really like without all these distortions? And the answer to that is yes. But science is often the worst offender of all for letting preconceptions govern perceptions. Scientists often reject data outright if it contradicts settled theory; they assume that the experiment was flawed if they don't just ignore it altogether. There are far more observations supporting, say, the existence of ghosts than there are supporting the existence of all kinds of phenomena firmly accepted by scientists—say neutrinos or quarks—yet the latter are almost universally accepted as real while the former are not only rejected but sneered at—simply on the basis that there's a physical theory for the latter but not the former. I hope I'm not loosening your hold on reality," Darling concluded with a mischievous but kind smile, apparently reading Grant's expression.

"No, of course not," said Grant, consciously relaxing in case Darling might clam up if he thought Grant was going bonky. "But—under the circumstances, how can I—how can anyone decide what is real and what isn't?"

"Ah! Now I have the pleasure of telling you that that is outside my area of expertise. I just do experiments on cognition. As to what is really real—cognitive psychology can't help you there. What you need is a philosopher, or a physical scientist, a physicist."

"Do you know any?"

"They keep some over at the Lake Building," said Darling. "I do know one of them, a guy named Ron Steiner. Nice guy. Tell him I sent you." He laughed again, a delighted laugh that made his face look happy, wise, and self-absorbed.

The Lake Building was a plain, square brick structure built in the era of limited college budgets decades after the triumphalist architecture of the central campus. Radiators ticked in its yellow-tiled stairwell, and the hall Grant emerged into was quiet and warm, with the soft but psychically intense hum of classes in session behind its closed doors. Guided by a directory, he followed the hall to an office with a plastic sign that said RONALD STEINER,

Ph.D. Dr. Steiner's office was small, but so cluttered that Grant had to scan it for a few seconds to be sure no one was in there. He wandered back down the hall. In an empty seminar room a bony, curly-headed youth was fiddling with some wires connected to an electrical device. Grant tapped on the door. The youth looked up.

"I'm looking for Dr. Steiner. Do you know when he might be in his office this afternoon?"

"I'm Steiner," the youth said. He had a soft backcountry voice and melancholy brown eyes, large bony hands, and sinewy arms. He wore a beige polo shirt that his mother might have bought him.

"Oh, Dr. Steiner. I'm David Grant." He stepped forward to shake hands. "I've just been over talking to Dr. Darling in the psychology department, and he gave me your name."

"How's Dick doing?" asked Dr. Steiner as he absently jiggled a jack connected to one of his wires. "I have a lab in here later," he explained. "This thing isn't working right. We're going to measure the speed of light."

"Ah," said Grant. "Well, would you mind if I ask you something while you're—?"

"Go ahead," said Steiner.

"Well—" Grant took a deep breath. "—this may be kind of abrupt, because I'm bringing you into the middle of a conversation I've just been having with Dr. Darling. But my question is, are there other worlds than this?"

"You mean other planets?"

"No, I mean—" Grant paused to consider just what he did mean. "I mean, is it possible that there are other—universes, I guess, that are like ours but not exactly like ours. Like, maybe, a universe where this state is twice as big as it is now, say, and landlocked, but where everything else is the same—or almost the same?"

"Sure. There might be lots," said Steiner.

"Can you tell me how?"

"All kinds of ways," said Steiner, unscrewing the jack from the wire he was holding. "There's a theory of quantum mechanics called the 'Many-Universes Interpretation.' Do you know about that one?"

"No," said Grant, but the name had given him a jolt. What had Kat said? But that had been a dream, he scolded himself.

"Well, do you know anything about quantum mechanics?"

"It has something to do with tiny little particles. And uncertainty."

"Right. Well, there's this mystery about quantum mechanics that people have been wondering about since it was discovered. All the big scientists have their opinions on it, but nobody has been able to figure it out for sure. Quantum mechanics gives you a picture of a world where things are all smeared out—where a particle is simultaneously a little bit in all the places it might possibly be. The equations only tell you the *probabilities* of things happening, not what *will* happen or *how* they go from being smeared-out probabilities to being one or another actual situation. Like the equations might tell you that a particle has a fifty percent chance of going one way and a fifty percent chance of going another. But the question is, what makes the particle go one way instead of the other? One answer is that the particle takes both paths, but in two different universes. So every time there are two or more alternatives for a particle or group of particles to take, the universe splits into as many universes as there are alternatives, with each universe containing one outcome. Which means, because there are so many particles in the universe, that every second the universe is splitting into trillions and trillions of new universes, and they in turn split into trillions and trillions more, and so on. We only see one because we are only in one, and so to us it looks mysterious how each particle chooses just one path.

"According to that interpretation, there are nearly an infinite number of 'parallel universes' to ours. The ones that have just recently split off are almost identical to ours. Some others, which split off long ago, look so different you couldn't even recognize them. And everything in between."

Steiner stopped talking and looked at Grant mildly and seriously. Grant tried to think of something to ask, or at least to decide what he thought about what Steiner had just said. "People really believe that?"

"It's one of the main competing interpretations of quantum mechanics."

"But—but how could we ever get to any of these 'alternate universes'?"

"We couldn't, if you mean physically."

"How else is there?"

"Who knows? Nobody knows how consciousness works, for one thing. Maybe it's a field phenomenon that isn't bounded by space-time.

"There's also a geometric theory of time that has alternate universes. This one English physicist thinks he's solved quantum relativity without superstrings." Steiner stopped working on the cable and looked at Grant gravely, as if he would surely be shocked by this. "That has to do with bringing together relativity and quantum mechanics," he explained, seeing that Grant was not entirely current on these startling developments. "Those are the two big theories of modern physics, and both of them predict experimental results almost perfectly. The problem is that they seem to contradict each other in some ways. Everybody knows they have to be made consistent sooner or later, but no one has been able to bring them together in a convincing way."

Steiner found a piece of sandpaper in a drawer and began pulling the bare ends of the cable wires through it, making them the shiny pink color of raw copper. "What this English guy says is that the only way to simultaneously solve relativity and quantum mechanics is in a theory where time isn't real. All that exists are trajectories on an infinite-dimensional surface called a 'manifold,' with some points on them kind of 'lit up' by a probability function so that they are actually manifested—they actually exist as physical realities. One of the trajectories contains our universe, and the ones right next to it contain universes almost exactly like ours, and next to them universes that are a little more different, and so on.

"But the cool thing he says is that there isn't really any such thing as time. It's just that each one of the points that is lit up on these trajectories is a single instant in a single universe—but that single instant comes complete with all the memories and traces consistent with the existence of causal precursors to it—so that if you were to experience that instant, you would *think* there was time because you would think you remembered the past. But all there really is is that instant with those memories."

SIXTEEN

HOLIDAY BY THE SEA

Grant went into the office every day for two weeks, but it soon became apparent that he had no work, even on the matters he himself had brought in before his trips to St. Elizabeth's. His requests for updates on his cases were met with respectful briefings and copies of all written materials. This upset him. If he were really in the loop, he would be deluged with questions, requests for guidance, challenges to his approaches, decisions to make, clients to soothe—but instead there was this effort to make him *feel* in the loop. He was invited to team meetings—where inevitably the partner who had been assigned in his absence held sway—so that he was made to understand ever so gently that his cases were under control, and that he needn't worry about them until he was fully himself again, which everyone confidently expected to be never.

But thinking it over, he had decided not to fight this particular battle yet. After all, he *had* just been in the bonko house. If it came to a showdown now about who should run his cases, there was a significant chance he would lose. When a few months had gone by and he was obviously okay again, he would just start issuing orders and setting strategy, and if anyone protested, he would complain that the firm was branding him with a lasting stigma, bringing to bear both liberal guilt and fear of lawsuits.

But this strategy of biding his time was unexpectedly hard to implement. On his old medications he could have dismissed the whole thing from his mind, watched the pale March sky over the river through his office windows, or dozed in his chair with the door to his balcony open a crack to let in a feather of deliciously fresh air. But on his new medications he was compelled to get up and do something.

Considering how to pass the time until he could step back into his old shoes, Grant thought of St. Clair. He remembered a warm overcast morning on one of his childhood holidays, standing on a fish-smelling pier and watching a darkening horizon with tiny jots of lightning over the gray deeps, fishing boats hurrying back to harbor over the oily-smooth swells, seagulls mewling in the air. At the same time he had strong memories of St. Clair as a quaint small town in the middle of a broad agricultural state. While the former memories were real and the latter delusional, he knew that he could not have told that without outside help. His talks with the two professors hovered at the edge of his mind, and now for the first time he remembered being surprised by the smell of the ocean on his trip to St. Clair with Kat.

He shrugged off these thoughts. He probably "remembered" a landlocked state because he had passed most of his life in the city, living as if the ocean really were a thousand miles away. A few days strengthening the memories of his childhood St. Clair beach holidays would be a good way to ease himself back to certainty, as

well as a pleasant vacation. He notified the appropriate firm ad-
ministrators that he was taking some time off—much to everyone's well-concealed relief, he thought—and the next day, after
checking into a bed-and-breakfast on St. Clair's outskirts, he was
taking a drive north between trees and flats of coarse grass on the
two-lane county route that ran up the coast, watery sun flashing
between tall trees along the road. After a few miles the trees gave
way to a low guardrail, and he was driving along a cliff a hundred
feet above the ocean. The ocean kept St. Clair warmer than the
city; at midday, the gusty, damp air was no more than chilly, shade
and sunlight sweeping over the earth from the fast-moving
clouds. He had a back window open two inches, and now in the
fresh air a raw, disorienting, earthy smell came, as if this coast had
been newly scooped, the land gouged away to let the ocean in,
and then quickly dressed up with woods, beaches, and piers so that
no one would know. Grant rolled the window up and held the
steering wheel tightly, ignoring this impression.

At the next opportunity he turned inland, on a narrow rural
road of patched asphalt. After a mile or two of woods and fallow
fields surrounded by rusty barbed wire, fruit orchards began to
appear, and an occasional farmhouse with a long muddy driveway. Breaks in the clouds swept vistas of sunlight across the orchards, lighting the bare trees vivid gray and brown against the
pale green of winter grass.

And suddenly, coming around a wide curve, he saw something he recognized. He screeched the Mercedes to a stop. Then
he backed up until he was on the shoulder directly across from
the narrow gravel road that ran into the woods.

He stopped the engine and got out, the refined *ding-ding* of
the ignition key alert buffeted away on the fresh wind that
seemed to fill the earth, along with the motion of the clouds,
trees, and grass.

It hadn't been a hallucination, then; this was a real place. Down that gravel road was Kat's mother's house. Kat or Thotmoses might be there; at the very least he could subpoena the Hatshep woman to disclose their whereabouts and assets. The anger he had worked with Dr. York to "release" came roaring back to him. A civil suit and a felony prosecution would be a suitable way to dispel once and for all the fear, confusion, and helplessness the father–daughter team had inflicted on him, he thought with grim satisfaction. It was time to turn the tables, to pull them into a world in which *he* was something of a magician, mega-damages and jail time locking them into a nightmare of *his* making—mundane, but just as awful as the one they had concocted for him. He nearly rubbed his hands together, which any lawyer who has read Dickens can usually stop himself from doing, though sometimes only at the last moment.

He got back in his car, spun his tires in the mud of the shoulder, crossed the asphalt, and jounced onto the track between the trees, his heart pounding with excitement and reawakened fury. Gravel crackled under his tires. He drove through woods, past hedgerows and stone walls, split-rail fences and grazing horses, narrow gravel drives with NO TRESPASSING signs, the occasional peak of a house among the trees. He came to a stop sign he recognized and took a right, following the road uphill. Near the top he turned into the Hatshep driveway, pressed closely on both sides by trees and vines, and emerged after a hundred yards onto the paved area behind the garages.

He got out of the car. A wave of sunlight passed over the red brick, gray tree trunks, and emerald lawns, the wind hissing in the trees and ruffling the grass like live things in an empty world. No one seemed to have noticed his arrival. He followed the flagstone walk. Over the tops of trees growing down the steep slope beyond the lawn, sunlight swept across a vast valley that looked like paradise.

Two people appeared, walking up the path from the terraced gardens, a nun and a monk in the robes of holy orders. The monk was dark and tall, long hair blowing about his shoulders, and the nun was small and fair, her blonde hair mostly covered by a hood. For a moment they seemed not to see him, but then the nun looked in his direction and said something. Then they ran across the lawn toward him.

They were Kat and the young receptionist from the Trans-Humanist Institute.

Grant was frozen. He had hoped, planned to find Kat, but the suddenness and strangeness of this left him for the moment flat-footed.

She reached the flagstone walk first and stopped in front of him, throwing back her hood, breathing deeply, her eyes search-ing his face hungrily. The receptionist-monk hung back a couple of steps. Grant realized vaguely that he had rarely seen Kat in daylight; it lit the depths of her eyes and made her skin almost sil-very, the wind blowing a couple of stray blonde hairs and the skirts of her midnight-blue robes.

"Aren't you going to say anything?" she asked, grinning. "I can hear the wind whistling in your mouth."

"Kat."

"And you remember my colleague, Andrei." The man stepped forward and put out his large, hard hand, which Grant shook re-flexively. His robes were the same midnight color as Kat's, but with a brownish tint instead of bluish.

"So you're here," said Kat. "It *is* you this time, isn't it? The one from the inland state?"

Grant had been struggling to recover his cool, menacing lawyer's demeanor, but now he gaped at her. Then he suddenly felt dizzy; his legs sagged.

A hard hand went under his armpit, another around his back. Andrei had stepped forward quickly to hold him up.

"Let go of me," Grant said, sprawling heavily into Andrei's arms. Then Andrei was helping him stumble across the lawn toward the house.

Kat supported him on the other side. "Stay here. Stay here," she said to him over and over, like a medic trying to keep someone from going into shock. Her voice seemed to come through a ringing in his ears. "Stay with me. Look at me. Have you been having a hard time? Poor Grant. Tell me about it. Come on, talk to me, Grant. No, don't close your eyes. Come *on,* Grant, don't be a dick!"

The novelty of a nun calling him a dick made Grant open his eyes and focus on her.

"You're here now, so everything's all right. I'm proud of you. I knew you could do it," she said. "You should be proud of yourself. Aren't you happy?"

"I might kill you. Maybe," Grant mumbled dizzily, trying to walk with his unsteady legs. "And sue you."

"Okay, but first you have to feel better. You can't sue anyone if you can't stand up, right?"

Someone opened the front door as they climbed the steps, and came forward with a concerned exclamation. Grant saw dizzily that it was Alex, Mrs. Hatshep's driver or secretary or whatever he was. With Andrei holding him up on one side and Alex on the other, and Kat closing the door behind them, they passed into the still, warm air of the Hatshep house.

Kat's robed figure ran off down the hall; Andrei and Alex walked Grant through a doorway into a small sitting room with leaded windows swung half-open over yellow flower beds that the wind outside disturbed only a little, so that the air through

the windows was sweet and almost warm. They helped him off
with his raincoat and sat him on a graceful old sofa with carved
legs. Sitting down made him feel better, and the sofa's faint smell
of venerable wood and upholstery seemed to reduce his dizziness
and make everything seem more real. The flower beds outside
the window blazed brilliantly as a shaft of sunlight passed over
them.

Kat hurried in, her arms full. Her nun's habit was gone; she
wore tight jeans and a shirt that showed an inch of her belly. She
handed a clipboard to Alex and a large bundle wrapped in cloth
to Andrei. "My mother will see you in a few minutes," she said
to Grant, as if that were important. She sat on the sofa facing
him, one leg bent under her, for all the world just like his old
girlfriend. "But first I'll try to help you."

Alex sat on the other side of him, watching him and making
notes on the clipboard. Andrei had unwrapped the bundle and
was setting up something on the sideboard under the other window.

"First I'd better make sure it's really you." Kat looked into
Grant's eyes and asked slowly and steadily: "Can you tell me the
name of a town beyond St. Clair? On the other side of St. Clair?
Where the ocean is now?"

"Mumford," said Grant without thinking.

Kat seemed almost to float out of her seat with excitement.
She grabbed his arm. "It *is* you!"

Grant realized that his hands were gripping the sofa cushions
as if holding him to earth. He tried to laugh contemptuously, but
it came out sounding a little crazy.

Kat studied him seriously. "Do you know how you got here?"

"I drove."

Alex took Grant's wrist. Grant yanked it away violently, half-
rising. Alex looked at him with an appealing smile, holding a

blood-pressure cuff, and after a moment's hesitation Grant re-laxed and let him roll up his sleeve and take his blood pressure.

A man and a woman in white aprons hurried in carrying trays covered with white linen, china, and silver; they set these on the coffee table. Alex, done taking Grant's blood pressure and pulse and making some more notes, poured tea. Grant gulped his gratefully, the dry, bitter taste giving him another hold on reality. By the time Alex had refilled his cup, murmuring soothingly, he felt almost well enough again to sue everyone in sight. He scarcely winced when Alex loomed around him and shone a doc-tor's examination light in his eyes.

"Do you remember the last time you saw me?" Kat asked. "In the little town? In Ontario?"

He stared at her, suddenly aghast again. He clasped his teacup between his hands.

She grinned gleefully, as if he had again passed some kind of test. "It's him," she said to Alex and Andrei. "He made it."

"This is a dream," said Grant mechanically. His insides were full of ashes. "Or I'm crazy again." Because how could the real Kat know about his hallucination or dream of meeting her in the little town? Or about the landlocked state he imagined he re-membered?

"No," Kat said. "No, no, no. Listen to me." She looked into his eyes, trying to hold his attention. "Grant, listen to me. I'm going to explain."

He leaped at her, drove her over backward with the table and tea-tray and crashed down on top of her, clawing and punching. It took Andrei and Alex ten seconds to pull him off, and in that time he tried his best to kill her. They twisted his arms behind him and dragged him up onto the sofa. Alex held his wrists, breathing heavily, and Andrei knelt by Kat. She was coughing gutturally and uncontrollably, trying to sit up, and suddenly she vomited over the broken crockery and spilled tea. Andrei held her, murmuring to her, and when he got up and helped her shakily to her feet, there was nothing left inside Grant but nausea and the terrible feeling in his hands of the delicate bones he had tried to crush.

The tea table was righted; a chair was set on its feet. The two kitchen people were cleaning up the crockery, tea, and vomit, clucking and clinking shards. Someone gave Kat a cloth napkin, and she wiped her face and blew her nose. Then she sat on the sofa next to Grant again. One of her eyes was bloodshot and swollen, and there were cuts and purple and red marks on her neck and throat. He couldn't look at them. He looked down at his knees instead.

She was crying, and her voice was shaking, but she spoke to him. "Are you all right?" She didn't sound sarcastic. When he didn't answer, she repeated the question.

"No." Though this was a dream or delusion, the feeling of her throat in his hands, his fists against her face horrified him, as if he really could have killed her. Alex released his wrists. He rubbed them automatically.

Kat was composing herself, wiping her face with the napkin, brushing her hair back, sniffling. "Look at me." He raised his eyes. "Did that make you feel better? If not, you can do it again. I'll tell Andrei and Alex to go away, not to interfere." She seemed completely serious. Grant stared at her. Then he cursed her bitterly, calling her every filthy name he could think of, repeating himself clumsily. He finally mumbled himself silent, feeling empty and numb.

"Okay. Now will you listen to me?" she asked.

When he didn't answer, she cleared her throat and swallowed painfully, then started to talk as if reciting something, a set piece she had memorized. As she talked, her voice got steadier. Someone came into the room and handed her an ice pack, which she pressed against her eye. "If it makes you feel better for now, you can believe you're dreaming, that this is a lucid dream. Okay?"

He said nothing.

"But just as in a lucid dream, it makes no sense to reject the rules of the world you're in. So let's proceed on that basis. This is a lucid dream, and I'm your numinal figure, and I'm going to explain something important to you. Okay?"

She repeated that until he nodded numbly. It was dawning on him just how bad this was. He smelled incense, and then something wet spattered on the side of his head, making him jump sideways, raising his hands to protect himself. Andrei was standing next to the sofa chanting under his breath, shaking holy water from an aspergillum, and behind him on the sideboard a little altar stood on an embroidered cloth, with a crucifix, candles in front of some precious-looking icons, a golden chalice, and a censer that was leaking smoke.

"Andrei is saying Mass for you," said Kat. "It'll help you. Right now I'm going to explain what's happening, and I want you to adapt to what I'm saying, just like you do in lucid dreams. Adapt without accepting. You're an expert at this. You've had to adapt to all kinds of sensoria, and you've learned to do it without being afraid or getting disoriented or paralyzed or trying to talk yourself out of it. I want you to adapt like that now. Okay?"

Don't panic, Dr. Gani had said.

"In the end, it'll be up to you to accept or reject what I'm going to say. You can ask any questions you want, examine anything you want, take all the time you need. I'm just asking for a chance to explain. Is that a deal?"

He nodded automatically, looking around. Andrei sprinkled him with more holy water, making crosses in the air over him and mumbling. Think, Dr. Gani had said; try to distinguish the real from the unreal. How could he start thinking himself out of this? What was real in this room? Or was he completely inside a hallucination?

Kat took his hands in hers; they were hot and damp, as if from her injuries. He pulled away with a jerk. Her hands felt so real; it was like rubbing your own hands together to stay in a dream; she was trying to hold him in the dream.

"Okay," she said soothingly. "Just listen to me." When she took away the ice pack for a second, he saw that her hurt eye was already swollen almost shut.

"Imagine that you have a lucid dream of being at home, in your house. You've had those, haven't you?"

He nodded.

"Okay. Now imagine it's a very long lucid dream, but finally you wake up. You're in your bed, in your bedroom. You get up and make breakfast, go out and get the newspaper, and sit at the breakfast table reading it. But then, just out of habit, you do a triple-read, and it turns out you're dreaming. You've just had a false awakening. Are you with me?"

Suddenly he was concentrating on her words, like a man holding on to something solid in a world of vertigo.

"So now you realize you're dreaming, and you decide you want to wake up. So you do. You go up to your bedroom and lie down and go to sleep in the dream, and then you wake up some-where else, say in a hotel that you've traveled to for work.

"You get up and shower, and while you're getting dressed you do a triple-read on your watch, and lo and behold, you're still dreaming. Another false awakening.

"So you wake yourself up. You're lying in bed at a girl-friend's house. You get up, get breakfast, et cetera, but then you realize again that you're dreaming. Do you see where I'm going with this? I know you've had this experience with maybe three or four false awakenings in a row. Well, now I'm telling you to imagine that this goes on indefinitely. Suddenly, *all* your awakenings are false. No matter how many times you wake up, the dream tests say you're still dreaming. Maybe it sounds a little scary, but you're all right in all the dreams. You're safe, you're in familiar places, the reality laws are familiar. You could decide to stay in any one of them, and it would be quite comfortable. So it's not really scary, just kind of confusing, and you're wondering when you're really going to wake up. Okay? Do you get that?

"Now add another wrinkle. Exactly the same scenario, except that now every time you do your triple-read and your other checks, you're *awake*. All the places you wake up in are equivalent, as they were before, but now your dream tests fail in all of them. When you think about it, that's just a tiny little difference from the previous scenario—the stability of some tiny little text on a watch, stuff like that. Right?

"Okay. One more wrinkle now, the last one. I want you to do your dream tests. Do your dream tests now and tell me the results."

Slowly, reluctantly, he looked at his watch.

It said KENNETH COLE—NEW YORK. He looked up at her bruised face, then down at the watch again. KENNETH COLE—NEW YORK. He looked out the window at the yellow flowers stirring in the breezes, then back at his watch. KENNETH COLE—NEW YORK. He looked at Andrei standing over him mumbling phrases from a book and punctuating them by swinging the censer on its chain so that fragrant smoke drifted over him. He looked back at his watch: KENNETH COLE—NEW YORK.

Cold fear poured in on top of the dread already filling him.

"Try the lights," Kat said.

He clicked the switches on the table lamps on either side of the sofa. They both worked perfectly.

"So?" asked Kat.

He shook his head.

"Okay," said Kat. "Any questions?"

One had been growing in the jumble in his mind. "Who are you?"

A soft voice said from the doorway: "Ms. Hatshep will see you now."

"Thank you, Carl," said Kat, and turned back to Grant. "I'll answer all your questions, anything you want, I promise," she said. Her voice was urgent, as if reminding him what to do in case of fire in a building that was already burning. "But now you have to remember what I told you, and adapt to the world I just described. Can you do that?"

"I don't—"

"My mother has business decisions to make. She won't waste time on you if she thinks you're not capable." She stood up. Behind her, Andrei was blowing out candles and wrapping the altar stuff up carefully in the gold-embroidered cloth, grave in his brownish-black robes. Alex stood up too, making a last note, and clicked the top onto his fountain pen. Kat leaned over Grant, hands on his shoulders, and he smelled the sweaty, sweet-sour smell of the fear and violence her small body had undergone. She murmured into his ear. "She's going to ask you to do something, and only you can decide on your answer. But I want you to know that I know you can do what she asks. I *know* it."

She pulled on his hand, and he stood up unsteadily. Clearly what was happening now had gone beyond lawsuits and prosecutions, he realized; it had moved on briskly to touch the very core of reality. He swayed on his feet, but then balanced.

Kat led him down the hall, Andrei close behind, perhaps to catch him if he collapsed. Grant suddenly wondered how he looked; he ran a hand over his hair and straightened his collar, though he had no idea why. Fortunately, he had twenty-five years' professional experience being blindsided, sandbagged, and ambushed; he could handle this. But it was a dream, he reminded himself, so it didn't really matter. Go along with it, as the numinal Kat character had suggested; don't panic, as Dr. Gani had suggested; there would be plenty of time later to figure things out.

SEVENTEEN

God-o-Gram

In the big drawing room where Grant had met her before, Tatiana Hatshep again sat on the sofa holding a lapdog.

"Good afternoon, Mr. Grant," she said as they came forward. Then she caught sight of Kat's face, and her eyes widened.

"Mr. Grant had a momentary transition crisis," Kat explained matter-of-factly. "He's feeling better now."

"Nice to see you looking so fit," Grant said suavely to Mrs. Hatshep. He could just as easily have screamed and crashed through the glass doors at the back of the room, but that would be uncomfortably like panic. Anyway, he wasn't going to break down in front of this woman, even in a dream.

Mrs. Hatshep studied him coldly, ignoring the pleasantry. "I'm not going to conduct a long introductory session with you, Mr. Grant, or try to ease you into this gently. You and I are both adults, so I will come straight to the point. We have expended substantial resources to bring you here because we want something from you—a service. And we're willing to pay for it—pay very handsomely indeed.

"A year ago our search program identified you as a potential candidate, and now you have graduated to candidate status. So now it's time for me to make you a proposition.

"We have modified your nervous system to allow you to travel to where the Universal Creator-Maintainer-Destroyer abides. We have done this because we need certain blessings from this entity, and we want you to act as our messenger."

"Come again?"

"We want you to go to what you might call God, and say a prayer for us."

"Ah," said Grant sagely.

"If you feel inclined to be ironic, Mr. Grant, I shall ask you to excuse me and come back when you are in a more businesslike mood."

"Sorry." He glanced at Kat; her frown made him try to be serious. "You want me to go to God and say a prayer for you. Right." He made what he hoped was an obvious effort to keep a straight face. He tried to think of something to say. "Usually when people say 'go to God—' "

"I don't mean anything like that. I mean continue the process of learning to translate your consciousness across houses until you are able to accomplish the ultimate translation. No more physical modifications will be necessary. All you need now is training. You've been given a gift that very few humans have ever possessed. We've rescued you from a prison cell and set the wide world before you.

"Aside from the benefits of the changes we have made to your brain—which are incalculable in themselves—the importance of this project is such that we also offer you whatever else is within our power to give—and that takes in a lot of territory.

Think about it, Mr. Grant. What is it you want? Power? Wealth? Knowledge? Women?"

Twenty-five years' practice thinking fast. Twenty-five years' practice springing the unexpected to keep the opposition off balance—

He pointed at Kat. "I want her."

It had the intended effect. Suddenly deprived of anything to say, Mrs. Hatshep looked at Kat. Kat looked blank, as if she wasn't sure she had understood.

"Give her to me, and I'll do what you want," he said. "I'll go talk to God or whatever."

Tatiana Hatshep contrived to look weary. "I should have said, anything within—"

Grant cut her off, his voice furious. "Don't you argue with me, you bitch. After you and your husband the circus freak and your daughter the whore fucked up my brain—"

"Mr. Grant—"

"Well, then, I guess we're agreed," he said, suddenly broadly cheerful, another lawyerly mood change to keep them guessing. "You give me your daughter, and I go see God."

Mrs. Hatshep regarded him with steely amusement. "It's impossible, I'm afraid. She has taken holy orders, and a vow of celibacy. Her earlier dalliance with you was one of her spiritual duties, but the time for that is over now. I'm telling you this so you won't be hurt when she refuses you. And so that you'll know how very much out of your league you would be if you had the ill fortune of getting what you've asked for. It would be like giving a lion to a piece of meat. A rump steak."

"Then you can get another God guy," Grant said, and realized suddenly that negotiating with Mrs. Hatshep had relaxed him, and that he was suddenly and perversely enjoying himself. But this was a lucid dream! Here he was, at last letting himself get lost in some good sensoria just when he was supposed to resist them. But he couldn't resist baiting the Hatshep woman, dream or no dream. "What do you do then, if Mr. God-o-Gram guy walks?"

"We continue our recruiting. Don't make the mistake of thinking you're irreplaceable, Mr. Grant. It takes time, but we've been finding and training candidates for many years now, and we know enough to rely on the percentages. The casino always wins, weren't you aware of that?

"Now if you'll excuse me, I have a meeting. Alex, would you please take Mr. Grant to his room?" Her tone was casual, but Grant was delighted at the sudden appearance of an appointment. He had shaken her, he guessed, and she needed a chance to regroup.

Alex conducted him up the marble staircase making polite conversation, as though Grant had just popped over for a hunting weekend. He showed Grant into a suite furnished with comfortable-looking antiques and hung with paintings, some that looked very old: portraits of beautiful women resembling Tatiana and Katerina Hatshep, and of high-cheeked, handsome men like Andrei. Big windows looked out over the wild gardens down the slope behind the house, in which, from this third-story height, Grant saw stone steps and gravel walks winding among the trees. After Alex left, Grant found his raincoat hanging all alone in the walk-in closet. The full-length mirror on the closet door surprised him by showing an elegant man in casual clothes, his hair slightly disarranged, but otherwise debonair.

He took off his shoes and lay on the bed fully dressed. He was satisfied. He hadn't panicked, so now he could wake up in an orderly fashion. He would talk to Dr. York about adjusting his medication to control his dreams or hallucinations or whatever this had been—though he had to admit that it had been fun.

A movement woke him, and he opened his eyes. At first he couldn't remember where he was. Deep blue twilight came through windows, making the room a dim blue gold. Kat was sitting on the edge of the bed.

He got up on his elbows fast, heart thumping with fear.

She jumped, then just sat looking at him. "You've gotten what you want," she said finally. "I came to tell you."

One of her eyes was shapely and clear, the other ugly, black, and swollen shut. Her beautiful, small body moved slightly with her breathing, and he could smell the sweet and sour tang of her sweat, the faint bile of vomit on her breath. An intense curiosity suddenly came over him. "Who are you?"

"I work for the church."

Suddenly it made a perfect, horrible kind of sense. "You're some kind of Jonestown-type religious cult that scrambles people's brains as part of your—"

"No, idiot. Do I seem like a religious fanatic to you?"

"That's how the Moonies start out on you. They send some normal-looking beautiful girl to accost you—"

"We're not Moonies. If you want to know, we're the Caucasus Synod of the Western Orthodox Church."

"Caucasian?"

"Caucasus. Some mountains in Eastern Europe. Where most of the people who live around here come from."

"What are you, Slavs? Armenians?"

"We're what they call a 'dispersed ethnic minority,' like the Gypsies or the Jews. The name of the church goes back to our original region, an isolated valley in the Caucasus that wasn't in contact with the rest of the world until a few hundred years ago.

"You've never heard of us, like most people. That's how we like it. It's dangerous to be different, so we don't advertise it. Look at what happened to the Gypsies and the Jews. We keep to ourselves. We live away from other people and mostly marry and mix within our own communities, which people think is because we're snobbish 'old money' families. Which I guess we are.

"Except we're a little more than that. More than an ethnic group, even. The main difference is that *Homo sapiens emporos*—that's us—have a greater ability to travel between houses—worlds, sensoria, realities—than *Homo sapiens sapiens*."

He stared at her blankly. "You're saying you're a different species."

"No. A different subspecies, maybe, but even that is open to doubt. But different enough to have a unique trait. A trait not shared with the 'mainstream' group, or at least not recognized by it."

"Oh, so rich people are a different *subspecies* than the rest of us. I hadn't heard that one. I thought it was just the Aryans."

She looked at him gravely. "It's the other way around. A different subspecies accumulates wealth to keep itself safe."

"And so fucking up humans is just like animal vivisection. Nothing to go to jail over."

"It's not like vivisection. It's the way we've survived."

"Explain it to me one more time, because I need a good laugh. You 'recruit' 'mainstream' people to go to God—"

"And say prayers for us. The closer you get to the Source, the more powerful your prayers become. And if you can get very, very close—"

"Prayers for what?"

"For the safety and prosperity of our people."

He stared at her. "And these prayers get answered, just like that."

"Hopefully. Answers to prayers aren't predictable, but the nearer you get to the Source—"

"That's insane."

"No more insane than your view of the world seems to us. We're both conditioned by our experiences. We have different sets of experiences, that's all."

"But—how could people not have found out about you?"

"They did find out. We were almost wiped out in the Middle Ages, before we went into hiding. We have our own folktales and history, just like the Gypsies. We've been lucky that our main difference isn't physical. In fact, we look so much like mainstream people that most of our own people today also believe that there is no difference, and some have even intermarried. The old folklore is considered superstition."

"The church doesn't approve."

"No. The church believes we should preserve our heritage."

He studied her, frowning. "Explain to me how a different species, subspecies of humans suddenly pops up out of nowhere."

"It doesn't. Several different human subspecies survived during the Paleolithic—the Stone Age—and there was interbreeding. Some isolated groups retained unique genetic features."

"In this dream world."

"We have proxies in all the loci—all the houses similar enough to contain us—just as you do."

"Of course. Silly me."

She ignored his sarcasm. "This is the part you have to listen to carefully. I'm glad you're relaxed about it, but make sure you let the information in. It'll save you a lot of confusion.

"First, this house, or locus, which is a similar group of houses, is very close to your previous house, only a step away, and shares nearly all its characteristics. The differences are contingent: St. Clair is a sea town here, but landlocked there, for example."

"Come on, Kat. This is a lucid dream, you said before."

"*Every* world is a lucid dream. Including the world you come from. A lucid dream in which none of the dream tests work."

"Bullshit."

"Second, every world is complete in itself, including its inhabitants. So there's a David Grant for this house as well as a David Grant for your former house, and David Grants in every house similar enough for there to be a David Grant."

"So I could meet myself here?"

"No. You *are* the David Grant of this world. The only difference is that you also remember being in a different world, though the memories are so similar that you conflate most of them, don't distinguish them in your mind. Physical travel between houses—alternate worlds—is impossible. You would have to somehow create a whole new body in the new house, and that would violate conservation of mass-energy. On the other hand, we believe that changes in memories—tiny electrical changes within the brain—are within the Heisenberg limits, so no physical laws are violated.

"When you travel, it's as if you introduce a memory stream from the 'you' in one house—what we call your 'proxy' in that house—to your proxy in another. Do you get it? There's a Kat Hatshep in your former house, and I'm her when I'm there—or rather, she's me when she gets my memories.

"Just by chance, you were born with a small injury or defect in a certain part of your brain. When stimulated, it causes you to have small seizures. Millions of people have the same thing; it's no big deal. But in your case these seizures happen to project in a very specific way into your posterior parietal lobe, the part of your brain responsible for metaphysical proprioception—locating yourself in a particular house. Because of this, you're a tremendous find for us, one in a million. All we needed to do was to strengthen your seizures a little and teach you lucid dreaming to give you practice navigating new sensoria. But your movements between houses aren't entirely conscious yet. That's why you've been noticing discontinuities in the last few months."

Grant had kept calm so far by doing what Kat had suggested before: suspending judgment and acting as if he was having a lucid dream. But the paradoxical weakness of this trick was suddenly evident: now that he needed to evaluate her explanation, he had to stop suspending judgment, turn his judging function back on. But once he did that, he was forced to make a judgment—was this world real or not? If it *was* a dream, he should have woken up long ago. He hadn't, and there were only two other alternatives: either Kat's explanation was true, or else he had gone crazy again and was wandering in a delusional world inside his head. And it was clear to him which of those alternatives must be true. Kat's explanation was good enough to engage his judging function but not good enough to satisfy it. He had gone crazy again, he knew, his injured brain taking refuge in an internal hallucinatory world where he was an extraordinary person, where Kat had come back to him, where he outwitted billionaires, where he would learn superhuman powers—

"God damn you," he blurted bitterly.

"What?"

"It's not real."

She knelt on the bed in front of him, hands on his arms. Her voice and face were urgent. "Grant, listen to me—this is part of the—"

"—first, it's too good to be true, but skip that part. Second, it's hopelessly self-contradictory. If there are—"

"Listen to me, damn it! Listen to my voice. You have to stay here, don't let yourself—"

"—the same people living in every world, how can you say someone 'travels' between worlds? It doesn't make sense—"

"—I already *told* you—"

"—and if you people already know how to travel between worlds, why do you need me? You shouldn't need me to do something you can already do better—"

"Stop!" she screamed. *"Stop! You're going to—"*

"I'm probably wandering somewhere on that country road, hallucinating," he screamed back in her face. *"Maybe I'll get hit by a car! And all because you god damn—"*

He came out of it, finally.

EIGHTEEN

LIFE AS A HEAD

He shared a nursing home room with a gaunt old man named Humphrey who couldn't shit. In the afternoons, when a rectangle of sunlight along the wall lit the room a merciless yellow, Humphrey would lie on his bedpan croaking frantically: "Uh! Uh! Push! Push!" while a gloved nurse's aide tried to dig dried turds out of his withered rectum. Then, wiped and dressed again in his pajamas, the meager, awful-smelling products of his daily ritual carried away in the bedpan, Humphrey would sit against his pillows serenely working his sunken jaws as if chewing, the sun's yellowish reflection lighting the skull under his spotty gray flesh, like an X-ray of his impending death.

It had taken Grant a long time even to realize that he was still alive. He had been in a coma, he understood later, and afterward had been on so many drugs that he had no idea it was him; he remembered only tiny, anonymous lit scenes in a vast darkness that was sometimes comfortable, sometimes painful, occasionally suffocating so that something struggled in it and someone yelled about something, and then the darkness became blacker, and swallowed it all up again, and he didn't care if it ever came back.

After this second death he was reborn one day in a hospital, but no one attended the birth. He could see again, and think, and he knew himself to be someone, but he still couldn't move, and there was no one there except someone breathing heavily in their sleep on the other side of a plastic curtain that divided the small fluorescent-lit room. He lay there for what felt like days. Finally a man in blue scrubs came with a sponge and a stainless steel basin of tepid disinfectant-smelling water and gave him a bath, lifting his arms and legs and rolling him onto his stomach, glancing into his face only once or twice, and then with the neutral look they use at the meatpacking plant.

It was a long time later that he even became curious about what had happened. By this time he remembered his name and vaguely remembered his life. He wanted to get up and go home, but they wouldn't let him; they kept him tied to the bed. He tried to scream, but he was too weak; so he cried instead, tears running down his face and into his ears, and a nurse wrote this down on a clipboard. His doctor was pleased.

But he wasn't tied to the bed, it turned out: he was paralyzed. He was a quadriplegic. He was lucky he could breathe by himself. Sure enough, he had been wandering in a hallucination in some woods near St. Clair, and unfortunately had wandered onto the road. He didn't remember how he learned this; all he knew was that he wanted to die. He begged the nurses to give him an injection of something that would kill him. The nurses wrote this down on a clipboard, and the doctor was pleased. He said Grant was exhibiting appropriate affect and could leave the hospital soon.

So they took him in an ambulance to the nursing home

where he would spend the rest of his days. He was nothing but a head on a pillow. His only views were those he could get by moving his eyes: the ceiling—whose topography of bumps and small smudges he learned by heart the first day—the wall with a decorative map showing the wide landlocked state, and his blank, masticating corpse of a roommate. At mealtimes a nurse's aide would prop him up and hurriedly shovel baby food into his mouth, wiping his chin with a damp washcloth as he struggled to swallow fast enough to keep from choking.

A Legal Services paralegal came by one afternoon, and Grant, sobbing, told him he wanted to die. The paralegal nodded seriously and made some notes, looking as if what *he* wanted was to get out of this bare, shit-smelling place where they kept putrefied Alzheimer's victims, "mentally challenged" individuals ranging from respectful cross-eyed dwarves who screamed solemnly now and then to the barely recognizable flesh remainders that lay in beds and breathed, and, hardest to take of all, the quadriplegics, alert but unable to do anything but sit or lie in this hell and wish they could move just enough to kill themselves.

The nurse's aides, who did most of the work taking care of the inmates, and who seemed to be replaced every two weeks, were angry ghetto blacks and dull-eyed hillbillies with alcohol breath. One of the former, a huge man with his hair in cornrows under a shower cap that made him look like a sadistic baker, liked to poke Grant painfully in the stomach with a huge finger while changing his clothes or giving him a sponge bath, murmuring "You don't fuck with me, man. I told you not to fuck with me." The nurse who saw the bruises on Grant's stomach and listened to his tearful report wrote something on a clipboard and went on tight-lipped to the next room, and nothing changed.

Nothing ever changed.

He was prescribed sleeping pills, antidepressants, muscle-relaxants, tranquilizers, antibiotics to fight bedsores, and laxatives so that the shit would dribble out of his necrotic body. About half the time the aides—who were responsible for administering medications—kept the sleeping pills and tranquilizers for themselves, and threatened violence if he told anyone. The big man with the shower cap also liked to pour Grant's laxative liquid onto his chin and watch it run down his neck, mumbling "I fuck you up, man. I fuck you up bad."

Large doses of psychiatric medication alternating with none at all made Grant crazy. During his occasional rational moments he knew that he often screamed and ranted when he was out of his gourd, which had doubtless made involuntary commitment an easy call for some judge. He knew how it worked from his pro bono cases. A paper signed by the doctor who stood by the foot of his bed reading his chart twice a month had been forwarded to a court, which had assigned him a guardian ad litem. The guardian had probably visited for a few minutes on one of his crazy days, concurred in the commitment request, and approved an assignment of his bank account to pay the nursing home in monthly installments. The installments would be twice as much as the nursing home received for the 95 percent of its patients who were on Medicaid, so it had every incentive to keep him as its guest. And so everyone had done their job, money changed hands, and everyone was happy, and the psychotic quadriplegic lying in his bed and screaming or crying was well taken care of.

He would die there.

Even after Grant realized that he would never get out of the nursing home, for a long time in his confusion he refused to think about Kat or his visits to the "other world." Whenever he stumbled across some stray memory of them, he would mumble and cry in fear, and sometimes would have one of his fits. He must not think about it; it was insanity; those thoughts had made him the way he was, led him to wander blind out onto a rural highway. But finally the realization came to him that it didn't matter now what he thought about. He was crazy anyway, and wasn't in danger of wandering anymore; he was going to spend the rest of his life in this bed, his sores hurting and itching, the sadistic or indifferent nurses and nurse's aides his only companions, unable even to turn his head by himself, gyrating drug doses making it impossible for him to think straight most of the time. If he could go psychotic and live in a fantasy world, he was under what amounted to a moral obligation to do it. Perhaps that was what people did in hell, he realized: went deep inside and lived in their fantasies. Perhaps the world the attorney David Grant had lived in before had been a fantasy retreat from hell, which had nevertheless come to claim him in the end.

So he started to think about Kat and the other worlds. He thought about them as much as he could, mumbling about them even in his most regressed states, trying to fit together jumbled memories and fantasies, to see her face clearly, remember those worlds so clearly that he could enter them as he had before.

But try as he might, he could generate only memories and fantasies. The complete sensorium, the lucid dream that went on and on, did not return.

It was ironic, he realized dimly: now that he needed his hallucinations, they eluded him. He was just crazy enough to suffer, but not crazy enough to be happy.

In his clearer moments, between turns of the overdose-and-withdrawal kaleidoscope, he was sure there must be a way to return there. Presumably his brain still had the damage Thotmoses had done to it. Given time, he could probably remember his lucid dreaming techniques. He could approach Kat's world the same way he had before.

Thinking this made him feel better than he had since waking up to his new life. Now he had a goal, a way to use his remaining faculties.

On an afternoon when his brain was quiet, and when—as on all such afternoons—there was nothing to do but smell the stink of the nursing home, watch the bar of sunlight creep across the wall, and listen to the monotonous screams of one of the vegetables down the hall, he realized that to make progress with his new project he had to get off his medications. They jangled his brain and made him unable to focus; they might also be blocking his hallucinations by some direct pharmacological action. Since he had no idea which drugs were responsible, he would have to reject them all—all except the laxative, which he knew he couldn't live without.

So the next time a nurse came into his room, he told her calmly in the weak and trembling voice that was left to him that he wanted to stop taking his medicines, all but the laxative. She continued writing something in his chart without looking up. As she went to notate Humphrey's chart, Grant explained that his meds were making him unable to think, especially when they weren't given consistently, which they often weren't. He opined that without them he would be less trouble, because he wouldn't scream or cry or spit out the food the aides tried to feed him. He told her that if she wasn't comfortable making the decision herself, he would like to talk to his doctor.

The nurse walked out of the room without even glancing at him, as if his voice were just part of the ambient noise of the place, and at noon the aide came around as usual with the tray of tiny paper cups of pills arranged by room number. As Grant tried to explain that he wasn't taking them anymore, the aide lifted his head and poured the pills into his still-moving mouth, followed by a tiny cupful of water. Grant didn't try to resist. He knew from his manic phases that the aide would call for help, and the process would just get more painful.

So ended his first and last attempt to discuss his care with the nursing home staff. To them he was no different from the grunting vegetables down the hall. A potato in a silo might just as well have asked for special treatment.

So if he was going to get sane enough to go completely psychotic, he was going to have to do it himself.

The nurse's aides who stole his meds thenceforth became his allies. It was the others, the honest ones, he now had to figure out how to outwit. He knew that he took three capsules and a large tablet in the mornings, two capsules and the large tablet at noon, and three capsules, the large tablet, and a smaller tablet in the evenings. About half the time some of these pills were hurriedly secreted by some professional. Grant would have to figure out how to handle the other half.

He had to learn how to hold the pills in his mouth until the aides left the room, and then get rid of them somehow. He thought about this, curling his tongue into different positions in his mouth, for several days. It was amazing how daunting the task seemed, and a few times he decided he couldn't do it; being a half-crazy head on a pillow sapped one's confidence. But finally he screwed up his nerve and tried to intercept his noon pills, tears running from his eyes. He managed to catch the big tablet and one of the capsules under his tongue. After the aide had left the room he swallowed them, astonished and overjoyed at his ability to do just that one thing, his tears turning to tears of joy.

After that he practiced covertly holding the pills every time he got them. None of the aides noticed; they probably wouldn't have noticed if he had turned into a rubber Godzilla doll. For a couple of weeks he swallowed the pills after the aides had left, telling himself he needed to be sure he could do the first step before going on to the rest of his plan, whatever that was. One evening he choked as five pills tried to crowd down his throat together; in his panic to swallow them he didn't realize until after they had gone down that it might have been a decent way to kill himself.

His new goal and his modest preliminary success gave Grant a shred of self-esteem that seemed to help him stay more cogent even when medications were raging through his body, though he was careful later to recheck any ideas he had at those times. He tried to be objective and analytical, to carefully work out a plan. As a boy he had read *The Count of Monte Cristo,* and remembered the Count digging a tunnel through the stone wall of his dungeon with a teaspoon, taking a decade over it, but getting out in the end. The Count, Papillon, Hilts, all had escaped from their dungeons through sheer patience, planning, and indomitable will. He himself would be the indomitable Head on the Pillow, the Head that would outwit the world of ambulatory flesh through sheer nerve, intelligence, and persistence.

The plan he worked out was this: the first time he spit out his meds would be on a night before the Brutal Baker aide had the early-morning shift. That way maybe the Brutal Baker would take them, leaving no saliva-softened pills lying around in the room for anyone to see. Grant would then be able to go at least twenty-four hours without brain medication. Maybe being clearheaded that long would let him think of a plan to avoid the meds completely.

So one night after the meds aide left, Grant maneuvered the

five pills out from under his tongue, twisted his lips toward the middle of the room, and spit them as hard as he could. It was half an hour until lights-out, so anyone who happened to wander in would see them on the floor; and if Grant got a reputation for spitting out his pills, that would be the end of his plan, because then his benefactors would hold his mouth open and watch them go down his throat every time. But by lights-out, the pills would have dissolved in his mouth. So it was a risk, but one he had to take.

Grant caught a movement out of the corner of his eye. His decayed roommate Humphrey had gotten out of bed and was standing in his pajamas looking down at the floor.

"Humphrey," Grant's wobbly, fluty voice said. Senile dementia was faint praise for what ailed Humphrey, but he still possessed certain skills in making a racket, which he used most often when anything the least bit unusual happened, anything out of the normal routine. "Humphrey, no! Get back in bed!" Faced with this unanticipated twist, all of Grant's tiny store of confidence vanished. So much for the quadriplegic weakling outsmarting everyone. He was so naive, so pitiful, unable to think ahead enough even to foresee that Humphrey would raise the alarm if he spit out his pills. He could do nothing for himself. He would give up, ask for more and more pills, and if they didn't kill him at least maybe he could forget that he existed, sleep the rest of his life away—

Humphrey crouched down with surprising agility for a corpse, leaving Grant's range of vision.

"Humphrey," sobbed Grant.

Humphrey stood back up, putting something into his mouth, and chewing it vigorously with his bare gums. Then he crouched down again four more times, and then went back to sit in his bed, a look of satisfaction and interest showing through his grotesque chewing.

Grant stopped crying, straining to watch Humphrey out of the corner of his eye.

From that night on, Humphrey ate all of Grant's pills. He never once looked at Grant, seeming as oblivious to his presence as he had been since the head on the pillow had arrived in his room. It was as though to Humphrey the pills sprouted on the floor like tiny colored mushrooms; and yet it invariably took only a second after Grant spit them out for him to be down on his haunches putting them in his mouth with great satisfaction. Degenerated as he was, he also seemed to understand the need for secrecy: more than once Grant had seen him jump into bed and present an innocent death's-head face to the world when someone unex-pectedly came down the hall—in fact, these were the only times Humphrey ever stopped his compulsive chewing, but nobody ever noticed. Furthermore, the pills never seemed to have the least effect on him; he sat all day just as he always had, working his ancient gums and mumbling to himself, sometimes yelling for a wife or daughter long gone to dust, sometimes demanding that the unmoved nurse's aides tell him what time it was.

For Grant, complete withdrawal from the pills was much harder than he had imagined. He spent a week suicidal and un-able to sleep, his bedsores and joints hurting intensely, tears and mucus pouring from his eyes and nose. He decided to give up twenty times, but always caught the pills in his mouth and spit them on the floor for Humphrey. Finally he felt better, though his sores still hurt.

Grant literally had nothing else to do but practice lucid dreaming, and now that his brain had been released from its clinging chemical web, he made rapid progress. Within a week he found himself in the basement of his grandmother's house, his body healthy and young again, and he cried so hard with joy that he woke himself up. Soon he was again by night a formidable lawyer and seducer, as well as a martial arts expert who often severely beat and sometimes killed with his bare hands the nurse's aide with the shower cap. He flew in the air like Superman. He cavorted with beautiful women. He walked with an Angel in a graveyard overlooking the misty ocean.

And every morning, after too short a time, he woke up.

That was almost more painful than not lucid dreaming at all. To return to this hell, wake to the brutal, stupid face of the aide in the shower cap, poking him and spilling his laxative onto his chin—but even worse, to know that this was *real*: to know that the basic laws of the universe were hellish, and that happiness, love, and beauty were dreams—that was almost unbearable. To this pain was added the anxiety of knowing that even these brief excursions from reality depended on Humphrey. Humphrey's color was poor—like the bottom of a dustbin—and Grant knew he could depart this earth any day. If he did, Grant's system would be finished. While Grant's pills had no apparent effect on him, when added to his own copious medication regime they couldn't be healthy. Once or twice he thought he heard Humphrey stop breathing in his sleep, an event that would wake him out of even his deepest lucid dreams. So far, though, Humphrey had always started breathing again, to arise the next morning like a gag resurrection.

Grant had to go into his permanent psychotic state before Humphrey's internal organs realized what was obvious to everyone else. But how? Every time he had gone crazy in the past, it had been involuntary. Yet there had to be some trigger. He racked his brain to identify it. His memory of life before the accident was spotty: the more he thought about it, the more it seemed like a story he had read about someone else, someone who wasn't a head on a pillow, but a big, handsome, successful lawyer and ladies' man. He struggled to remember what had made him crazy, asking himself, What am I missing now that I had then?

He turned the question over in his mind as the bar of sunlight crept depressively up the wall, half-listening to Humphrey's harsh snoring as he took a nap. For example, the night in Kat's mansion: what had he possessed that he had suddenly lost talking to her, sending him back here?

He knew the answer. His heart pounded painfully in the delicate birdcage of his ribs. He remembered it now with crystal clarity. Kat had persuaded him to treat the mansion sensorium as a lucid dream. That had allowed him to suspend disbelief. As soon as he could no longer suspend disbelief, he had plummeted back to earth. Belief had been replaced by disbelief, and that had brought him here.

If he wanted to go back, he had to once again suspend disbelief. Or would that be enough? It was now no longer a matter of maintaining a hallucination that was already there, but getting from the real world back to the hallucinatory world, like achieving escape velocity against a psychological version of gravity. Don't say "hallucinatory world," he told himself. "Hallucinatory world" means it isn't real, and if you keep telling yourself it isn't real, you'll never believe it is.

He had to believe in it. Suspension of disbelief might not be enough, and he had no time for half measures. He had to Believe.

He spent the rest of the afternoon trying, but by evening had hit a wall. Belief wasn't a matter of willpower or expedience, as the evangelicals made out when they urged you to accept Jesus so you could be saved. You believed things because you thought they were true, not because it would be nice if they were true, or because it would be beneficial to believe in them. It wasn't something you could talk yourself into—or rather, if you did, you had to actually convince yourself; there could be no faking. When your attitude was that you wanted to delude yourself back into a hallucinatory world so that you could go psychotic and escape reality—well, that wasn't going to work. The whole thing was a catch-22.

Right?

Could the sensorium he had visited have been a real world? he asked himself as a nurse's aide shoveled baby food into his mouth at "dinner." Was there any possibility of that? That was the way back, he realized suddenly, as the aide mopped his mouth with a washcloth and laid him back down in his bed. He had to convince himself through rational argument that that world had been real.

But how could he?

He thought about that. There was the fact that all the usual tests—triple-reads, mechanical malfunctions, spinning, and so on—had come up negative. Of course, they were tests for lucid dreams rather than unrealities of other kinds. And the fact that the sensorium had gone on and on without waking meant only that it hadn't been a lucid dream, not that it hadn't been a psychotic hallucination. His training had taught him how to detect the former but not the latter.

Which brought him to the question, how would you detect a hallucination?

He had already found an answer to that: if it vanished when you no longer believed in it.

But what if that was true of this world too?

The ceiling light went off, together with most of the hall lights, meaning it was ten o'clock, bedtime at the nursing home. A frustrated shriek came from down the hall, as it did every night: one of the vegetables resented being put to bed so early, as

if it harbored a small patch of normal teenage brain tissue somewhere in its swollen or shrunken head.

There was a rustling of sheets and a contented grunting.

"Good night, Humphrey," Grant quavered to his benefactor.
As usual there was no reply.

Too preoccupied to sleep, Grant continued to think into the
darkness. Nonsense, he told himself, picking up his train of
thought—this world didn't vanish when you didn't believe in it.
That was what made it real.

But how did he know that? Had he ever stopped believing in
it? In the same way he had stopped believing in the other sensorium, in a visceral, bone-deep, final way?

What was at the basis of his belief in the "real" world,
anyway—in the fact that it was the one and only real world? He
thought hard about that, trying to strip away all bullshit and lazi-
ness; when your brain was your last controllable organ, you
couldn't afford to use it carelessly.

It couldn't just be that you believed in the waking world because you saw it, heard it, touched it; you perceived dream worlds
the same way. It also couldn't be because other people experi-
enced the waking world too, because people in your dreams
seemed to experience the same world you did.

There was the fact that you always woke up from dreams.
On the other hand, you could just as easily say that you always
"woke up from" waking when you went to sleep and dreamed
again; how could you decide that one side of the wake/dream
dichotomy was more real than the other? And some psychotics
presumably *never* "woke up" from their delusional worlds. And
besides, you couldn't really say that you would never "wake up"
from the waking world, only that you hadn't so far—which was
the same thing you could say in any dream.

No, the waking world's reality had to do with its *continuity,* he realized, the fact that it was always consistent, was always the same when you came back to it from sleep, from psychosis, from a drug trip, from amnesia, or from anywhere. In the waking world, even if you were absolutely convinced that your car keys were on the hall stand, if you had actually left them in your jacket pocket, that was where you would find them. Waking reality was stable and consistent and long-lasting. That was how you knew it was real; or even if theoretically you wanted to say that it wasn't real, the fact that you always came back to it and that you lived most of your time in it made it a good idea to treat it as real. If you cut off one of your fingers in the real world, you would experience living with nine fingers in most of your future sensoria.

But how did you *know* the real world was always the same when you came back to it? Or rather, how did you choose between the different worlds that you perceived—the worlds of waking, dreams, psychosis, et cetera—and decide which one was consistent and stable and long-lasting? You had to rely on your memory. In non-lucid dreaming you lost your memory of the waking world and had "memories" of the dreaming world: that was what made you believe while you dreamed that the dream world was the one and only real world. And when you woke up and realized it had been a dream, your memories of a world that looked just like the one from before your dream—and before and after all the other dreams you had ever had—told you that *this* was the real world.

So memory was the thing that defined the real world. What you remembered as the continuing story of your life was what defined the real world.

This thought seemed to lend solidity to another idea, one he had toyed with idly when he was learning lucid dreaming: What if in a lucid dream your memories of this world, the waking world, were wiped out and other memories substituted, so that they continued even when you woke up? And what if these new memories told you that in the *real world* text changed on two or three readings, and that lights and mechanical devices didn't work reliably? What if you woke up from such a dream convinced that *this* world was the dream and the other the real world? Your tests would confirm that, and you would wait to "wake up," which you could do by going to sleep in what you now thought of as the dream.

And now apply all that to his present situation. What if the world he was in right now, the world in which he was a head on a pillow in a nursing home, were that kind of self-reinforcing lucid dream, one which convinced you that the waking world was a dream and the dream was reality? Or what if it were a psychotic delusion, with the same characteristics, except that unlike a dream it went on and on, never interrupted? Surely a psychotic delusion could be unpleasant as well as pleasant—in fact, wasn't it more likely to be unpleasant, given that a disease caused it?

What if this world was the hallucination, and Kat's world real? Or what if he had had a false awakening, and had yet to really wake up?

He had been thinking so hard that he hadn't noticed how still the room had become, its darkness heavy with an intrusive silence. At first he tried to ignore it, but he found himself listening tensely. Something was wrong. He realized suddenly what it was.

There was no sound of Humphrey breathing.

That labored wheezing and snoring always erupted when Humphrey slept. He had "breathing problems," the nurses said, for which he was taking numerous medications. And on top of those, numerous other medications not meant for him, Grant happened to know.

"Humphrey?" Grant whispered. He strained his eyes toward Humphrey's bed. A black hump showed where Humphrey lay, but still there was no sound. Grant suddenly understood what this meant.

Strangely, he didn't panic. It was too late for that. He had to go now or not at all. There would be no more Humphrey to eat his pills, so by this time tomorrow Grant would be medicated back out of his mind, whether he decided to swallow the pills himself or make the aides force them down his throat. So it was now or never. He strained his eyes toward the window: the splash of greenish streetlight on the wall was yet untouched by any dawn blush. He had no other way to tell what time it was, but he had to assume the worst—two or three hours until the aides came in to serve breakfast and morning medications.

He felt very calm, and suddenly free of the swaddling self-pity that was more debilitating than any drug. *Think.* That was all he could do, but it was all he needed to do. Figure this out. Escape or be imprisoned here until he died.

In this calm, his mind suddenly felt free, flexible, powerful. The professors he remembered consulting with Before had told him there could be alternate worlds. Now that he had given himself permission to believe in them, only practical questions remained. How had he traveled between them before? His mind ran to the last time he had entered Kat's world. He had decided to vacation in St. Clair. And somewhere between leaving his bed and breakfast and seeing Kat, he had made the transition.

But where? How?

He painstakingly went over everything he remembered from that day, forced himself to recall everything he had seen and done, trying to identify discontinuities, disorientations, or anything that might signal a movement between worlds. He could remember none. Sweat was beginning to tickle on his face and neck as he sensed morning coming. He forced himself to relax, resisted the temptation to rack his brain, tried to let memories and impressions flow. It had been a beautiful day, the air as fresh as he had ever breathed; it had been windy, clouds scudding across the sky, sweeping vast tracts of sun and shadow across a wide landscape, the wind bringing the smell of the ocean—

The ocean.

His feeble heart sped up with excitement, and his eyes went to the dark blot of the map on the wall. There *had* been a discontinuity, but it had happened long before that day in the countryside outside St. Clair. It had happened the day he realized St. Clair was on the ocean, that morning in his St. Clair hotel room, on his last assignment for his law firm. Before that day he had remembered St. Clair being landlocked; after that day it had been on the coast. Now it was apparently landlocked again. Of course, he also remembered living his whole life in a landlocked state several states away from any ocean, but if that was a bogus dream or psychotic memory—

He tried to still himself. What had caused the discontinuity? He went over that morning carefully in his mind. He had had a dream, he remembered. In it he had decided to cross a boundary between his old life and St. Clair, which he saw in the dream as being on the ocean.

But he had often dreamed of other worlds and woken up back in his own. If that dream had caused him to wake up in a different world, *how* had it done it?

He glanced at the greenish bar of streetlight on the wall. Was it his imagination, or was it beginning to be suffused with the slightest shade of blue, as if the sky—invisible from where he lay—were beginning to lighten at the horizon?

What about the time *before* the St. Clair transition? How had he done it then?

The video game! He had played the video game and passed out, and when he woke up he was in another world!

What had the video game done? How had it caused the transition?

The last thing he remembered playing it was a shape on the screen that waved and fluttered like a weed in the wind, like the weed growing up by the fence in the dream he had sometimes—

Suddenly it clicked.

The waving, fluttering shape in the video game; the weed waving and fluttering in the lucid dream he had had that night in the St. Clair Holiday Inn; the IV Thotmoses had put in his neck that had made him see the weed waving—

A shiver went up his twisted spine, shaking his fragile, hunched body. Kat had said something about waves, electrical waves in the brain that could be produced by epilepsy, and if the seizures were in exactly the right place, the waves could shut down the parts of the brain that connected you to the current world, and then your consciousness would be free to go elsewhere, if you could believe in the "elsewhere" and picture it clearly. Grant knew that some epileptics could trigger seizures simply by thinking of a particular thing. Was Grant's trigger the image of the weed fluttering and waving?

He was filled with exhilaration. He was a head on a pillow, heart pounding in his narrow, delicate chest, his thin, twisted arms trembling uncontrollably, just a fragile skeleton hung with deteriorated organs, and he couldn't move, but this was his hour of destiny. Even a head on a pillow could fight.

NINETEEN

CROSSOVER

Grant came to himself still in bed in the dark, but he had no time to feel the despair of failure before he saw something moving under his covers. Something had crawled under there with him; he could feel it. As terror tore through him, two huge snakes burst up out of the bed; he gave a choking scream, and more huge snakes burst out, throwing him painfully to the floor and waving around him until he saw that they looked like arms and legs, and then realized that they *were* arms and legs—and then that they were *his* arms and legs.

Moving!

An exultation burst through him, shaking him even more than the terror. Tears blurred the hands he held before his face in the dark. *His hands,* large and thick and strong—nothing like the skeletal, curled-up claws that had come into his range of vision when the nurse's aides gave him a sponge bath.

"Grant?"

Kat was sitting up in bed, looking down at him in alarm.

Heart pounding blindingly, he put his hands on the floor: instead of washable tile, he felt rug.

The last thing he remembered was closing his eyes and summoning the image of the windy, sunny day, the low chain-link fence with the weed that the mowers had missed growing up next to it, waving and swaying in the wind, its leaves fluttering—

Kat switched on the bedside lamp and looked down at him searchingly. "Grant? Are you all right?"

"I'm all right," he said, looking at his hands, opening and closing them. "I'm all right."

"You've been away," she said softly, slipping her legs out from under the covers, opening a drawer in the night table, and then coming down to crouch next to him, pulling apart the Velcro fastener of a blood pressure cuff. She was wearing a T-shirt and faded blue pajama pants, and he thought she was the most beautiful thing he had ever seen, despite the bruises on her neck and the swollen-shut eye. "Haven't you?"

"I've been away," he said. He looked around and realized that he had a parallel memory of this room, of being here just a few hours ago, crying and screaming— "How long was I gone?"

"You've been here all the time. I gave you a tranquilizer because you freaked out." He remembered that suddenly too. She pushed up the sleeve of his sweaty shirt and strapped the cuff around his arm. "How long do you remember being away? Where were you?"

He tried to explain in a few stumbling words, before he realized what she had said. "What do you mean I've been here all the time?"

"I'll explain everything," she said soothingly. "Are you okay? Are you going to lose it again?"

"I'm okay," he said. "I'm okay."

She read the blood pressure monitor, then shone a penlight in his eyes. Then she put the penlight and cuff back in the drawer and picked up the antique telephone on the night table. "Lake? Sorry to bother you so late. Would you have Deirdre bring us some tea and cakes? Yes, he's up." Then she turned back to Grant. He could smell the warm, clean animal musk of her body. She stood up, pulling on his hand, and he stood too, clumsily. She went to the closet and put on a silvery-blue dressing gown that looked tasty as cake frosting, and then they sat on the edge of the bed, she watching his face intently. "Do you have a headache or feel nauseated? Any odd visual effects, like little squares or part of your range of vision darkened?"

"No."

"Then we can probably wait a little while to get the medical team to examine you, though they won't like it."

"Okay." He sat dazed, looking around

"And we have to keep talking so I'll know if you decide to go into shock."

"Okay. What were we talking about before? Before I left?" As he asked the question, he knew the answer; it was one of his parallel memory streams. "You were explaining what's happening to me. Let's go on with that."

"I mean talk about the weather or something nice. I don't want to get you going again just yet."

"No," he agreed, but then added slowly: "But I'm better now, I think. I mean, where am I going to go? I just brought myself back from there. If I get upset, I'll just stay here and be upset."

"Well, I don't want you to, okay? If you feel like you're getting upset, I want you to tell me right away. Agreed?"

He nodded. There was a soft knock, and a shy girl in an apron came in carrying a tray heavy with tea things and a plate of tiny frosted cakes that looked too precious to eat. She put it down on the small table between the two bedroom armchairs and withdrew silently. Grant suddenly felt starved. They sat in the armchairs, he eating cakes greedily and slurping tea, Kat watching him, arms hugging her knees. The single bedside lamp lit the room dimly, throwing shadows behind their chairs. After a while Grant leaned back, holding his teacup and saucer, and looked at her expectantly.

She took a deep breath. "Where was I?"

He searched his parallel memory stream. "You were about to explain why, if you—your people can run rings around us regular people in traveling between worlds, why you need a regular person to help you talk to Jesus or whatever it is."

"Are you sure you're ready? Don't you want to lie down and rest?"

"I've just been lying down for a year. I never want to lie down again."

She nodded. "What I was trying to tell you before was that we're wired differently. *Sapiens sapiens* brains have very narrow limits on traveling, but the controls are superficial. Our limits are much broader, but the controls are much stronger. You'd have to fundamentally rewire our brains to give us access to a wider range. But paradoxically, for you, disable a few key areas and presto, there are essentially no limits.

"We search for people like you, whose travel-limiting faculties are damaged, but who are still sane. People born with damage to the limiting areas often end up crazy if there's no one to teach them how to travel, because then they travel randomly through unconnected stories. Your preexisting damage wasn't quite great enough to disconnect you without a push, though when I honey-potted you, you jumped proxies the very first time. I've never seen anything like it."

" 'Honey-potted' me?"

"When we first dated. I wanted to see if the memory stream from the locus where we had sex would show up in any of your other proxies. You went for it so fast that I took you right away to let my mother have a look at you. Usually it takes months and a lot of pushing to get even a good candidate to travel for the first time, but you went off like a rocket, though of course you didn't know what had happened. Do you remember being confused about whether or not certain things happened, or where things were? You were cycling back and forth between loci without knowing it. You were trying to treat alternate memory streams as if they were one consistent stream."

But Grant had picked up on a different point. "Usually takes months? How many times have you done this?"

"Dozens, if you mean me personally. It's not a game, Grant. This is how we've survived for hundreds of years, though it's secret even from most of our own people nowadays. It's so rare to find someone who has the potential to help us that we don't stop to ask. We open the doors in their brains and let them decide afterward."

When he finished his tea, she insisted he rest. She left the room for a few minutes and returned wearing her nun's habit and carrying the mobile altar wrapped up in the embroidered cloth. She set it up quickly, lit the candles and incense, and said a long Mass over him. Two men Grant hadn't seen before, also wearing clerical robes, came in partway through this, and examined him thoroughly with lights, monitors, and palpations while she sprinkled, incensed, and mumbled over him. She finished shortly after they left, put everything away, took off her habit, and lay down next to him in the dark. He couldn't sleep. Fear kept him awake, his heart beating fast, sweat beading on his face. Was he still really lying paralyzed in the nursing home? And if he fell asleep here, would he wake up back there, in a world where he was about to be drugged out of his mind again, so that he could never escape? Now that his elation had worn off, it seemed impossible that his return here wasn't too good to be true.

And even if it *was* true, his doubting it might actually destroy it, the way he had destroyed the nursing home world by talking himself out of it.

Relax. Accept where you are, he told himself.

He lay sweating, tense as a spring.

He must have fallen asleep after all, because when he woke the curtains were drawn and the sky was clear and cheerful, though mist clung among the trees of the terraced gardens, and the slanting morning sunlight fell on mist in the valley, where tiny columns of smoke rose from distant chimneys. Grant opened a window; the chilly air smelled like pine and damp dirt.

The Caucasus Synod Western Orthodox Church was a large, squat, spired building of rough gray stone three blocks from the village's single traffic light. Kat parked one of her mother's black SUVs in the gravel lot and they climbed stone steps to the huge arched doors, one of which stood open. Kat was in her jeans and belly shirt again, and a leather jacket. They entered a dim high-ceilinged vestibule with stone walls and a dark wooden floor. Kat knocked on a door at the right, and went in.

Dr. Thotmoses' office was large, bright, and high-ceilinged, with a shiny oak floor and a smell of wood polish and sweet tobacco. Kat led Grant to an enormous desk, the only piece of furniture he had ever seen that looked big enough for Thotmoses. A bald man in clerical robes was leaning over Thotmoses' shoulder and pointing to something on a paper. He was one of the men who had examined Grant the night before. As soon as Kat and Grant came in, he shook hands with them and left, closing the door silently. Thotmoses came around the desk to greet them. He wore a clerical collar but no robe, just his usual rumpled suit.

"Mr. Grant," he said, folding Grant's hand in his huge, dry one. "This is certainly a day for celebration. Sit down. We were worried about you for all of two hours. But Kat tells us you now remember spending a year in a nursing home before returning entirely under your own power. This is very auspicious, I must say." He opened a humidor of expensive-looking cigars, which Grant declined. "I won't ask you to describe your sojourn in detail, as you will be thoroughly debriefed by our medical and psychological staff, including Father Amon, whom you just met. But we have a few preliminary issues to clear up, including the little matter of your employment contract." He went back around the desk and sat down, giving Grant his bland, professional smile. While he looked and sounded the same as Grant remembered, in this office Thotmoses seemed self-assured and charming, not the elderly crank he had been back at the Amana Building, which seemed lifetimes ago now, when Katerina the sister in holy orders had impersonated a perky, perfect girlfriend.

"But even before that, of course, the first order of business must be an apology for deceiving you and putting you through so much uncertainty and fear. I want to express my deep regret for that, and to say that if there is anything I or any of us can do to make amends, you need only let us know. Unfortunately, the sort of people we need to recruit cannot be approached directly with a proposal as unusual as the one we are making to you. And we can't waste our chances of success, because only once in a great while do we identify anyone whose neurological idiopathy reacts to our modifications in just the right way. I want you to know how unique you are. You're one in a million now, and soon, if you continue your excellent progress, you'll be literally one of a kind."

Grant suddenly felt peculiar. "So how many people's brains do you wreck for every one that—reacts the right way?"

"We give them the gift of life beyond the confines of their single world," said Dr. Thotmoses. "They have it forever, to do with as they wish, whether or not they are able to help us."

"But how many never learn to use it? Your 'gift.' How many just end up crazy?"

"A small, very small percentage," Thotmoses said.

"Fuck," said Grant.

"Perhaps," said Thotmoses tactfully, "this is a good segue to the next part of our discussion. The subject of which is: what can we give you in return for your services?"

"And what's with the church getup? You think sprinkling holy water around makes what you do okay?" Grant suddenly felt disoriented; the feeling had been popping up all morning, whenever it struck him that he was treating this world—or "house" or "locus" or whatever it was—as real. Kat glanced at him anxiously, as if she could read his mind.

"The church 'getup' has to do with the fact that we are a church. What we do involves what you might call deeper levels of reality, which is a domain where God cannot be ignored. We sprinkle holy water around and say Masses to call God's blessings onto our endeavors and onto the traveler undergoing these strenuous dislocations, and also to expiate the sin that you rightly observe is part of our struggle to survive." Melancholy passed over the huge man's face, deepening the creases around his mouth. "Think of me as a military chaplain if you like, blessing soldiers who do terrible things because it is their job to defend their community."

"But we are getting off the point. This is the employment contract part of our discussion. I want you to stop thinking of us as vivisectionists and imposters, and start thinking of us as people with whom you can develop a rewarding relationship. A very, very rewarding relationship. People who will give you what you want in exchange for your giving us what we need. What we need is to send you on an adventure that few people know enough to even dream of. And in return, we'll give you anything that's in our power to give. A pretty good deal, I would say."

"I already told your wife. I want her." He gestured at Kat.

Thotmoses' laugh seemed genuine. "Delightful, your performance with Tatiana. She is rarely caught off guard. You are an extraordinary man in more ways than one, apparently. But I'm completely serious, Grant." It was the first time he had called him anything but Mr. Grant. "We are rich, very, very rich. There is almost nothing we can't give you."

"I'm serious too. I want her."

"You already have her, as I understand it," Thotmoses said tactfully.

"I mean forever. To have and to hold, in sickness and in health."

"Let me explain something, Grant," said Thotmoses, leaning his elbows on the desk. "No, please let me finish. You want to strike at us—I understand. It's a phase—agitation, rage, desire for revenge—all perfectly normal. Early on, our recruits often exhibit this affect. Underlying it is fear. We've already manipulated you inexcusably through sexual bait, drugs, and trickery. Rage is a primitive way of banishing fear, asserting control.

"And you're right to be afraid. We are no kinder or less ruthless than other people. Your reaction is a sign of psychological health. But don't confuse healthy feelings with beneficial action. As it happens, your fear is not objectively justified in this case. Our agenda requires you to genuinely like us, or at least sympathize with us. You're no good to us unless you can go to the Source of Fate and sincerely plead our case. Appearances count for nothing there; truth counts for everything. If you dislike us, that dislike will be your message, and we will be hurt rather than helped by your intercession. Which means that we not only have to train you, but we have to bring you around to our side. Get you to love us, if possible. Which means that we will place our resources at your complete disposal. Which means in turn that you are a very lucky man."

Kat seemed about to say something, but held her tongue.

"To have and to hold," Grant said, fury taking him. "You *used* me—"

"Have *you* ever used anyone, Mr. Grant?" Thotmoses interrupted smoothly. "Be honest, because this is important to your moral outrage. What about the girl at the department store where you met Katerina?"

"Oh, so now you're the Ghost of Christmas Past. You people don't leave anything to chance, do you?"

"I am someone who has had to face the paradoxes of sin and survival. And yes, once we saw that you were a prospect, we researched you very thoroughly."

"Is that what you call it? How long were you spying on me before you sucked me in? And I may have jilted people, but I didn't burn holes in their brains."

"That's true. On the one hand, you did no physical damage to them. On the other hand, the damage you did do was simply to satisfy your casual desires. By contrast, the damage we did to you was necessary to ensure the survival of our people.

"If you work with us, you may find out that we are not that different."

```
┌──────────────┐
│   TWENTY     │
└──────────────┘
```

Honeymoon

Grant and Kat were married in a small, funereal ceremony in the
gardens, attended only by Alex and a couple of other senior
household staff, Andrei, and a few elegant, young-looking septu-
agenarians Grant was introduced to as family friends. Grant, in an
agony of confusion and apprehension now that he had actually
gotten what he wanted, had asked Kat pointedly whether she
would be defrocked or whatever they did to nuns, but she said
she had received dispensations long ago for much worse things.
Mrs. Hatshep wore a severe black dress and veil to the wedding.
By contrast, Dr. Thotmoses, on her arm and wearing a tuxedo
that must have taken ten yards of cloth, was as polite and abstracted as ever, as if the marriage of his daughter was no greater
matter than any other formal occasion he was obliged to attend.
Kat, beautiful in a long white dress, was pale but smiling. The
ceremony seemed real enough, though, and one of their wedding
presents was a remodeled carriage house at the far end of the

gardens, on a steep slope with an even better view of the valley than the main house.

On the first morning of his married life, Grant woke up early as Kat carried two steaming mugs of coffee into the bedroom, set one down next to him, and sat on the edge of a chair facing him, elbows on her knees. She wore a blue bathrobe, and looked tired and on edge, but she gave him a smile. "Time to go to church."

Dr. Thotmoses gave Grant a long orientation in a room with a chalkboard in the basement of the church, Kat lolling in a chair reading a magazine. At lunchtime they went out to one of the pricey restaurants in town—this one in a restored Colonial farmhouse—for expensive sandwiches; it reminded Grant of the innumerable lunch meetings with clients he had had in his old life, the familiarity of it almost dispelling the feeling of unreality that had stolen over him that morning.

When they got back to the church, Father Amon and a junior-looking cleric came in and gave Grant a battery of psychological tests, Thotmoses going off to take care of whatever business church officials take care of. By the end of the day Grant was tired, but he didn't know much more about his first training session than what Kat had told him that morning: "You pinpoint a place and time for me as precisely as you can, down to the day. Then you travel there using the technique you worked out in your nursing home. Meanwhile I travel to my own proxy in the same locus and then drive or fly or whatever to where you are.

"Think of it as a honeymoon. You pick somewhere from your past that you love, at a time you love. We can mix business with pleasure."

"I thought we'd go lie on a beach somewhere for a couple of weeks, then spend a month in Europe . . ."

"Not part of the contract." She grinned at him. "You're be-ing overpaid as it is."

To Grant's chagrin, he and Kat slept in separate beds, like middle-aged parents. That night, as she sat cross-legged on hers in Babar pajamas, watching, Grant lay in his while Father Amon and two assistants taped monitoring electrodes to his face and chest, and fit a kind of wired headband onto his head, snaking all the wires out to laptops they had set up in the living room. "We're starting from bed now to ease you into this, because traveling feels like falling asleep at first," she explained. "Keep in mind that dream-ing is different from traveling—Grant, are you listening?"

An anxiety that had been making him feel short of breath all day was now nearly overwhelming. Thotmoses had insisted that he start his training at once, before the memory of the technique he had worked out faded, and that was all very well, but Grant still felt disoriented and vulnerable, not ready. For one thing, he couldn't dismiss from his mind the fear that he might go back to the nursing home. Thotmoses had reassured him that travel was "volitional," which meant that you went only to the places you intended, and then only if you held their images steadily in your mind before exercising your "precipitating stimulus." This Grant tried to do now, but his hands were sweating, and he could feel his heart thumping in his chest. He had given Kat and Thot-moses the nursing home address and the dates he thought he had been there, so that Kat could rescue him in case of mishap.

As soon as Father Amon and his mendicants had followed their wires into the living room, quietly shutting the bedroom door behind them, Kat switched off the lamp and sat against her pillows.

Grant closed his eyes and tried to get into a comfortable

position without disarranging his monitors. A fold of the pillow-case made a bump under his head; he smoothed it out. His T-shirt was binding under his arms: he pulled it down. Then he noticed that there was a crick in his lower back; he tilted his pelvis and pulled in his stomach to relieve it.

Kat began giggling as he pulled his cover down a few inches so it wouldn't push on his throat. "Is Little Lord Fauntleroy comfort-able?"

He rolled his head back and forth to loosen up his neck, and let out his breath to relax. Then he turned his damp palms out so that his arms lay more comfortably, and flexed his shoulders slightly. "Okay."

He tried to relax with a few deep breaths, then closed his eyes and brought clearly into his mind the place where he and Kat had agreed to meet. Then he pictured the windy, bright day with the high overcast that made shadows vague, the public park with the slightly frowzy flower gardens surrounded by a low chain-link fence. At a place along the fence was a tall weed that the mowers had missed. The weed waved and fluttered in the warm breeze, waved and fluttered—

Wearing jeans, his old sweater with the beige and maroon stripes, and his gray Soviet Army–style overcoat from Aunt Dee's sec-ondhand store, David Grant walked along a quiet neighborhood street six days before Christmas, his worn hiking boots squelch-ing in inch-deep slush. Usually the midwinter thaw didn't come until January, but today the temperature was in the high thirties, though the snow-heavy sky was low and iron-gray. The air was windless, damp with the smell of water and snow, and melting snow tapped in the downspouts of the Victorian houses and tin-kled in street drains. Grant walked slowly, hands in his pockets, lulled by the gray stillness and the relief from college toil that the first day of winter break had brought.

It seemed that one minute he was walking quietly, looking around and wondering idly how he would describe this day if he were a writer, and the next minute he had the memories of a forty-nine-year-old lawyer version of himself alongside his own memories, and half of him was astonished and afraid, while the other half knew he was here to meet Kat, and a thrill of excitement came over him as he realized that this was a dream world—no, an "alternate house," a *different* world.

The clashing feelings made him stop walking and gape dizzily at nothing. There was no one else on the street, and the houses looked gray and sleepy. A car turned a corner two blocks away, and came slowly toward him down the very middle of the street, tires hissing thickly in the slush, an old man driving.

A girl came along the street toward him, wearing jeans and a blue parka, and as she got closer, he saw with a start that it was Kat, but young, the girl he had met in his grandmother's dream basement.

She looked into his face attentively as they approached each other. "Are you all right?"

At nineteen years old he seemed even bigger in comparison to her than he did at forty-nine. He opened his mouth to say something but burst into tears instead. Kat put one hand on his shoulder and the other on the back of his neck, and made comforting noises.

"It's okay," she said. "Everything's okay. Do you need me to tell you what's happened? Or do you remember?"

"I remember."

"You'll get used to it. After you do it a few times you'll get used to it."

"What about *him*?"

"He probably won't even remember. He'll block it out or re-member it as a dream or a fantasy. People don't remember things that don't fit, don't make sense. But unless we stay for hours or come back over and over, the most he's likely to do is dream of us."

"Why am I saying 'him'? It's *me*. I'm two people," Grant said frantically, looking at his hands.

"Shhh. Don't yell, Grant—maintain. It's okay. You're all right. You're saying 'him' because that's what people do. Your brain is used to getting memories from all over the place, all kinds of different places and times and events, to stick together into one self, so that's what it's doing now. Almost everybody identifies with the traveler memories because there are more of them, and they frame the local proxies' memories, so they have sort of a stronger center of gravity."

"This is the young me, right? He just got memories from an older me somewhere else, in some other world."

"Right! You got it."

"So I won't meet myself. There's no other me in this world anywhere."

"Right."

"And you too?"

"Right. I left St. Clair yesterday to come here and meet you today."

She took his arm and they started walking again.

"You knew I was going to be here?"

"When I got the memories from the locus where we planned to come here."

"And the people in that world—the people who are you and me—"

"They're still there."

"And they're conscious? They're really us?"

"They're our proxies there; we're our proxies here. We have proxies in all the alternate universes in which we exist."

"They're conscious? Just like we are? Then how come—how is it that we were them just now and we're not them now? Or . . ." His voice trailed off.

"There are two theories of traveling. Do you feel like hearing them now?'

"Yes."

"Okay. There's what they call the Spark Theory, where all the different Grants in all the worlds—'proxies,' we call them—have only one consciousness between them, and that consciousness can only be in one house at a time. So your consciousness travels from house to house, taking its memories with it—or stays stuck in only one house if you don't know how to travel.

"In the Spark Theory, the Grants in all the other houses are just automata—biological machines that act exactly like the Grant proxy would in those houses, but have no consciousness. So if you're conscious in a house, that's all you know for sure; I could be a biological automaton, acting just like Kat-with-consciousness, though I'm actually Kat-without-consciousness. Though in this case I'm not. Though that's what Kat-without-consciousness would say in this situation, because she acts just like Kat-with-consciousness in every way. In fact, they're identical biological machines, except for the consciousness element."

They walked in silence, Grant struggling to get his mind around this, one of his feet cold where slush was leaking into his boot.

"Theory number two is the Memory Theory, which says that all the proxies in every house—all the Grants, all the Kats, all of everyone across all the houses—have consciousness. What travels is memory. So that the David Grant in this house suddenly gets the memories of the David Grant in another house. The memories of his life in the other house are grafted onto his mind, introduced into his brain. That violates no physical laws because the physical brain changes are very tiny, within the Heisenberg-Planck uncertainty threshold. Under the Memory Theory we 'travel' between worlds by remembering them."

Grant tried to digest this, but he still felt stuck way back at the beginning, still trying to believe what he was seeing. "What's the difference between this and a dream? You looked like you look now in the dream where I first saw you. If I hadn't, I wouldn't have recognized you in the store, and none of this would have happened."

"This is real. Dreams can be memories, but they're not real. Like your kid self may dream about us tonight if he represses the memory of this."

"So you came to see me when I was seventeen, and I only remembered it in my dreams?"

"Maybe, but not necessarily. I could have come to a different locus, and your dream could have been a non-local memory."

"Come again?"

"Non-local memories. Remember I told you what dreams do? You can tap into the memories of your proxies in nearby loci. There seems to be a morphogenetic field of some kind that wraps around all the worlds, and it contains memories you can tap into under some conditions. Sometimes in dreams your mind mixes them up with its own weird fantasies.

"Remember telling me about the dream where you first saw me at your grandmother's? You told me the place and date you had dreamed about, so I traveled there and went to visit you. So when you remembered that locus in your dream—which I knew you would because you had told me you remembered it—I was there, I was part of it. But I don't know whether I came to the same locus and you blocked it and only remembered it in dreams later, or whether I came to a nearby locus and you dreamed it by tapping a non-local memory. It doesn't matter anyway."

He stopped walking and stared at her. "But—when I told you about the dream, you had already been in it. If you hadn't been in it, I wouldn't have recognized you and I would never have told you about it."

"Right," she said, smiling up at him, her breath steaming in the damp, cold air. Her face was pink with cold. "It all works out. That's how I knew it was the right locus to go to, because I was in it. And you told me the time and place; otherwise I wouldn't have been able to find it."

"That doesn't make sense," he said angrily.

"Yes it does."

"No it doesn't."

"Yes it does. Causation only works *inside* universes, not *between* them. 'Don't mistake contiguity for continuity,' my father says."

He stared at her blindly, his mind a whirl.

"What's the matter?" she said in alarm.

"I just thought of something."

"What?"

"Do you people live forever?"

"No," she said, puzzled.

"But if you're old, you can switch back to a world when you were young, right?"

"Yes," she said. "But that's different from not dying."

"But you—you can always be living in a young body if you want."

"True," she said. "What are you getting at?"

"Well—well, for us, you can't move out of your body. You stay in one world where—" He gestured helplessly. "—where time is linear. When you get old, you get old, and there's nothing you can do about it. When your body dies, you're trapped and you can't get away."

She shivered, perhaps with cold. "Aren't you glad we met?"

Over the next weeks, Grant traveled to a different locus nearly every night, Kat accompanying him, explaining, soothing, directing him back to their bedroom a couple of times when he started to panic. Thotmoses had explained that a recruit's "continuity index" was always dangerously low at this stage, when he took many short jaunts to practice his technique. Father Amon's monitoring was necessary to make sure that Grant didn't lose his sense of reality, of the thread of his story. Kat was the other safety precaution. When they traveled, her voice was his handhold on sanity; and when they were home he had sex with her as much as he was able, as if by burying himself in the warmth of her body he could hide from the terror of the infinities that pressed around him. He knew that she drugged herself whenever they did it, which meant she was drugged much of the time. But she never refused him; whenever she caught him looking at her hungrily—aroused by some unconsciously graceful movement, or the way she moistened her lips and looked up at him seriously with her beautiful eyes—she would smile sadly and slip away, returning a few minutes later to undress and lie submissive as he took her. The couple of times he put his hands on her without warning, she pulled away with barely concealed panic.

Grant knew, of course, that she had married him as part of her job, and was vaguely aware also that he had insisted on it more out of a need to assert some kind of control than because he loved her. But he needed the safety and release of tension her body gave him. She was beautiful and warm and she smelled good; he could feel the beating of her heart. He didn't want to think. Sex let him not think, let him shut everything out.

One night he climbed into her bed and started to kiss her, held her when she tried to get up for her shot. She was saying something with a shaking voice while he kissed her mouth. He pulled her against him, her writhing muscles and the hammering of her heart exciting him, his mouth going down to her neck.

There was an intense, gashing pain in his ear.

He yanked backward with a yell, both hands going to his ear, eyes so full of water he didn't see what hit him in the face with another scarlet flash of strong pain. He tumbled onto the floor and scrambled clumsily backward, blinked enough water out of his eyes to see Kat kneeling on her bed grasping a candlestick-holder, her hands shaking.

"Get up, you bag of shit," she said in a grating snarl that belied the shaking hands. "You *never* touch me, you understand? I'll kill you next time you touch me, you fucking ape." Her face was twisted with rage and contempt. She still had some blood on her chin from biting his ear.

Alex was washing one of the SUVs under the bright halogen lights mounted over the garage doors. A few crickets creaked in the dark as Grant came down the flagstone walk, hands in the pockets of his jeans, wearing a sports jacket against the spring evening's chill. "Alex, will you take me to the Amtrak station?"

Alex looked surprised, but smiled and threw his rag into his bucket, dug out his keys, and got in the driver's seat. Grant wondered whether he noticed the bruises on his face in the half light.

"Shall I tell them you'll be home for breakfast?" asked Alex as he let Grant out in front of the small, restored railroad station with its quaint spire and clock, obviously wishing he could ask what was going on.

"Sure," said Grant, and closed the door. He didn't mean it sarcastically. He was too jangled to organize a good parting speech. His stomach still trembling, he walked into the cozy brightly lit lobby.

Even though it seemed like an odd, ancient relic, his credit card worked at the ticket counter, and half an hour later he was on the train. There were only a few people in his car, rocking gently as it rattled over rough tracks and around curves. Grant sat with his head bowed, drained, but his mind still going, trying to decide whether what he had done made any sense.

He realized now that he had walked out assuming Kat would come to her senses and come running after him, begging him to stay. She and Thotmoses had told him how important he was so many times that he had started to believe it. He wanted her to plead with him, he realized, so he could spit in her face, make her crawl for the contempt in which she held him and his inferior human type.

But maybe they assumed *he* would come crawling back when he realized what he had done. Could he escape death with what they had taught him already? Or were there other things he had to know? If so, he would *have* to crawl back, no matter what. But what if they wouldn't take him? The thought made the bottom drop out of his stomach. Or maybe this was really a lucid dream or psychotic delusion after all. Maybe this episode—Kat turning crazy, he storming off—was his diseased brain pulling itself closer to reality in preparation for resurfacing, maybe back to the nursing home. His heart pounded, and he touched his throbbing ear delicately. Even if everything Kat had told him was true, his fear might pull him back there. Always at his side, she had been his defense against doubt, keeping him steady and focused. What if he got lost without her, went crazy, wandering the worlds, unable to stabilize any of them or believe in any of them?

He had nothing to fear except fear itself, he told himself

firmly. But he knew that he *was* afraid, and so had good reason to be fearful.

Coming home gave Grant two contradictory feelings. When the cab dropped him off at midday, and he stood in his driveway, damp gusts bringing the smell of rain from the low clouds, the place looked for all the world as if he had only been gone for a weekend; yet what he had lived through since he had last been here made him feel like a ghost returning to a former life.

He let himself in. He didn't realize until he saw his furniture and smelled the familiar smell of the house that he had been half-afraid someone else would be living there, that he had become a kind of Rip Van Winkle, returning to a world where he had no place. But everything was untouched. He walked into the sunken living room and opened the blinds. The house seemed comfortable and quiet, though small and low-ceilinged; he remembered bemusedly how proud he had once been of its size and elegance. He dropped onto the sofa with its reassuring smell of leather, untied his shoes, stretched his tired toes. Actually, it was what you would call snug, he thought contentedly. He knew he would get used to the illusion that the small rooms didn't contain enough air for breathing. He got up and opened the sliding door to the patio a couple of inches, then lay on the couch. Here he was suddenly back to his old comfortable life, and it felt good. He didn't have to ever move from here again, he told himself. This world was as real as they came, either really real or just as real as he wanted it to be. Maybe he would go back to work, though he didn't need the money. And once he felt stable enough in this world, maybe he would see about poking around in some others again. He owed Kat and Dr. Thotmoses nothing. This was better for him than their crazy plan that he "go to God," if that wasn't all just a fable.

If traveling was too hard without Kat, fine: he would stay home. A couple of tears welled from his eyes and ran down the sides of his face. He wiped them away with his sleeve, smelling the salty twenty-four-hour body odor on his shirt. He was done with them, and good riddance. He believed in the other worlds, he realized with dull surprise as he drifted off to sleep. He believed, but that didn't mean he had to travel to them. Except maybe when he was old and wanted to be young again. That seemed too good to be true, yet it seemed it *was* true. Like a dream . . .

TWENTY-
ONE

GARDEN OMPHALOS

Grant stood by the waist-high chain-link fence of a frowzy public garden on a bright, windy, high-overcast summer day, just
stood there dreamily until he realized where he was. He was *here,*
his departure point for traveling between houses. If he walked a
dozen yards along this fence, he would come to the tall weed the
mowers had missed, the one that waved back and forth in the
breeze— He made himself think of something else; visualizing
the weed was how he traveled; he had learned how to arrive just
out of sight of it so that there would be no danger of being
swept away before he had time to properly visualize his chosen
destination. The fact that he had come here on falling asleep
didn't mean anything: he had gotten used to starting his travels
from this place, coming here to let the waving weed—his "precipitating epileptogenic stimulus"—disable his brain's neurological barriers to traveling. Should he wake up, return home? He
had decided at the very least to take a rest in his familiar world

before he thought of traveling again. On the other hand, he didn't want to program his brain to avoid this place, because he would need to come here if he ever did decide to travel.

The afternoon was warm and sleepy, the wind making a somnolent rushing sound—now rising, now falling—in the young pines and maples in the garden beyond the fence, in the hedges, scraggly rosebushes, and flower beds. From the middle distance he could hear the yells of children and see among the trees the sparkle of a swimming pool. It was relaxingly familiar; he felt the anxiety draining out of him. Now that he was here, there didn't seem to be any reason he shouldn't wander around a bit. He could go home anytime using the traveling skills he had learned.

The public garden and swimming pool were on a hilltop, and on the side nearest him was a parking lot of cracked gray asphalt about a quarter full of comfortably aged family cars, contrasting with his own shiny BMW. A narrow blacktop ran down a grassy slope, disappearing at the bottom among trees, beyond which Grant glimpsed quiet, hilly suburban neighborhoods. He had lived in one of them as a child, his local proxy's memory told him; now he had an opulent downtown condo.

A sidewalk led from the parking lot to an open gate in the chain-link fence. A bulging woman with pale, suety legs was coming slowly along this sidewalk, patiently leading by the hand a tiny girl who was singing to herself. Both wore flowered bathing suits. The woman watched Grant carefully, and he realized that he must look strange: a middle-aged man gawking around as if he had just arrived from another world. He pretended to be reading the faded sign prohibiting alcoholic beverages, skateboards, pets, and motor vehicles of any kind. It also said that the park was closed after dark, though anyone could climb over the fence, he remembered from his own childhood. In this locus he had never left town, had returned after college and law school, gotten a job with a local firm—

He let the woman and tiny girl move slowly through the gate, and gave them time to progress along the gravel path, the girl's singing getting louder and more emphatic, as if drawn forth by the swimming pool that was now at hand. Finally, having given them a long head start, he followed.

The wind was less in the garden, screened by trees and hedges. As he crunched along the gravel, the warm, gusty fragrance of flower beds and pine was gradually cut by the sharp smell of chlorinated water, a smell that even after forty years gave him a thrill of excitement, the same excitement that filled the yells of the children playing in the rectangle of sparkling blue.

The pool was inside another chain-link fence, this one seven feet tall to prevent all but the most determined youths from drowning after hours. The woman with the suety legs was now sitting on a pool chair under one of the faded blue beach umbrellas, taking off her daughter's sun hat. A couple of other pale mothers tended their toddlers in the shallow end; a small boy shining with water and holding an inner tube with a horse's head around his waist was trying only half-successfully to observe the rule against running, leaving a wet trail on the sun-baked pool terrace; a bigger boy in knee-length trunks jumped off the diving board cannonball fashion, his skinny body making an unimpressive splash. All as it had been in Grant's own middle-class childhood, as it had been in the childhoods of countless children in late twentieth-century middle-America, which existed somewhere out among the worlds.

A low, white-painted cinderblock building on the opposite side of the pool had signs saying MEN and WOMEN. Grant followed the sidewalk and entered through the Men's side. No one gave him a glance. The pool chairs under the umbrella next to the suety mother's were free of towels and clothes; he went and sat on one of them. He reclined it comfortably and closed his eyes, the breeze stirring his hair. He didn't need to go to God, he realized; just this was enough; the sense of the eternal existence of this day somewhere, this eternal warm, breezy summer day at the suburban swimming pool, innocent and depthless as sunlight sparkling on water.

"Excuse me."

Grant opened his eyes. It was the mother in the flowered bathing suit, standing by his umbrella. Her daughter sat on the concrete in the shade of the next umbrella, absorbed in making a plastic horse run in and out of a plastic bucket turned on its side, and narrating to herself. With a momentary feeling that he must have done something wrong, he said in a voice that sounded more defensive than he meant: "Yes?"

"Who are you?"

She said it not as if she was about to tell him that the pool was for members only, but curiously, as if she wanted to know.

"David Grant," he said, recovering his manners and straightening in his chair. He was about to add some pleasantry when she said, "You're a traveler, aren't you?"

"I beg your pardon?"

"A traveler between the worlds. Or the 'houses,' as they call them."

He gaped. "Who are you?"

"Maryann Shelby. May I sit down?"

"Um—of course." A jolt of excitement went through him. Kat and Thotmoses had told him they had trained other "candidates," of course, but for some reason he had never imagined actually meeting one. "You're a—you know how to—"

As Maryann Shelby sat down, her little girl looked up to get a bead on her, then continued with her horse game. The woman's poise and the steadiness of her brown eyes were disorienting, incongruous in her flabby body, which had the self-righteous protectiveness emitted like a pheromone by the mothers of very young children. It was as if an actress playing a mother had suddenly stepped out of character. "Not now. Now I mostly live here. May I ask who recruited you?"

"What? Um— Can I ask why you want to know?"

"Are you still working for them?" When he still hesitated, she asked with mild surprise: "Am I the first traveler you've met? David, if you're going to wander around out here, you're going to have to get used to the expatriates."

"What do you mean?"

"Almost nobody goes all the way for them. Very few even try." She studied him shrewdly. "You've just quit, haven't you?"

"Yes."

"Good for you. Almost everyone does. As soon as they find out what's really going on, they drop out and take off on their own, pursue their own agendas." She sat dignified and composed, hands folded on the round table under the umbrella. She laughed suddenly. "I don't look much like a cross-universe adventurer, I know," she said. "It's just that I realized after a long time that this was the most supremely happy day of my life. So I spend a lot of time here."

"Here," he echoed, trying to get his bearings.

"Yes. It doesn't look like much, does it? But it has everything. Love—" She glanced at her little girl, who was now lying down with her plastic horse clasped to her chest, in a twitching counterfeit of sleep. "Comfort. Leisure. Good weather." She smiled at Grant again. "I've seen you here several times, looking around as if you just arrived, then just leaving again suddenly.

There's a particular look the travelers have. Or maybe in some way people who have multiple parallel memory streams can sense them in others. Does your local proxy live around here?"

"Downtown."

"Do you visit because it's such a beautiful day?"

"No. It's my—departure point."

"Oh!" she said with seeming surprise and pleasure. "Well, that makes sense, actually. Some days are just unworldly; they contain something other days don't. This day has a feeling of—" She seemed to study the afternoon with narrowed eyes. "—eternity. You can conceive of it going on and on forever. You must have felt it once, and come back to it."

"So you come here, to this day, over and over?"

"Not always, but often. Like a comfortable chair in your favorite nook in the garden. I was recruited by Piotr Thotmoses and Andrei Hatshep."

Grant felt struck by a thunderbolt. "Andrei! Did he have a sister named Katerina?"

"So it *was* them!" said Maryann Shelby excitedly. "It's so nice to meet you, David! Like meeting an old friend, or at least a fellow-member of an exclusive club. She *was* his sister. I met her, of course, but she wasn't involved in my training. It was Andrei and Dr. Thotmoses for me. Of course, for you it would have been Katerina. Unless you had been homosexual—then we would have shared a lover as well as our training. How exciting! How are the old gang? As rapacious as ever? How did you figure them out?"

"I'm not sure I *have* figured them out," said Grant slowly. He wasn't sure what to make of the Shelby woman. Could she be another of Thotmoses' tricks, or some kind of test? He looked around the swimming pool reflexively.

"How do you mean? You're on your own here, aren't you?"

She looked around the pool too. "Or is your handler hanging around here somewhere out of sight?"

"No," said Grant. "I'm on my own. Kat and I had a—disagreement, and I walked out. Out of the training program and everything else, I guess."

"Oh, I see, a romantic tiff. How interesting! You'll have to tell me about it; I'd love to hear about someone walking out on Katerina. How long had you been training?"

"It's kind of hard to say—because I've been different times in different worlds, I mean."

"I understand you. But you caught on, anyway, however long it took."

"Caught on to what?"

"What you caught on to. That you were being had."

"Well, I figured that out, yes, but that's not why I left. I mean, they make no secret of it, do they? They were pretty up front about it with me."

"Oh, yes, they're terribly, disarmingly up front," said Maryann. "After they reel you back in from the first shock of betrayal, and the second shock, and the third shock. 'Yes, we tricked you and screwed you and we're using you, and because we've admitted it you can trust us from now on' is the only way to restore any kind of working relationship, wouldn't you think? You don't mind my saying this, do you? If you still feel loyal to them—"

"No, no, please go on." A melancholy comfort had begun to replace his surprise. What the Shelby woman said made sense, and it was an enormous relief to have someone to talk to about it.

"They're very smart and they've had a lot of experience. They know they're beautiful and fascinating, which makes it easy for people to overlook their ill-treatment. So did Kat marry you? Andrei married me."

Grant stared at her.

"And they have Mrs. Hatshep pretend she's terribly against it—"

"They—that happened to you too?"

"It happens to everyone the Thotmoses team recruits. As I said, they have a system. So she did marry you?"

In spite of everything, Grant's heart was like a stone. He tried to keep the feeling out of his voice, but it sounded ashen anyway. "Yes. But one time when I tried to have sex with her she—hit me. With a candlestick." He put his hand up to his face tenderly, but there were no bruises or scabs on this proxy.

"Really?" she asked, deliciously scandalized, as if they were talking about an office romance. "But I'm amazed she would risk it. Their recruits are like gold to them—that much of what they say is true." To his surprise, she reached across the table and put her cool, plump hand on his. "Don't be sad, David. They take everyone in. Katerina and Andrei have probably seduced more people than Wilt Chamberlain. But in the end, they're stone cold."

"But they have to be, don't they?"

"Oh, yes," said Maryann, with fierce mockery. "Because burning people's brains and sending them up the pipeline to beg God is the only way the poor darlings can survive. Because they don't have the killer instincts of us strong, scary *Homo sapiens sapiens*. You *have* come out early, haven't you? Well, it's not your fault. It's hard to tell what's true and what's not when they've just taken your reality to pieces. But you would have figured it out eventually."

"You don't believe them."

"You've seen their methods, and what they're like when they're angry. Does any of that suggest that they evolved from peaceful vegetarian sloths? And now you're going to tell me that they have to send us because their brain structure limits how far they can jump houses," she said as Grant opened his mouth to say that. "Well, I haven't done any studies on their brains, but I've talked to people, expatriates like us, who don't believe that stuff about them being a separate subspecies. It's just as likely they're a bunch of people who figured out how to do this some-how, and invented an elaborate story to tell their trainees. I've talked to people who've seen them as far out in the worlds as you can go and still get back. And that's the point."

"What is?"

"You can't go all that distance, all the way up near the Source of Fate, and stay human. That's why they send us. It's like send-ing dogs into collapsed buildings to find survivors. Why should they risk their beautiful, rich, clever selves when they can sacri-fice us? We're like dogs to them: some of them love us, but when push comes to shove—"

Grant stared at her. "So they can go as far as we can? Up to wherever it is and all that?"

"If they're modified the way they modify us, I would bet yes. People who've been around a lot longer than I have are al-most sure of it. They use us because, hey, it's a tough job, but somebody's got to do it."

When he opened his eyes, lying on the couch in his living room, it was night, not even a glow on the horizon showing where the sun had gone down. One of his arms was asleep, and the night air through the slightly open glass door had made the living room chilly. He sat up groggily. Light came from the direction of the kitchen. He thought he had left it on until he heard the clink of a spoon. His heart jumped. He got up, rubbing his arm and blinking sleep out of his eyes.

The kitchen light seemed blinding. He stood in the doorway

squinting. Kat sat at the kitchen table with a mug of tea, grinning up at him.

"You look great," she said. "I can smell your breath from here."

"So you came."

"Isn't that what you wanted? For me to crawl to you, swear I'll never do it again?"

"I'm not sure that'll be enough."

"Of course not. Do you want to beat me up again, or—?"

Anger rose in him suddenly. "No, that's all right. Just make yourself comfortable, sneer at me until you feel a little rested, and then *get the fuck out of my house.*" He was breathing hard suddenly, and he realized that his hands were clenched.

She jumped up, knocking her chair over. "You fucking asshole!" she screamed into his face. "Why did you have to do that? The one thing that would get your tiny little *sapiens* brain all twisted up. Oh," she minced mockingly, "she won't spread her legs for me, so I'll rape her! Oh, she doesn't like that—!"

Head spinning with rage, he grabbed her arms. "If you don't like *sapiens*," he gritted, hustling her out of the kitchen and down the dark hall to the foyer, "then you should stay away from them. You should stay away from them."

"Get your hands off me—! Get your *god damn*—!"

They scuffled by the front door, he smelling her violent animal musk. She managed to pull away and stand against the door, breathing hard, eyes gleaming desperately in the dark. "Don't you understand?" she quavered. "Do you think I'm superhuman? You think only you can go to mental hospitals and get totally fucked up?" Sudden tears ran down her cheeks. "Come back, okay?" she sobbed. "I'll do what you want, anything you want. It'll never happen again, I swear."

"I don't want it as part of your job."

"Then what do you want?" she shrieked insanely. *"What do you want?"*

The crazy rictus of her face drove him back a step, but she seemed to have exhausted herself; she leaned back against the door again and sobbed helplessly with sick desperation. "It'll never happen again. I'll do whatever you want," she said brokenly.

The rage suddenly drained out of Grant. He stood slump-shouldered, feeling the cool slate of the floor through his socks, head throbbing as if he had a hangover. He tried to think. Finally he asked a question he had puzzled out on the train: "Why do you care what I do? You said the houses include all possible universes. So if that's true, there are houses where I work with you, and houses where I don't. If this is a house where I don't, so what?"

"Because in this house whether or not you work with us is important. It's my whole life."

"But—you can move to some other house. Where I *do* work with you."

She stared at him. "Sure. I could go house to house, to wherever good things happen, regardless of whether they have any consistency, until my continuity index goes to zero and my life has no story, and I go insane. Just go wherever it feels good. Break down all meaning, all causation, all goals."

He was silent.

"People can't live like that." She had stopped crying. The opportunity to work, to explain something to a recruit, seemed to steady her. "We're not aliens. We need to live lives with stories, with meaning, just like anyone else."

"Why? Just as a game? When you know you don't have to?"

"Think of your old life, before you learned how to travel. Why did you work and strive to achieve things, knowing that in the end you would die anyway? Why did you bother? Was it just a game? I mean, you could have been a heroin addict and stayed at home the rest of your life feeling good, waiting for death that way, right? The outcome would have been the same." When he didn't answer, she went on. "This is *real,* Grant. Each of the houses is *real,* and is all there is. There are important things, things we have to do. The fact that there are an infinite number of houses is an abstraction, but this is *real,* and in this reality we need you. *I* need you."

"I have to sit down," he said dully.

They went back to the kitchen and sat across the table from each other. She clasped her cup of lukewarm tea with slightly trembling hands as if to warm herself, face red and beautiful eyes bloodshot. One of them still had faint blue marks around it from where he had tried to kill her a few weeks or months ago, telling him that they were in the same locus where that had happened. Her beauty was almost enough to make him forgive her, he realized, but now the thought stirred anxiety and anger in his gut.

"Do you know someone named Maryann Shelby?"

She looked startled. "Yes," she said cautiously. When he kept his eyes on her, she went on: "She was a recruit we tried to train. She didn't work out."

"She says she left when she found out the truth."

"Where did you see her? Is that why you—?"

"No. It wasn't until just now. She was at my departure locus. It's a place I lived when I was a kid, it turns out. There's a park with a swimming pool. I wandered around in there and she was at the swimming pool. She figured out I was a traveler somehow." Then, suddenly worried, he added: "You won't go after her, will you?"

"We don't 'go after' people. It's too much trouble, and there's no reason to anyway. We anticipate a certain amount of attrition."

"How much attrition? Percentage-wise?"

She shrugged, studying him anxiously, her forehead wrinkled. "What did Maryann tell you?"

"That you folks could go up to the Source of Fate or whatever you call it just as well as we can, but you prefer us to do it. And that going up there damages people."

"That's not true."

"None of it?"

"It doesn't damage people. It changes them, but what do you expect? Going there isn't a minor thing. It's an experience that a lot of people would die for."

"What about the other part, that you can go up yourselves. Is that true?"

"Well, as far as it goes," she said slowly. "But you—and Maryann—don't understand. I wish we had had a chance to talk to her before she took off, if that's what was bothering her."

"Maybe the best strategy," said Grant heavily, "would be to talk to people up front. Act with a minimum of decency. Otherwise there's quite a large disillusionment factor when they find out the way I did—especially when it's the tenth fucking time you've fed them a pack of lies." He was trying to get angry again, but he just felt dull and empty.

"We can't do that. If we had 'leveled' with you a year ago, you would have run like hell. We had to show you first and tell you second. I think you understand that, and that's why you decided to accept what happened. Well, you know what? There are some more things we're not telling you, for the same reason. It's the same reason you don't tell toddlers about sex. They wouldn't understand it, and it would just scare them, and probably interfere with their development. But say one toddler who thinks she's precocious finds out about sex and tells other toddlers about it. That's in essence what Maryann did to you. You blame us for hiding the truth, but it's something we want you to learn at the right time, when you're equipped to understand it.

"This is going to sound funny, Grant, but you have to trust us."

"Trust you." He stared at the table, trying to think. The heaviness in him was turning to utter exhaustion and a faint nausea, and it felt better not to move too much. "Because you're so pretty and rich and smart. When you're perfectly happy lying to me, and you see my kind as a sort of farm animal—"

"We do *not* see you as a farm animal. You're more like a Messiah to us. You know how people treat Messiahs? They try to propitiate them, flatter and bribe and persuade them. There's nothing more selfish than a person facing her Messiah. So stop bullshitting me, Grant. You're in a position of strength, and you know it. What do you want? You can have anything. *Anything.* You want to rape me, starve me, torture me? You want money, or a harem, or drugs? You can have anything you want. Just tell me. *Tell me.*"

TWO

MARRIED LIFE

Kat was as good as her word, but by the time they had been back in their honeymoon house just a few days, he knew that he had made another irreversible mistake with her. Whether because she thought he might want sex without notice or because she could no longer bear living with him any other way, Kat was now drugged nearly all the time, her face slack, eyes dull, pupils so dilated that her irises often looked black. She had changed her wardrobe too; she now wore short skirts and lace stockings like a prostitute, leather with hot lingerie underneath, filmy, clinging nightgowns. But she was like a doll, a "poseable action figure," submissive and willing, but inert.

But Grant's dismay at this change in her was eclipsed by dismay at himself. Something had snapped inside him, some fiber of rationality or forbearance. It was impossible to accept what had happened to him; the real world had been yanked away, and he was falling through an abyss with nothing to hold on to. Before,

Kat had been his companion, his helper, his security. But Kat had withdrawn into a chemical haze, and now he was all alone, falling through pieces of stories, incomplete episodes, scenes that didn't fit together, things brushing against him, words in his ears, visions in his eyes.

Maybe it was this disorientation, or rage at the glimpse he had gotten of her contempt for him, or revenge for her withdrawal into the drugs, but he began to treat her in a way that seemed to him nearly insane. Now that he knew she would let him get away with anything, and now that the woman he knew had hidden herself away, he felt almost incapable of not pushing the envelope, devising new things to try on the beautiful doll that lay unfeeling on the bed for him.

She deserved it, he told himself savagely. She had seduced him, set him up to have his brain scrambled, kept him from getting help, and now maybe he was a hallucinating paraplegic, or a toy for some sick rich people on a hidden estate, or a madman, or no one at all. Anyway she couldn't feel anything, he told himself when the flames engulfed him. Sometimes afterward he would hold her enervated body and sob. But his guilt at torturing this sad little doll didn't seem able to break the addiction to perverse adventure that was at least a handhold on reality now that the old Kat was gone. No one ever said a word about it, though they could hardly have missed the changes in her. Father Amon and his people did their monitoring as though she wasn't there; Thotmoses never remarked when she showed up for Grant's lectures obviously snowed to the eyebrows.

She was now quiet and submissive outside the bedroom too; she seemed to exist only for his comfort. She ate little, and grew thin and pale, and Grant, watching her from the corners of his eyes, asked himself: What if she dies? The question tormented him. She rarely said anything unless he talked to her: she served him his meals, rubbed his back when he was tense, never left the house without him, and, of course, gave him sex whenever he wanted it.

At the same time, his training accelerated. He seemed to have developed a split personality: focused and disciplined at work; sadistic and pathologically impulsive at home. As Kat declined, Thotmoses took a more active role. After a few weeks, Grant had learned to travel while awake, or at least to distinguish sleep from the transitional withdrawal of consciousness that traveling involved. Increasingly now he traveled alone. From the start he had had a skill for directing himself, finding in lucid dreams the house he was aiming for, and later holding its image, its *feeling* clearly as he watched the waving weed by the chain-link fence.

One day Thotmoses told him, "We've decided on your next step. We want you to explore your departure locus, exclusively. Spend as much time as possible there. Stay away from the epileptogenic stimulus so you won't travel by accident."

"What's the objective?"

"Exploratory. The departure locus obviously has some special significance for you: you were drawn there almost before your training started. We hope to find out whether this has any implications for your further development."

Grant had been a lawyer long enough to recognize a non-answer. But having no better plan, he began to wander around his departure locus, always on the same summer day, warm, breezy, and bright, though as the afternoon wore on a haziness diffused the sunlight so that shadows became vague, and some subliminal barometric sense seemed to pick up a feeling in the air that made him glance often at the horizon; but nowhere was there any sign of either calm or storm, only the pale, bright haze and the warm, gusty wind. Only once did he finger the keys to his new gray BMW and consider driving back to his apartment, but he quickly decided against it. His local proxy—which had driven here this Sunday afternoon to see the old neighborhood—was deadly familiar with the apartment and downtown, the streets, bars, restaurants, clubs, his office building, the theaters and halls—a twenty-five-year stint in this small city had numbed him to all of it; he was sure that whatever he had come here for wasn't anywhere back there.

Instead, he started to take walks in the hilly neighborhoods surrounding the public garden. At the bottom of the road that led down from the parking lot was a quiet intersection with streets climbing away in three directions. The first day, Grant chose at random Larch Street, whose sidewalk was so steep it was almost like a staircase stained by the tart-smelling fruit of crab apple trees. After a few blocks of small, neat houses with small, neat yards, Larch leveled off, and Grant took a cross street that curved uphill again. Soon he was breathing hard, sweating despite the breeze, and the crab apple trees had given way to mature oaks and elms growing well back from the sidewalk over flower beds, shrubs, and big lawns. To his right, the yards sloped upward; on his left houses, trees, and fences closed off the downhill view, so that only the sense of being high up remained, as if, oddly, this suburban hill had brought him to a place where the light was clearer, where sounds seemed to leak away into the air, giving the impression of emptiness you feel on mountaintops. At its summit, the street ran level for a hundred yards, and Grant had the sudden illusion that beyond the houses and trees on one side or the other there *was* nothing but sky, that the world fell away just a dozen yards from him, fading into the silent, hazy, bright sky.

Maybe it really did, he thought with a jolt. Maybe that was what he was supposed to find here.

A white Colonial on his left had a wide lawn with overhanging trees and a pink reflecting ball on a pedestal. There was no one on the street, and the house looked empty, its inhabitants off at work or somewhere. Grant crossed its lawn, seeing in the reflecting ball a pink, convex world in which a rapidly swelling man moved toward an abrupt horizon where purplish leaves fluttered. Under the trees the yard smelled damp and mulchy. In back there was a second-floor deck, firewood stacked on flagstones underneath. A small, patchy back lawn sloped down to a high wooden fence, over which poked leaves from the next garden. Grant pulled himself up on the fence so he could look between the leaves. Beyond was a sunny back yard with a swing set, a pale brick rambler, and beyond that a glimpse of another sloping street, reality continuing innocently beyond sight after all.

There was no telling for sure how far it really went, but at least it had the decency to continue where you actually looked, keeping up appearances. Grant walked back out to the street, expanding calamitously and then shrinking away again to nothing in the pink ball.

TWENTY-THREE

Himself

As the weeks went by, Grant looked forward more and more to his walks in the departure locus: they seemed to calm him, focus his mind, as if he had finally found a real place to rest his feet. Back "home" he became quiet and preoccupied, as if the center of gravity of his reality—his "default locus"—had begun to shift, pushing to the periphery the world where he and Kat shared a house at the end of Mrs. Hatshep's gardens with laptops, wires, and psychological testers, making it a place visited but not lived in. As his attention withdrew from her, Kat began to gain weight and get some color back, though she continued the dutiful wife, unobtrusive but always available—and always watching him.

He began to venture farther and farther on his departure locus walks, staying longer, often not leaving until evening, when the first drops of rain from a storm that piled up in the late afternoon began to fall. Eventually he reached the limit of how far he could walk and still be back to the weed before the downpour. Still there had been no revelation, nothing out of the ordinary except the occasional odd feeling as he watched flowers nod in the wind in someone's yard, or stood on a sidewalk on the highest point of a climbing street. He would have to stay in the locus longer so he could walk farther, it seemed. It need make no difference how long he was away from the house he shared with Kat, because of course the point at which he "returned"—when the local proxy received the memories or consciousness, whichever it was, from the other locus—was entirely up to him. He had asked Thotmoses why he needed to return at all—why he couldn't spend his "off" hours anywhere he wanted—back home in the city, for example, or at some beach bar in Tahiti. Thotmoses was firm, however: now that his continuity index was climbing back to healthy levels, the last thing he should do was spike it again. The mind needed a causally plausible sequence of events to function properly. Whimsical travel outside such a coherent storyline caused disorientation, feelings of unreality, eventually psychosis. Even the most seasoned travelers made sure that their lives made some kind of firm sense; such discipline in a trainee was even more important.

The next time he traveled to the departure locus, he visualized himself an umbrella, and found himself by the chain-link fence holding it. That didn't violate any physical laws, he knew: he had simply shown up in a locus where his proxy carried an umbrella for completely causal reasons—such as having listened to the weather report, which he now remembered doing at his downtown apartment.

So that afternoon when towering thunderheads blew up like sunlit cliffs, gradually turning the daylight pearly, then misty white, then flat gray as they moved ponderously across the sky, Grant continued walking, beyond the farthest point he had reached so far. Soon the wind died, leaving still, muggy air, and he could hear now and then the faint wet grumbling of the storm. When the first raindrops started to fall with a cool downward gust, the deep light making the green of the trees dark and rich, he still hadn't turned around; he opened his umbrella and kept walking.

At first the rain was soft, as if the small drops floated thickly down from just above the trees. But they gradually got bigger and came down harder, until rain roared in silvery-dark curtains all around him and light from windows glittered yellow in spattering water on the sidewalk. Thunder boomed loud and ominously behind him, and he suddenly remembered reading about people caught outdoors in thunderstorms, whose names also appeared in the obituary columns. He hadn't thought of that; taking an umbrella had seemed ample forethought. He needed to get indoors, he realized, or risk going to God prematurely.

An enormous, splitting crack of lightning blinded and deafened him with a bang he could feel on his skin.

He ran in terror toward the nearest house, flooded lawn squishing under his feet.

The old man, Mr. Kinepolous, gave him a slightly musty towel to dry his hair. Grant had lost his umbrella somewhere between the sidewalk and the front door, and had gotten soaked in the time it had taken Mr. Kinepolous to put down his newspaper, get up from his armchair under the lamp, and shuffle into the front hall. Mr. Kinepolous's tiny bathroom was done in white and green tile, the floor in white and black tile, in a zigzag pattern that must have been elegant just after World War II. While Grant dried off, Mr. Kinepolous got him a cup of coffee, and gave it to him in the living room with a tremulous hand that made the black liquid ripple.

"It's very kind of you," Grant said, still holding the towel. "I'm sorry to—"

"Oh, no," Mr. Kinepolous waved a thick gray-haired hand dismissively, closing his eyes. He was hunched and bald, with a sagging, fleshy face and enormous ears, large gray pants, and a threadbare sweater. "Sit."

Holding his cup of coffee and the towel, Grant sat on the museum piece Mr. Kinepolous indicated—a sofa of some 1950s design. Everything in the tiny living room was the same vintage: the coffee table, two lamps, the radio, Mr. Kinepolous's armchair—this worn to the nap—and Mr. Kinepolous himself. He lowered himself stiffly into the armchair, let out his breath, and crossed his feet in down-at-the-heel slippers. "I'm a widower," he said. "So I don't mind the company." He had a very slight accent, and he talked slightly too loudly. "Listen to that," he said, rolling his eyes upward as a booming roll of thunder reached a crescendo, shaking the house. "Maybe it'll break this heat, anyway. You live in the neighborhood?"

"Downtown."

"Ahh. You can use the phone if you want to call someone to come pick you up." He waved backhanded at the ancient rotary instrument on the lamp stand next to him.

"Well, actually, my car is at the park. I was just looking around when it started to rain."

"Park?" asked Mr. Kinepolous. "Which one?"

"I don't know the name. It's a few miles from here."

"A few miles," Mr. Kinepolous murmured, putting his thick hands on the arms of his chair and wrinkling his already wrinkled brows. Then began a painfully slow discussion—a monologue, mostly—with long pauses while Mr. Kinepolous screwed up his face or closed his eyes, locating each city park in his memory, and sketching out a geographic plan of the city as it had been many years ago. There were a hundred parks, Grant guessed, but listening to the rumble of thunder and the rain drumming on a roof somewhere up the narrow staircase off the front hall, Grant didn't feel impatient. Finally Mr. Kinepolous ended his monologue with: "Anyway, you can stay here tonight if you want. I'll fix you up a bed on the sofa."

"It's very kind of you," said Grant.

"Oh, no," said Mr. Kinepolous, closing his eyes and waving dismissively.

With painful slowness, Mr. Kinepolous made up the sofa, mumbling directions to himself from time to time and seeming not to hear Grant's offers to help. A short time later he said good night and fumbled with the lamp switches, then went upstairs, and Grant lay alone in the dark. He could hear Mr. Kinepolous moving around upstairs, a small thump or the squeak of springs. The pillow he had his head on was lumpy and a little smelly, and the sofa was too short, so that he lay with his feet propped on one of the arms, but the warmth of the old man's hospitality had made him relaxed and sleepy, as if he had found somewhere safe after so long.

Of course, as soon as he fell asleep he found himself standing by the fence at the little public garden half a day's walk away, on yesterday's windy, warm afternoon. He could have gone back to Kat and Dr. Thotmoses or started walking again, either toward Mr. Kinepolous's house or in some other direction, but instead he decided to wake up on the sofa where he had fallen asleep. He liked Mr. Kinepolous, and besides, waking up there would improve his continuity scores, which Thotmoses was always nagging him about. And he might be able to get all the way across the city from Mr. Kinepolous's house if he started early enough.

So he moved slowly along the chain-link fence toward the

weed, visualizing Mr. Kinepolous's tiny post–World War II living room with the antique radio and sofa, the antique upright piano in the corner, the 1950s lamps and armchair and telephone, Mr. Kinepolous's voice in his ears describing the city as it used to be . . .

When he woke up it was morning, which is a good time to wake up, though it doesn't matter so much if you've just come from a coordinate where it's always afternoon and you can go anywhere at any time. He lay on the sofa in Mr. Kinepolous's tiny living room, sunlight coming cheerfully through small open windows on each side of the mantelpiece. In the morning sunlight, the room didn't look nearly so old or decrepit. Grant got up, dressed, folded his sheets and blanket, and walked into the short hall, which led to a small, neat kitchen at the back of the house, a screen door showing a tiny, neat back yard. For an elderly bachelor, Mr. Kinepolous certainly kept things up. Grant went back out into the hall, which had what looked like a new runner down the middle of it, to the foot of the stairs.

"Mr. Kinepolous?" he called timidly, twice. There was no answer. Mr. Kinepolous must have gotten up early, as old people do, maybe gone out for a walk. Or maybe he was asleep. Either way, Grant was in a hurry to get going. He went into the green-, white-, and black-tiled bathroom and made such toilet as he could with the primitive unguents on hand, then left by the front door, meaning to memorize the house number and street name so he could visit Mr. Kinepolous on his way back.

But he never did that, and he never saw Mr. Kinepolous again. Because when he stepped through the front door, his heart started to pound so hard that the world tilted as if he would faint, and he had to put his hand on the doorjamb to keep himself steady.

The day was as beautiful as he had sensed from indoors; the kind of day children take for granted and which reminds grown-ups of childhood: soft, cool air, yellow-white sunlight, puffy clouds floating serenely in clear blue sky, giving a breath and memory of youth even to the very old, a feeling that age is unnecessary and unnatural; that you could walk through a door somewhere or an arbor in a garden, or pass through a dream, and be young again, young and beautiful and strong, with the whole world before you and life ahead of you.

But looking at the street from the top of Mr. Kinepolous's two front steps, it took Grant only a second to realize that he was not where he had fallen asleep. That is, the basic geography was the same—the street ran level for another block, then sloped steeply down just like the street that had brought him here—but there was a difference. It was as if he had unexpectedly woken up in an old movie. The houses along the street were different: the split-levels and Cape Cods with aluminum siding had changed to tiny, neat brick houses with tiny, neat yards, and the bulky black or dull green cars parked in driveways or at the curb were archaically rounded. There were ornate cast-iron streetlights every ten yards, painted a fresh gray green. A man in a baggy suit and a hat with a band walked along the sidewalk slowly, as if enjoying the morning.

It came to Grant suddenly where he was and how he had gotten here. The antiques he had visualized as he had approach the fluttering weed—the Buck Rogers radio, 1950s telephone, the 1950s furniture—focusing on it had brought him back not only to Mr. Kinepolous's house, but back to the day of that furniture. Quite by accident, he had traveled to Mr. Kinepolous's street in what looked like the 1950s. He did triple-, quadruple-reads on his watch, and stepped back inside Mr. Kinepolous's front hall to switch the light on and off—but quietly, in case the young Mr. Kinepolous or his wife were upstairs. The tests told him he was awake.

Awake in a world where his causal proxy was a small child. He looked suddenly down at his hands and body: they were an adult's, the same hands and body he had brought here in the rainstorm.

But they couldn't be.

He looked around again, to make sure he hadn't made a mistake based on a man with a hat and a couple of antique cars, but the new-looking obsolete neighborhood convinced him. He stepped down onto the front walk and snapped a twig off a spindly rosebush that had been induced to grow in a narrow flower bed. His body seemed solid enough. If he wasn't dreaming, then something very strange was happening, something for which Thotmoses and Kat had not prepared him. Was it this they had wanted him to discover by wandering around in this locus?

Entranced, he went forward to take a walk in this exotic world. He didn't think his khaki pants, polo shirt, and Hush Puppies looked too out of place. The man in the suit and hat was just coming level with Mr. Kinepolous's house when Grant reached the sidewalk, and he looked at Grant with forthright curiosity, but smiled and said "Good morning" in a corny accent.

Grant turned down the sidewalk and walked slowly through bright sunlight and cool tree-shade, smelling the damp from the gardens and the curbs that the sun was just drying up. A few birds twittered, and a rounded black car passed slowly, its unfiltered exhaust smelling chokingly of half-burned gasoline. A small one-story brick building was built right up to the sidewalk just where the street began to slope steeply downward. As Grant approached, he saw that it was a garage where two men in oily jumpsuits were working on a car, and next to it was a small shabby shop with a barber's pole, and next to that a store with a carefully hand-lettered sign in its window that said CANDY AND SWEETS.

Up the sidewalk toward him came two boys in shorts, probably no more than five or six years old, pumping their small legs stoutly to climb the hill. The one on the right was blond, crewcut, and freckled, but the one on the left had olive skin and brown hair, full lips and cautious, curious dark eyes.

In that instant an intense flash of recognition made the street whirl around Grant; the Candy and Sweets store, the blue sky where fairy-tale clouds floated close to the top of the hill, the concave world below far away, so that he seemed to walk in the quiet, sparkling air of the sky—

TWENTY-Four

HIMSELF AGAIN

As he might have expected, Dr. Thotmoses' champagne was a
hundred years old, mellow and sweet with age, and just tasting it
seemed to go to Grant's head, a froth of ecstatic bubbles directly
to the brain. After a long and improving Mass in the chapel, of
which he hadn't understood a word but from which he was still
damp, Grant sat with Kat and Dr. Thotmoses in Thotmoses' office at 9 A.M. and sipped it from flutes so delicate they seemed almost edible. Grant didn't like to drink in the morning, but Kat
and Thotmoses had been so excited at his adventure that he
found himself excited too, as if something really extraordinary
had happened, and as if he himself were extraordinary, which
seemed worth a drink. Also, someone the size of Dr. Thotmoses
getting excited was a little overwhelming; his enormous arms
and hands making room-sized gestures, his voice booming.
There was a small refrigerator built into the sideboard behind his
desk, apparently well stocked.

Kat and Thotmoses didn't talk as they sipped, but it didn't seem to be because champagne of this vintage deserved undivided attention. Instead, they both gazed at Grant like treasurehunters at some trove they had finally found, giddily happy but also afraid it was too good to be true. Finally Kat threw her arms around his neck and started to cry, and Grant found himself holding her tenderly, kissing the top of her head, Thotmoses smiling approvingly and a little foolishly at them. Grant's second glass of champagne tasted even better that the first, and after his third, its age and majesty had loosed his and Kat's tongues, while Thotmoses, who was probably far too big to get drunk on three glasses of champagne, kept grinning like a schoolboy.

"But you told me," said Grant, jabbing his finger at them, "*you told me* you can't do that. You can't go to a world, house, locus as someone other than your proxy. Because that would violate physical laws. So it must have been just a dream—lucid dream."

"Then how do you explain," said Kat, sharing his armchair now, "how your memories can end up in a proxy in another locus? Memories have physical substrates," she tapped her head tipsily. "So you have to create an uncaused effect in every house you travel to."

"But you *told* me—"

"Uh-uh-uhh," she said wickedly and musically, wagging a finger at him. "You shouldn't believe everything you hear."

"What we told you was true," said Thotmoses. "Our calculations indicate that the changes to brain substrates resulting from memory changes may well be within the Planck limit, so no physical laws would be actually violated."

"But if a whole new body appears—"

"It's just a matter of getting enough energy from somewhere."

"But—"

"From where, we don't know. But the whole universe appeared from nowhere, they say. Small particles are constantly blinking in and out of existence because of quantum fluctuations.

"We don't understand everything about traveling, not by a long measure; and one of the things we don't understand is what you just achieved. Perhaps the projection of seizural waves into the posterior parietal lobe wipes out and then 'reboots' the orientation association area so thoroughly that you can travel to loci where the most fundamental physical laws are different, allowing, for instance, the appearance of an entire adult human body as the effect of a cause external to the locus. If this explanation is correct, it is odd, to say the least, that such radically different physical laws can support worlds so apparently similar to ours in appearance and history. You would expect worlds structured by fundamentally different laws to look fundamentally different. Or maybe there is another explanation.

"In any event, what you have done is travel as what we call a 'ghost proxy.' The name is confusing, because as far as we can tell this proxy possesses just as much physical agency as any causal person in the locus. But it's also like a ghost because it's a *separate version of someone who already exists.* The few—very few—trainees who accomplish this feat do it almost invariably by returning to some locus that has a nostalgic or neurotic hold over them from childhood. They can then actually meet their causal proxy, just as you did.

"This, of course, is a very shocking event."

Back at the house, Grant's head was still whirling, but less pleasantly now that the champagne was wearing off. His mouth tasted bad. He went into the bathroom and was almost done brushing his teeth when he became aware simultaneously of the smell of cologne and the feeling that someone was standing in the doorway. He turned his head to look, then straightened up very slowly.

It was a large, well-set-up man in khaki pants, a polo shirt, and Hush Puppies, with an expensive watch and a good haircut and something haunted about the eyes.

It was himself.

He quietly came into the bathroom, shut the door, and watched Grant with some amusement.

"Close your mouth," he said. He had a deep, gentle voice. Grant hadn't known he had such a nice voice. "Sorry to scare you, but you learned about ghost proxies today, right?" He paused while this and a thousand other things spun through Grant's mind. "I need to tell you something. About Kat.

"You know some of it already. She was raised to be a kind of geisha for the secret society inside their church, as part of their 'recruiting.' What you don't know is how hard it is on her. She's hundreds of years old, subjectively, and she's circled back and played her role so many times, with so many people, that her mind is going. Sex sickens her, and men disgust her. She hates how they smell. Women are only a little better. She's tried to kill herself. The drugs are the only things that keep her alive when she's working.

"She told me about a dream she had. She was in a beautiful garden, but she was barely able to walk because an ape was with her. She was taking it for a walk, but its leash was tied to her wrist. It yanked at her arm, grunting, loping, and shuffling, and she could barely drag it along. She looked down at her tied arm and saw that it had begun to turn hairy and coarse, as if being tied to the ape had infected her; and then she realized that the ape was pulling because it wanted to drag her back to the bedroom she shared with it, to mount her as it did a dozen times a day. She knelt on the path and the ape mounted her, then and there, and she vomited, and her vomit was blood writhing with maggots."

After he had left, Grant stood looking at nothing for a long time, vaguely aware that his reflection in the mirror was stock-still.

"What's the matter?" said a voice next to him, making him jump. Kat stood in the doorway, studying him with eyes turned lavender blue by the lavender of her dressing gown.

"Nothing. I have to take a shower."

He took one, scrubbing himself twice over with soap, and then put on a lot of deodorant and rummaged in the medicine cabinet. He had never thought twice before about the large selection of men's cologne in there. He looked at the bottles doubtfully.

"Which of these colognes do you like best?" he called through the open bathroom door.

"What?" After a second she came down the hall again.

"Which of these colognes smells the best?"

She leaned against the bathroom doorframe and studied him dully. "What's happened?"

"A ghost proxy. Of me. Told me about you. About the dream with the ape. Which one?"

"Either the skinny blue bottle or the green."

He smelled them both cautiously, then put on the green.

She stood looking at him sadly. "It's my job," she said finally, dully. "I'm sorry."

TWENTY-FIVE

HIMSELF YET AGAIN

The breakthrough with his ghost proxy and his revelation about Kat seemed to accelerate a change that had been growing inside Grant. As Dr. Thotmoses had predicted, sheer repetition seemed at last to have made his new life real to him, while his increasing skill at traveling brought a feeling of control. He now began to work with an intensity that in his previous life he had reserved for the arts of seduction. Kat, left alone at last, gained back the rest of her weight and began to look like the old Kat, though quieter, as if keeping watch from a hidden position.

For the first few weeks Thotmoses had Grant wake up over and over in Mr. Kinepolous's house in the 1950s, to stabilize whatever neural pattern his brain had stumbled upon to accomplish the ghost proxy trick. Dozens of times Grant walked the 1950s sidewalk and saw the dark-haired boy who was himself coming up the hill.

Thotmoses, Father Amon, and their team debriefed him

exhaustively after every session, ran their tests, and monitored his sleep, diet, and mood, running and rerunning his continuity index and other measures. After about two months of this, Thotmoses finally seemed to relax, as if some bullet had been dodged. He set Grant a second task: to "ghost" a locus he knew very well. Grant picked the locus where he was a lawyer and lived in the suburbs and chased women.

At first he wondered why Thotmoses had given him such an easy assignment; by now traveling to a locus he knew that well was like falling off a log. But he soon discovered that this very familiarity was the problem: he identified so closely with his causal proxy there that the first several times he tried it he returned *as* his causal proxy, the same way he had traveled before his ghost proxy breakthrough, injecting into his causal proxy brief shots of puzzling memories.

"Be careful," Thotmoses advised him. "If you do that too often, he'll start to adopt the alternate memory stream as real, and we don't know where that might lead. Don't be headstrong. Figure out exactly how you're going to manage it before you try again."

Slouched in a leather armchair in the cool church foyer after one of these sessions, Grant's frustration suddenly turned to surprise at himself; he had become so accustomed to traveling that being thwarted like this seemed unnatural. What had seemed absurd six months ago had become possible, then feasible, and then routine, like an aboriginal bushman adapting to city life, or an astronaut to zero gravity. Human beings dominated the earth because they had evolved over geologic time an organ that could adapt to radically new environments over weeks rather than eons—and adapt so thoroughly that even the memories of their previous lives quickly became hazy and unfamiliar. Thotmoses' explanation of the physics of traveling, which had seemed bizarre before, now seemed so obvious that only a crank could deny it. It was simply necessary to take seriously the scientists' insistence on the reality of alternate parallel universes, and then to learn to negotiate them, like a child learning to walk. Refusing to do that was like accepting Newton's gravitational equations but then being astonished when things fell to the ground. In fact, what was strange was the *inability* to travel, the insistence on mentally translating the trajectory of one single house into a closed, inescapable box whose sides were space and time, like an agoraphobic hiding in his house and refusing to come out.

He tried not to remind himself that the creation of a ghost proxy—an apparition of flesh and blood—should still be impossible even under this broader view of reality.

"Try to wake up in a place where you can see your causal proxy," Thotmoses suggested after Grant had moped around the Hatshep gardens and the church for a couple of days. "If you can see him, then you're not him. But make sure he doesn't see you; otherwise you risk creating causal paradoxes, which are sometimes messy and occasionally disastrous."

"Like the guy who came to see me in the bathroom?"

"That was innocuous," said Thotmoses, waving a huge hand. "Notice that you pick the earliest possible time *after* you learned about ghost proxies to ghost yourself, making sure that no significant anomalies would occur. Obviously you will have had excellent instruction." His face creased into a smile.

Grant took more turns in the garden, and finally decided that he would try to visualize himself napping on the couch in the days after he quit work, and at the same time visualize himself separately standing in the hall watching himself. It was tricky, because it involved visualizing separately both an image of himself as he looked on the outside and an image of his consciousness from the inside, without putting the two together as they had been his whole life, and then maintaining that unfamiliar split as he invoked his epileptogenic stimulus—

But it worked. He stood in the hallway of his suburban house, and a gray, exhausted-looking version of himself lay dead asleep on the couch, drooling a little. He stood fascinated, wondering how close he had come to losing his mind in those terrible weeks after Kat and Thotmoses had disappeared.

Thotmoses again insisted that Grant repeat this new step over and over to stabilize it. So for a couple of weeks he regularly arrived in the hall where he had made his first visit, but he had napped on the sofa so often in that locus that he could never be sure it was the same day or time. It was nerve-racking not knowing if his causal proxy would wake up and see him; and a couple of times as he was sneaking out of the house, closing the front door silently behind him, he heard his causal proxy call "Kat?" in a hoarse, broken voice that gave him the shivers. As soon as he could, he took to arriving elsewhere, either in the basement, where his proxy almost never went, or outside the house.

Without informing Thotmoses or Kat, he had set himself a task in his former default locus; just to have something to do there, he told himself at first. Since the day his ghost proxy had told him about Kat, he had left her alone. Now he slept in a separate room, and dropped his eyes whenever they met. But another question that needed answering had occurred to him. He started traveling to an alley across the street from a fashionably shabby apartment building in one of the city's most exclusive faux-bohemian neighborhoods, where his ex-girlfriend Stacy lived. He lounged on the sidewalk on different days at different times of the year.

Finally, he found a bright, chill November noon not long

after he had found Kat, when Stacy left her building. He turned away to hide his face. He didn't want a causal paradox; he just wanted to know something. He was too far away to see whether she looked well or ill, but she was dressed with her usual calculated carelessness, dark hair in a ponytail. When she was gone, he used the key he had never returned to let himself into the building and her apartment. She kept a journal, he knew, in which she carefully recorded everything she did, and her "impressions," just like a real poet. He found it on her desk, a fat three-ring notebook of printer pages. He sat down in her expensive, messy living room and flipped back through the weeks.

He had left her at Macy's, hadn't even come back to tell her he was going. There had been no sign anything was wrong, and she had been shopping, so the time had gone by without her noticing at first. She had found a denim shirt that flattered her while looking like some rumpled thing you had just pulled out of a drawer. It was $275 of careful design and tailoring, an artifice to make men love you, because men loved women who were beautiful without trying, which showed how much they knew about beauty and about women and about love. Along with her satisfaction at finding the shirt there was the usual vague shame at her talent for shopping, the middle-class skill she had learned from her mother in Kansas City on many mother–daughter outings. Stacy had no pure pleasures. Whenever her expert eye fell on a rack of clothes, together with the hunter's elation a churn of revulsion came into her stomach; she seemed to scent her mother's faint, tasteful perfume just covering the warm, aging female smell of her body, which seemed to be the smell of Stacy's own body no matter how much she washed, no matter how roughly she treated herself. Her mother's carefully coifed hair, debutante half smile, tasteful, expensive clothes, her mother smiling pleasantly at the breakfast table when Stacy knew that her father had come home drunk at two in the morning, her mother smiling pleasantly as she grew old and lost her looks and lost her husband, smiling pleasantly for the grim reaper—

Stacy would scowl unconsciously so as not to look like her mother, and feel the shiver of revulsion, and shop. She couldn't resist pleasure, even though all her pleasures were mixed with the same revulsion and helplessness. Because pleasure was the only thing left, wasn't it? Except for poetry, which she wrote to try to drag herself out of the muck where she had been born, defective and shameful, a hollow thing.

Grant had left her at her most vulnerable, when she had surrendered like a drug addict to the sickening pleasure of shopping, like an addict shivering over the picture in her head of Grant seeing her in the shirt and some tight pair of jeans, getting the look he got when he wanted her, and coming at her full of want and not to be denied, so that she could fight and struggle against him and scream with rage, the only time she could show her real self, so that afterward she felt better, and could relax in his arms, and sometimes feel like a real person for a while.

It had been the sex he wanted, she had realized after he disappeared—sex and the ego satisfaction of dating a girl in her twenties. He had never liked her poetry—he had pretended, but she wasn't a fool, even though he thought he had fooled her. She had been in love with him, had wanted him to love her, and the poetry was herself as she wanted to be seen. But he had politely ignored the poetry, had used her as men have used empty women since the beginning of time, for sex and status, and then dropped her without a word. When someone better had come along, she guessed—someone maybe with a real personality under her skin, or who wrote good poetry, or who was poised and mature, not just a pretender, someone who really did pull rumpled shirts out of her drawer and really didn't care what she looked like. Someone real instead of a façade built to cover up her mother's debutante rictus and her father's drunken whoring, the sickening provincialism of her small town, a mediocre education and deadeningly conventional ideas: to cover up a mediocre, conventional Midwestern girl who wrote florid, stilted poetry that only served to show what a cliché she was. Her one saving grace was that she had been born beautiful, so that she could hold men for a while and pretend they loved her, until they saw through the beauty to the hole underneath. Then they left her, vanished without a trace, and she holding a shirt on a hanger and waiting for half an hour, forty minutes, an hour in the Women's Wear department, then wandering the store looking for him with the shirt still bunched in her hand, finally humiliating herself at the Customer Service counter asking them to page him and waiting while he didn't come, then dropping the shirt and shakily leaving the store, her stomach trembling, her body empty inside, head aching with tears she couldn't cry.

"If I succeed, carry your prayer, Kat gets some credit, right?" Grant asked abruptly one day, slouched in an armchair in front of Thotmoses' huge desk.

Thotmoses studied him, and Grant thought there was a sudden gleam in his eyes, quickly covered up. He spoke calmly. "Among those with esoteric knowledge, she would be a kind of folk hero. But its success would be dear to her even if no one else ever knew; she has given up more than you can possibly imagine to do this work."

"Then I want to do it."

There was a silence while Thotmoses seemed to do his best to see inside him. Finally he said, "You will be completely on your own. We won't be able to help you. You've already gone

where we can't follow, but this destination is immeasurably farther."

Grant nodded, fear flowing into him, a silent, cold stream.

"Of course, you are free to turn away at any time, go off on
your own and forget us. Nearly all of our recruits do just that."

"Why? Are they afraid?"

"We don't know. Once this phase begins, they're beyond our
reach. We don't think anything bad happens. But I would say
that if they are afraid, it is a fear of changing—changing too
much, beyond one's own recognition. Of becoming something—
no longer entirely human."

Grant sat thinking, and the study seemed very silent, as if not
only Thotmoses but also the building they sat in waited for his
answer. "How will I know when I'm ready?"

"You have been ready for months, ever since you stabilized
your ability to travel as a ghost proxy. We were only waiting for
you to make your decision."

Thotmoses opened a drawer, took something out, and put it
on the desk. Grant didn't recognize it at first; then he saw with a
shock that it was a large black automatic pistol.

"Take it," said Thotmoses, gesturing it toward Grant as if he
preferred not to touch it. "It's for you."

"Why?"

"Katerina will tell you. She takes over now." He smiled.
"I'm at the end of my usefulness, I'm afraid."

Crickets sang in the deep blue dusk, and out the open windows
of the darkened living room Grant could see the black shapes of
trees, and faintly smell pine and soil on the chilly air. He sat on
the couch, the pistol Thotmoses had given him cool and heavy in
his hand. Kat sat in a chair by a window, knees pulled up to her
chin, and he watched her golden profile staring out, motionless.

She wore a pair of overalls, and the contrast with the effortlessly fashionable clothes he was used to seeing on her made him realize that none of it had been effortless. It reminded him of Stacy, and he felt sick.

Finally she spoke softly in the dark, her voice cool and dreamy. "Do you remember a long time ago when we first met? You told me you used to think there was a path that led in a direction away from all the directions on earth, through worlds ranged along a dimension of stories. Leading in one direction to hell and in the other to heaven, and our world somewhere between."

"Yes."

"Even then, you saw something almost no one else can see. Now that your training is done, you should be able to find that path. When you find it, you must follow it upward, toward what you called 'heaven.' Do you remember? Do you understand?"

"Yes."

"I've never been there, of course. Only a very few people have. You will have to find your own way."

"What about the gun?"

She turned her face toward him. "Have you fired it?"

"No."

"You should fire it now, see it work. Pick something and shoot it."

He knew right away that she wasn't joking. He looked at her in the dark with a sinking feeling of shock and sadness.

"Shoot something," she said.

He looked around. On a sideboard by the hall door an antique Chinese vase reflected a gleam of deep blue. Grant held up the heavy gun, steadied it, and squeezed the trigger. There was a deafening, blinding explosion, and the gun bucked in his hand, and he could barely hear the splinters of the vase hitting the walls. The darkness and stillness after the shot seemed fractured by its violence, split with noise and destruction.

"Again," Kat said.

He looked around again, ears ringing, the afterimage of the flash hanging before his eyes. He squinted through it at the gray outline of the quadraphonic LP turntable faintly visible in the deeper darkness of the Oriental cabinet. He held the gun tight with both hands this time and grimaced as he squeezed the trigger twice, and the turntable leaped in sparking pieces from the cabinet, leaving a tendril of electric-smelling smoke behind it, and the cabinet itself with a jagged tear.

"Again," said Kat.

"That's enough," Grant said. "I don't think there are any more of your mother's wedding presents in here."

Kat uncurled herself and got up, with a grace he guessed was in her whether she chose to put it on or not, like a cat's grace. She came toward him in bare feet and sat on the couch facing him, one of her feet curled underneath her, the other touching the floor. Her eyes on his were intent, steady, as if she were concentrating to see him, or trying to hold his will steady with her own. "I'm done now, Grant, finished. Do you understand? This—your recruitment—was my last. No, don't apologize—everything you've done has been exactly right—it's I who have declined. I had one success, many years ago, and it was hard too, very hard. This job takes its toll; I've known that since I started.

"I've gone through my life a dozen times, always recruiting. But I can't do it anymore. If I fail this time, I fade away. In a few years, no one will remember who I am. I can't live with people, not in the normal way. I'm very old, but I'm still not a person, not really. So what will I be if people forget me?

"But if my last recruit succeeds, carries our prayer to the Source of Fate, I won't need to worry. Do you understand?" Her beautiful eyes looking into his were sick, vulnerable, expecting nothing, giving nothing; eyes that lived in the cold spaces between the stars. The sadness Grant had felt before came over him. She was manipulating him again; they had never really been close; he had never really known her.

"Are you ready? Is there anything you want to ask, anything you need to do or say before you go?"

"No. Oh, wait a minute, yes. You know the proxy that came and told me about you? Don't I have to go back and do that to avoid—avoid a—"

"An anomaly, yes. Go ahead and do it, and then we'll talk."

So he did it, sitting on the couch, visualizing himself in the bathroom that day brushing his teeth, and himself looking at himself from the doorway, then letting the weed by the fence wave and flutter in the wind, wave and flutter—and then the transition, like a combination of a momentary sleep and being lifted on a Ferris wheel and turning the page of a book, until he was standing in the doorway looking at himself leaning over the sink rinsing toothpaste from his mouth.

Soon he was back in the deep blue dusk.

"Okay," he said.

She waited until he had steadied himself on the sofa and in the house again, and then she began to talk softly. "What I am going to tell you—you won't like. But there isn't any other way. You just went back to close a loop and prevent an anomaly—a thing both happening and not happening in the same locus. That is crucial, normally. But there is one exception." She took his right hand, which held the gun, and lifted it so that it was between them, a cold, heavy thing between their two breathing bodies. "You have to take a gun like this to your departure locus, where you meet the two boys on the hill. You have to kill the boy who is you."

The darkness, the violence from the shots, her awful eyes, whirled around him sickeningly. He felt as if he would vomit. "What? No, I can't." He dropped the gun to the floor with a thud. "That's me! That boy is *me!*"

"Yes."

"But—why? And if I kill myself, who'll grow up to kill me? It's impossible; it will make—"

"Yes; an anomaly. The most fundamental kind."

"But—," he said, "it'll screw things up. Anomalies are bad, right? How can a locus contain two contradictory things? Something's got to give."

"Don't worry about the locus. In the fundamental geometry, everything happens. Everything's already there, in alternate worlds. You can do nothing to change any of it. It is on a higher level entirely, something so much higher that it makes free will look like a sculpture that never changes. Don't worry about screwing things up. It's *you* who has to change.

"There is no other way, Grant. We don't know exactly why, or how, because we can't follow you to the other side of it, but we know it's the only thing that works.

"Now you know everything I know about traveling and about the Source of Fate. You wanted me to tell you everything, remember? Well, that's the last thing I know."

TWENTY-
SIX

God and Atom

He stood at the top of that hill in the quiet morning sunlight, and until the very last second, he hadn't made up his mind. When he raised the gun, it occurred to him idly that the anxiety on the dark boy's face when he caught sight of the big man at the top of the hill, which he had thought amusing before, had been completely justified. He squeezed his eyes shut and squeezed the trigger.

He didn't seem to hear the gun or feel its kick, so as he opened his eyes, he was able to hope he hadn't done it, hope more than he had ever hoped anything in his life—

The boy's body lay twitching on the sidewalk, blood sprayed behind it where its head should be, as if someone had tried to complete a headless boy by painting an expressionist mural, shards of skull like pieces of hairy nutshell glistening in it. The shot still echoed in the street, and the people on the sidewalk were still spinning round with silent screaming faces. The blond boy was standing still, looking at nothing and hoarsely screaming, all his fingers splayed out as far as they would go. Grant sat down heavily and vomited, the gun falling out of his hand.

Yet he was still standing up, and the two boys were watching him cautiously and curiously as they sidled toward the candy store. He hadn't done it after all! Thank God! It had been a nightmare picture of his imagination. He hadn't—!

But he sat slumped in his own vomit, feeling that he would pass out, and the blond boy was screaming, screaming—

And he was standing there, and the boys were sidling into the candy store—

Then something very bad happened. A catastrophe so intense that he forgot all about killing the boy.

He stood watching the candy store door close behind the two boys, sitting in his vomit as people ran across the street toward him; stood in the quiet morning sunlight; felt hands pulling at him, heard voices shouting furiously; turned to follow the boys into the candy store—

Last thoughts flickered in a mind made to hold only one world. *The anomaly—the impossible switchback—grown-up shoots the boy who will be the grown-up so he doesn't grow up so he can't shoot the boy so the boy becomes the grown-up who shoots the boy who doesn't grow up and doesn't shoot the boy who grows up to shoot the boy who doesn't grow up—*

He fought to stay in existence, struggled to stay on the surface of an ocean crashing with tidal waves from two directions, two worlds, drowning him—

—to shoot who grows up to shoot who doesn't grow up to shoot who does shoot who doesn't shoot who does who doesn't who does who doesn't does doesn't does doesn't doesdoesn'tdoesdoesn'tdoes/n't-does/n'tdoes/n't—

Two universes squeezed into a mind only made for one, and burst it—it was *his* brain exploded on the sidewalk—

Then everything got worse.

Very much worse.

Because he saw suddenly, his torn-open mind helpless to ignore it, that there weren't two universes. It was very much worse than that. There were an infinite number of universes, each of them complete and all-consuming, implacable and heavy with being, each separately taking up his whole mind, every last corner of it—

He tried to swim on an ocean now rising in thousand-foot waves; mountain ranges crashed on him, and the dead frozen spaces between the stars, the pumping organs of creatures, the insides of suns, and boiling mathematics, bottomless music, fear, calmness, winds; rocks and bones and slime and fire and vacuum crashed on him, and there were so many directions, he was upside down everywhere, knew everything and nothing, was everywhere and nowhere, infinitely big and so small he couldn't stop shrinking—

No one, not even God, could have stood it. He collapsed like a spiderweb under a ton of bricks.

Gave up. Sank.

Drowned.

Drowned; but didn't die. In his moment of surrender, he wasn't obliterated as had seemed inevitable; he saw that there was a way to stay in existence. And that gave him hope, and he tried to exist again, crest the waves, but as soon as he did, everything crashed onto him again, as if his tiny struggling had attracted the attention of the infinities, which rushed to stamp him out.

He must drown, die, be no more, be nothing but an open thing, an awakeness with no self, an open eye that was a con-

sciousness as dead as vacuum because it had no subject, was just a
phenomenon like gravity or light, vast as all the universes.

He drowned, died.

And glimpsed a way to survive, and couldn't help trying to
be a self.

Was crushed, drowned, died, surrendered.

Faintest hope to exist.

Crushed.

Drowned, incinerated—everything except one thing so small,
it effectively didn't exist—just one single molecule of want: a want
to be small. A single remaining blasted seared molecule that was
just a simple chemical yearning to be small again. Not big as all the
universes—not even God could stand that; not an infinite Eye
open over all worlds, all possibilities, all histories. A want to be tiny
and asleep: so small he was nothing; so fast asleep he was dead.

These things were outside time; but a story must move, so it
must be imagined that iterations converged. A trillion dashings
to pieces; a trillion faintest glimpses of something that could be
limited; a trillion efforts to exist; a trillion dashings to pieces. And
every iteration seeming infinitesimally to move him, so that the
infinite orthogonal axes turned inward into something that was
just infinity curved upon itself to make a funnel, darker and
darker as it narrowed. Narrower and narrower, darker and darker,
until he woke up in his bed at the nursing home, a head on a pillow, and it was morning, and they had just discovered the dead
body of an old man in the next bed.

"Dead," a big Jamaican woman named Margaret was telling another nurse's aide, standing over the old man's bed. "He threw
his pills on the floor. Maybe he threw up, you know."

Grant was crying with joy. The women's voices in the small
room rubbed on him like corduroy, and there was a smell of shit!

He couldn't move! And he was tucked into this narrow bed under blankets that held him like a cocoon. It had all been a dream, a psychotic nightmare brought on no doubt by his cleverness in not taking his medicine for a month.

Margaret noticed him crying. "There, there," she said. "It's not you that's dead, man." She laughed wheezingly with the other woman.

"Those—those are—*my* pills," Grant got out between his sobs.

"These pills right here on the floor?" Margaret said, surprised. "You spit them out?"

"Y-yes."

They would bring him more pills, and some of them would make him sleep, go into a motionless, noiseless burial in something dense and dark that didn't let him move. Something that pressed all around him, making him as small as possible, and unconscious. And when he woke up, there was only this room to see, and anyway, he could always close his eyes. Except for his eyes, he didn't have to take responsibility for moving at all. He sobbed with relief and happiness.

"There, there," said Margaret sympathetically.

A little while later a harried-looking doctor came in with the day-shift nurse, leaned over the old man, felt his neck, shone a light in his eyes, put a stethoscope on the skinny chest under the faded pajamas, signed a form that the nurse held out for him, and left. A little while after that two male aides wheeled in a long metal cart and unfolded a black plastic body-bag. They pulled the covers off Humphrey, then worked the bag under his body while flirting with the two big female aides, the four of them laughing, and then they half lifted, half rolled the body into the bag, and zipped it up over a face that didn't look too

much more dead than Humphrey ever had, and slid it from the
bed onto the cart.

The aide Margaret who had been comforting Grant must have
told someone he was crying, because soon after they had taken
Humphrey away, the gray-faced nurse returned, opened a plastic
packet, and without a word swabbed Grant's arm and stuck him
with a needle. She was walking out the door then and he thought
he was saying something to her, perhaps thanking her, but he was
suddenly dizzy, and then—

Everything got very much worse.

The first thing he noticed was that he was still awake. That was
annoying; he had wanted to sleep, though he couldn't at that
moment remember why.

The second thing he noticed was that he was inert, in a completely silent, still place, buried in a kind of blackish mud that
held him motionless, but without any feeling in his body. So he
was asleep; that was good, but how to get rid of consciousness? If
he could have moved, he would have squirmed into a more comfortable position, stretched—

The third thing he noticed was an infinite number of universes rolled into a ball near him, and giving off a faint light. It
was as if the universes had been filed away as a card catalog
curled into a sphere. Even worse, the sphere was not entirely separate from him. He had somehow gotten very close to one of the
cards, so that if he focused, he saw only that card, the universe in
it; but all the rest of the universes hummed and whirled restlessly
nearby, and he knew that one wrong move would bring them all
down on him.

That brought everything back, and Grant panicked. It was

like finding yourself buried in mud next to a nuclear bomb. He couldn't move, couldn't struggle, shout, or cry, or even close his eyes to shut out the sight of the ball.

So he went mad. His mind, formerly exploded by the infinities, was now rent by its own shrieking fear, now in its panic burst through to places not meant for it. The chanting moans of the dead came from below him in the ground, and he knew they were creeping up through the dirt. His paralyzed body was crawled over by cockroaches, maggots, and centipedes, which wriggled into his mouth and ears and eyes and into his brain and lungs. His body rotted and swelled and burst there under the ground, and the clawed, rotting hands of the dead reached up through holes and tore his flesh and cracked his joints, dragging pieces of him down into their holes to eat.

He woke from the injection the nurse had given him screaming fit to burst the arteries in his head. The harassed and irritated doctor was called again from his rounds, and examined Grant as quickly as he had the old man's body. This one was presenting with delusional panic, probably schizophrenic in etiology. But he was a quadriplegic and immobile anyway, morbidity high, and the nursing home staff would be angry if he didn't shut him up or if he prescribed anything that would add to their workload. So he prescribed heavy doses of a hypnotic, to be administered at six-hour intervals by injection. It was kinder anyway, he thought vaguely, hurrying back out to his car to continue his interrupted rounds; no one would want to be conscious in such a state.

So from that time on, Grant was buried deep in the mud place with the sphere. He would have agreed with everything the doctor had thought except that it was kinder, because he was *awake*—had trained himself to be awake even in deep sleep, and now he didn't seem able to stop, and that was the worst possible

torture, worse than dying, because he was tormented by the unnatural horror of the universe ball.

He couldn't wake up and couldn't go to sleep, couldn't move
or stop thinking, could neither really live nor really die. So he
went mad, and he stayed mad for a long, long time, smothered by
writhing insects, eaten by cadavers, his mind devoured by voices
that laughed and screamed at him and told him how disgusting
he was, and how his punishment was to be awake forever.

But fortunately, the human mind—unlike the universes—is
finite, and there is a limit to all its products, even madness. Eventually, after Grant had been driven shrieking through all the paths
of horror in his mind, he wound up one day back where he had
started, lying inert in the black mud place with the universe ball.
Then the chanting moans of the dead, and the insects all over
him, and the smothering held no more fear because he had already been where they had taken him, and so they faded away,
and he was left to lie in the dark with the ball and think.

And what he thought in the end was that it was no use staying here. It wasn't so bad, and it was snug, but nothing was ever
going to change. And it came to him that long ago and far away
he had made a promise to do something for someone, and had set
out to do it. Someone had thought it was important. Had it been
him? The more he thought about it, the more his attention was
drawn to the sphere, which at those times seemed to whirl, as if
the leaves of an infinite book were whirling before his eyes, each
leaf deep and elaborately etched. There was one part of the whirl
that caught his attention, and one part of the part on one of the
uncountable pages that engaged him, and a story came into his
mind, of a man standing at the top of a hill and two boys walking up it toward him. He tried to remember where he had seen
it before, and why it was important, but he had no success until

he tried to trace the man's steps backward in his mind to find out if he had any memory of where he had come from, and into his mind came the image of a day of wind and hazy, bright sunlight, and a tall weed next to a fence that waved in the wind, waved back and forth, its leaves fluttering—

TWENTY-SEVEN

The Ball of Doors

David Grant stood in quiet morning sunlight on a hill above the convex town curving away below, near a sky where puffy fairy-tale clouds floated. He remembered who he was now, as if he had never forgotten. He shuddered with relief. It was bliss to stand here, soothing and sweet to stand here in this soft air and be able to move and breathe and see and hear. And he had almost decided to stay in the motionless prison of his sedated quadriplegic body! It was some measure of how unbearable the crashing universes had been that live burial in a drug-induced paralysis had seemed desirable. He shuddered again, and looked at the scene around him—around his ghost proxy, he realized, as he saw the two boys walking up the hill toward him. In sudden fear he lifted his right hand, but there was nothing in it. Relaxing again, shivering with relaxation and relief, he watched the boys sidle into the candy store, keeping their eyes on him, a bell jingling on the door.

He had stood in just this place dozens of times and watched the same scene, but there was something different now, something nagging at him as he stood relaxing in the sunlight. Something drawing his attention, he realized, like gravitation from an invisible black hole.

The universe ball.

It was a heavy sphere of silver and crystal in his solar plexus, and yet at the same time all around him like a spherical map of the heavens, whirling and yet rock-still, infinite and infinitesimal. Involuntarily his attention turned inward to it, and it seemed to spin up with an intense hum, infinitely dense, infinitely heavy with information. He remembered now: somewhere along the way his mind had wrestled the universes—or his perceptions of them—into a ball, and had somehow put them to one side so that, as long as he remembered to govern his senses, he was able to keep them quiet, though the ball pulled at him with a kind of psychic force.

For the first time in a very long time, a thrill of excitement went through him. Could this ball of doors be how Kat's advanced recruits traveled after they went beyond her sight?

He sat on a sidewalk bench in the brightening, warming morning. It was strange: he was so far from home, out beyond the limits of what should be possible, a stranger to himself—and yet he felt comfortable and a little sleepy, as if he belonged here. Perhaps he belonged everywhere now; perhaps his feeling of solidity came from having inside him a ball of everything multiplied an infinite number of times, as if he were the center not only of the universe but of all the universes. His attention strayed to the gravitational presence in the middle of his body, and the ball responded, emerging from impalpability with a rising hum as if directly stimulating his brain's sensory centers, spinning faster and faster like an infinitely massive gyroscope, a finely silver-seamed ball of crystal that glowed with cold blue light.

He pulled his attention away from it with an effort, a chill going through him. The explosion into his senses of two simultaneous inconsistent realities when he had killed his child self had broken open his mind, and now the chaotic perception of multiple universes was an ever-present danger. He was not the center of the universes, he reassured himself; he was a negligibly tiny mote in one of them who had merely approached some kind of door, or ball of doors.

The ball seemed to shrink and slow its spinning, fading again except for the gravitation-like influence, which he was beginning to get used to, like a man standing in a strong wind. His ability to ignore it pleased him. It was a jewel of endless facets and limitless depths, of layer upon layer, chasm upon chasm, story upon story, and he knew that anyone who had not already been driven mad by it would be helpless before it. He had another advantage too; a purpose, a focus that would keep his attention in small places, where he could not be destroyed by the infinities. He would work single-mindedly to find the "upward path," if only because he wanted to indulge in the luxury of existing as himself for a while.

The dappled shade of a tree had crept over him, and a little breeze stirred, keeping the climbing sun from feeling too hot. He was at the center of the universes after all, he saw suddenly, or rather one center among an infinity—a place cozy in its own eccentric localness, from which vantage point things could be organized: some closer and others farther away, some earlier and others later, some more important and others less; a place where you could sit and watch and not have everything happen at once, where you could take things one at a time. A point of view was another gift that kept you safe from the infinities, a solid place to set your feet while you figured out what to do next.

But with a lifting feeling, he realized that he already knew what to do next; in fact, he had known all his life. He had to move from the lower to the higher, from one rung to the next, to the body or face or voice or scene that would take him closer, even a tiny bit closer, to the celestial regions.

He had been trying to find those regions all his life, and maybe the urge that had driven him from lover to lover had been basically correct—or at least had given the illusion of movement, which back then maybe he had believed was the only thing possible. He had lacked the necessary tools or any real understanding back then; but he guessed now that his instinct to follow his *feelings*—the hunger that whispered that there had to be something better—had been right. Because what else could tell you whether one thing was closer to the celestial than another?

Maybe later he could figure out how to use the universe ball, but for now he would *feel* his way to the next rung on the ladder. It was the only way he knew.

Smelling the raw exhaust of a passing 1950s car, and squinting slightly against the sun, he emptied himself of thoughts and words, let the *feeling* of the celestial, the yearning for it, fill him, just as it used to . . .

And out of the feeling grew the morning when he was nineteen and had come to the little town in Canada.

He closed his eyes, preparing to let the weed wave and flutter, but before he could do that the universe ball hummed in his solar plexus with infinitely fast rotation, and he saw the image of the Canadian town emerge from the spinning, and it blew over him like a wind.

TWENTY-EIGHT

CLIMBING

It was near noon, but you could only tell because the uniform whitish overcast was brighter overhead than at the horizons. The summer air was neutral and windless, with a feeling of stasis, timelessness, as if the weather itself had paused, its pressures, temperatures, and humidities all balancing for an hour; or as if this was the first day of a new dispensation of serenity and equilibrium, come upon this little town first in the whole world. Beyond the bridge over the irrigation canal the town seemed as still as the weather. The trees made only the vaguest shade over cars parked along the streets in the pale gray air. Grant looked down at himself; he was still wearing his khaki pants and polo shirt. He had traveled here as a ghost proxy.

He paused on the bridge, the cool smell of water and silt coming up from the canal, its greenish-brown surface reflecting the sky and the underside of the bridge with only the slightest wobble. A few birds sang their tranquil midday songs. Three decades ago he had walked a few blocks into the town and then turned back, eager to get a ride to Toronto before sunset, but a memory had lain uneasy in him long afterward. Would he have found Kat if he had looked a little longer? The question made no sense. There was a locus in which the nineteen-year-old found Kat, and there was another where he turned back and caught a ride to Toronto.

It struck him suddenly that this same nineteen-year-old might arrive here any minute. His heart sped up, and he quickly crossed the bridge. His experience with anomalies had put him off them for life; but the universe ball in his solar plexus spun up, humming with voracious appetite, like an animal emerging from its cave, eager for feeding time. He strode along the cracked, weathered sidewalk, turning right at the first cross street instead of left, which was the way to the house where he had met Kat in his nineteen-year-old body.

He walked aimlessly through the village, and when it started raining late in the afternoon, he was at the bottom of a steep hill, the smell of onion grass coming from the damp, overgrown lawn of a brick Cape Cod nestled under a huge oak, a spindly tea rose leaning over its picket fence. Across the street was a small playground, out of which a woman hurried, pulling two reluctant children by the hands. A car went by slowly with its lights on in the darkening air; someone up the street stood in his doorway and called his pets or kids, warm yellow light glowing in the house behind him.

Big oaks grew behind the playground, their branches sheltering its inner half. Grant sat on a bench there in greenish-gray gloom, breathing cool, damp air, listening to the rain patter in the leaves above him, and on the swings and slide and monkey-bars. Ghost proxy though he was, a chilly damp penetrated his shirt; he crossed his arms to keep warm.

Thunder rumbled, and the curtain of rain thickened, glimmering dim silver like streaks of optic fiber piping celestial light down from the high regions; he felt an occasional cold drop through the canopy above him. It was a beautiful, melancholy place, and in its way celestial, with the smell of wet leaves, the sound and gray-silver glitter of the rain, but he wondered idly what would it be like on a clear evening. He remembered the painting of a village he had seen once, a village in the evening with the lights of houses shining gently beneath the stars, the sound of crickets, the air limpid and clear, like an evening out of childhood—

He realized suddenly what he had done, but after a momentary start calmed himself so as not to lose the vision; he relaxed back into it, letting it fill his head and chest with its aching loveliness. Then he touched the universe ball ever so slightly, so that it hummed intensely, throwing up a doorway that blew over him like wind—

He felt the moment of falling, disconnection, a jolt of intelligent sleep, as if everything had been taken apart and put back together again so quickly that there was no way to prove it had happened, but now there was no rain and the quality of the light was different—blue, still, smoky—and beyond the edge of the trees above him was an indigo sky in which stars twinkled. He walked out onto the sidewalk. He was in the village from his vision, from the painting.

It wasn't really so different from the little town he had seen during the day; or rather, if he had been asked to point out the differences he would have had a hard time. There were still the big trees with houses nestled under them, the street running past as before. But at the same time everything was different. The light was different, and the darkness, and the sense of space, in an indescribable way. Crickets sang in the mild air. He stood and watched as dusk gradually deepened to night, door lamps of houses near and far along the street and in the next street giving the still night a kind of spacious mystery, gentle circles each illuminating a door or some steps or the corner of a house, like portals to some of the billion stories of the world, or bits of dreams scattered about. Foliage spread above the lights like inky greenish clouds, except where some leaves hanging down into a circle were lit a dark green that made you think of trysts lasting far into the early hours. The air was dry as from a beautiful summer day, just beginning to be touched with the humidity of night, faintly aromatic of lawns, bushes, and lilac. A car hummed by in the distance, and the cheerful, quavering voices of two old ladies walking arm in arm came down the hill, one with a flashlight that at every moment revealed some new peril on the sidewalk to be warned of and clucked over: a crack, a rock, an uneven place. They passed across the street without noticing Grant, and tottered with slow conviviality into the dark.

He knew what he had done. He had climbed a rung on the ladder to the celestial. Anything you could visualize was actual, and so existed somewhere among the worlds, and so was real, and so could be visited. That was no surprise. But the important thing was that he hadn't traveled randomly; he was sure he had moved along the Upward Path, even if only a tiny step. He had sat in the early 1960s sunlight and daydreamed of the numinal town he had seen as a teenager in the 1970s, and had traveled there. Then he had taken the most beautiful sight in that town and let it lead him to a vision of this even more numinal village, and he had bootstrapped himself here! If he could do that over and over—find something in each locus that brought a vision of something higher—then he could climb.

He felt like jumping and yelling, but he didn't. It would disturb the quiet, and there was no use getting mixed up in conversations or explanations; and besides, the place intimidated him; it seemed a little too good for him, like an astonishingly wonderful girl that one dates, wondering how long such luck can last.

And, he realized, it was too soon to celebrate: he had taken only two steps so far. He had to search this locus for something that pulled him further upward, something in this already numinal world that led him to a clear vision of an even higher one.

He followed the sidewalk in the soft, beautiful night until it ended on the outskirts of town, where the speed-limit signs had higher digits and the street became a worn asphalt road running off into wide, flat lands in the greater mystery of night. Occasionally a car rushed by, its wind momentarily flattening the grass and lofting dust into the air; then as the sound of it faded away, there was only the creaking of crickets and sometimes the quiet hoot of frogs. He turned back and walked down streets of sleeping houses, then through the small commercial section with its closed shops, their dim nighttime lights casting his walking shadow on the deserted sidewalk: a hardware store, a pharmacy, a flower shop, an ice cream shop.

He rested on grass behind a bush until dawn, then walked around the village all day, like one of those bums you see sometimes pacing purposefully and mumbling to themselves. In that town he *did* feel like a bum, someone from a lower world, ungainly and coarse, flesh-deep with grime. The morning sky was clear, and the town as beautiful in sunlight as it had been in dusk. He saw a fairy-tale cottage overgrown with ivy half in sunlight and half in the shade of a huge oak; a neighborhood where birds sang songs he thought he had never heard before; a wide noontime residential street, empty except for a large gray cat sunning itself on a car, and three children walking along the sidewalk, deep in confidential talk. A dazzling blonde high school girl at the ice cream shop gave him two big glasses of water and watched him drink them approvingly, like a mother watching a child take medicine, looking as though she wanted to offer him food too.

In the afternoon the day turned cooler, a fresh breeze smelling of vast clean territories bringing clouds across the mountains on the horizon, so that by evening it was almost chilly, and slow gray clouds checkered the sky, giving the village a cozy feeling of having a roof with skylights. Grant was looking for somewhere to rest when he came down a residential street in the hour before the streetlights go on, and saw a fir tree growing near the sidewalk, the air under its branches dusky blue-green shadow, and when he saw it his mind was flooded with what he had been looking for.

Borne in on him was the memory of the small city where he had lived with his parents. On their block one autumn evening in transparent blue-gray dusk he had seen a fir tree growing in a front yard, and the color under its branches had brought over him a sudden immeasurable comprehension. The cool smell of grass, the chill of the air outside his denim jacket, the mystic light, and a melancholy loneliness mixed with the delicious feeling of being alone had brought him a vision of that street as a borderland between the safety of his house and a dizzying vastness, a tiny edge of which he could glimpse, and the intoxicating knowledge that even his house, the life he lived with his parents, was a tiny facet of a jewel-colored dusk whose heart was mystery. It was as though something he had been looking for all his life was finally about to arrive; as though a knowledge of the meaning of things was about to come to him, this feeling of vast comprehension its foretaste.

A yearning came over Grant. Watching the color under the tree's branches, he touched the universe ball—

TWENTY-NINE

WANDERING

David Grant's ghost proxy stood on a corner in an old suburb on a chilly evening he had left long ago. Everything was suddenly familiar: the sidewalk and lawns scattered with yellow leaves; the elderly white houses with their big yards; the long 1970s cars parked along the curbs. Across the street was where the six Devlin brothers lived, mean drunks but otherwise doggishly friendly, most of whom had gone into the army and come back strong as knotty trees; halfway down the block was the house of Ann Kunkle, the lissome, friendly, squeaky-clean Catholic girl with whom he and all the Devlin boys had been in love; a mile down, you would come to the park where high school kids went in their parents' cars to make out; a couple of miles in the other direction was the small university where his father taught. Grant suppressed an urge to walk the half block and visit his parents; he had to remind himself that he was not just a grown-up version of the boy he had been, come to visit the old neighborhood. In fact he *had* visited a few years ago in the locus where he was a forty-nine-year-old lawyer, and his disorientation had been severe. The neighborhood's isolated, sheltered feel had disappeared along with the old trees, which had been replaced by saplings spaced along new white sidewalks; traffic lights on the widened streets herded cars to and from a supermarket three blocks away; his parents' big white house had been replaced by two narrow "development homes" with standard garages and carefully measured lawns. But for the street names, he might have thought he had come to the wrong place, an alternate world in which he had never existed.

Of course, breaks in causation were always disorienting, whether they resulted from jumping worlds or from returning to a place after a long time and finding that cause and effect had continued working in your absence. If he had stayed in this town and gone to the university here, as his parents had wanted, married a local girl, had a family, and watched the town change day after day, nothing would have seemed strange. Instead he had chosen to leave, to look for better things.

Of course, there was a locus where he did stay, did marry a local girl, did do all those things. And, he realized, a slow excitement building in him, he could live in that locus if he wanted, or in any of them. He could go back now and seize the alternate destinies he had passed by, marry the right girl, live in the right place, find the right work, have beautiful children—

But he already *had,* he realized, or would, or was doing. There was nothing even remotely possible that he didn't do somewhere in the geometry of the universes. He would accomplish nothing by doing the things he regretted not doing because somewhere or other he *had* done them.

The only thing his traveling through alternate destinies would change was the memory stream of this particular ghost proxy. Yet to him that was everything, he reflected. It was memory that made you who you were, that made you anyone at all, or even any*thing* at all. The tragedy of death was that memory died: the story of a few small things important to one person vanished. But that wouldn't happen to him now—or rather it would, had, was happening to all of his causal proxies, except that his proxy in one locus had learned how to snake his stream of memories in and out of the worlds so that it never had to be lost, but just got longer and longer, and it happened that that set of memories was *him*. There was also the question of whether his ghost proxy body actually aged, given that its very defining characteristic was that it was not causal, and thus perhaps not within the realm of time. Whether or not that was true, one way or another it seemed that he had been freed from the inconvenience of dying. It was a thought almost too big to contemplate.

Yet his brain—the brain of the ghost proxy he traveled as now—included only an infinitesimal fraction of the memories of all his possible lives. Why shouldn't he give himself the pleasure of living in a history in which good things happened to him? In which he married Jana the surfer girl, for example, or found an Angel in the town where he had spent his solitary college years, as he had fantasized. If he lived those histories, then they would become his memories, and their happiness would become part of him forever.

But there was a problem, he realized, standing motionless on the sidewalk in the cool blue air. It came to him clearly for the first time that somewhere along the line *he had lost track of the connection to his causal proxies.* When was the last time he had inhabited one of them? Traveling as a ghost proxy he had *become* a ghost proxy. His "ghost" body—solid, but not connected causally to any local world—appeared now in every house he traveled to. He had never *learned* how to travel to causal proxies, he realized—it had just happened spontaneously when he was learning to jump houses—and he had no idea how to go back to traveling that way. Unbound from his causal proxies, he could go anywhere, but—and now his heart sank—what if he could no longer inhabit causal proxies? Unless he could get back into one of them he was destined to be an outsider, watching his proxies marry Jana or find the Angel, but never able to be anything but a watcher, a wanderer, a ghost.

The full comprehension of his enormous liberation and loneliness struck him for the first time, the exhilaration and sorrow of the soul set loose, the self freed from death, which, after all, is the final protection against the unbearable infinities.

He wandered all that night, until finally, breath steaming in a cold blue dawn, hands in his pockets, he walked through the empty, exhausted streets of the small downtown, tall buildings echoing occasionally with the sound of a car passing or the raucous laugh of a drunk, through the industrial areas with their long, dark factory buildings and warehouses behind chain-link fences, shattered bottles on the sidewalks. It struck him that this locus looked *less* celestial than the little village he had left to come here. But his feelings had led him, his exaltation at seeing the blue-green shadows among the pine-tree branches lifting him up out of even the numen of the village. Had his method failed, or was this world despite appearances somewhere higher on the Upward Path? He was so deep in thought that he almost didn't notice the light. Smoky light of dawn that seemed to draw a cloak around him, tuck him away in a cozy pocket of space, reminding him suddenly, irresistibly of the little house tucked away in a suburb in the seaside town where in his dreams he had lived with the surfer girl. . . .

He turned onto the dead-end street in the smoky purple-gray light at the very beginning of dawn, which made the trees and bushes around the houses a very deep, shadowy green, like a jungle. The air was damp; he couldn't tell whether its haziness was all from the dim light or whether there was a touch of mist as well. He was coming home from—well, nowhere, another world; he had no history in this one. He had tried to travel here as his causal proxy, but after a dozen tries had given up. Instead he had done the next best thing and come at a time when his causal proxy was away.

The small brick house was on a dead-end street off a quiet court. There were steep stairs to the front door, which opened when he turned the knob. He felt a moment of anger. He had told her a hundred times to lock up when he was away, but she often forgot. She was barely twenty; mistress to the ocean, she rode upon its back; goddesslike in her innocence, she didn't seem to understand that she could be hurt. She lay facedown on their futon in the bedroom, blanket thrown carelessly over the lower half of her. The window was open and the room smelled of damp grass and the sweet, warm, musky smell of Jana's sleep, of her youth and strength, her body cleansed by sunlight and the ocean and by the daily exercise that had created the smooth sheath of muscle beneath her flesh. He sat watching her sleep until the light brightened gradually to morning, and he thought she might wake up. Then he let himself quietly out of the house, setting the lock as he shut the front door behind him with a click.

He sat quietly near the back of the bus, watching the dark-haired twelve-year-old at the front staring absently out his window at the city skyline framed by dramatic storm clouds. There were only a few other people riding at seven thirty on a Saturday morning: an old lady in a nurse's uniform; a man in painter's overalls reading a newspaper; two girls murmuring to each other and giggling, wearing shirts and skirts like school uniforms. The stuffy air smelled of damp metal and rubber.

He had debated whether coming here could cause an anomaly, but had concluded that it wouldn't. He bore a resemblance to the boy, of course, but he wouldn't draw attention to himself; he intended to do no more than lurk in the back of the bus to resolve something he had always wondered about.

Gusts shook the trees planted along the sidewalks, and it looked like it might start raining again anytime. The bus lumbered along, splashing through puddles, stopping occasionally for traffic lights on the nearly deserted Saturday-morning streets, until it pulled up at a bus stop and a man got on, and as he did, Grant saw the twelve-year-old's head turn to look at him.

Grant looked too. He was a large, broad-shouldered man with graying hair, wearing a raincoat the same khaki color as Grant's—but then Grant started almost out of his seat.

It was himself.

Grant grasped the metal bar at the top of the seat in front of him, staring: there was no mistaking, it was definitely himself, or else someone who looked identical, down to the clothes he was wearing.

Panic overcame Grant, making it hard to breathe, and he put his head down to keep from fainting. Three versions of himself on this bus—he had caused an anomaly—he would be drowned any second by the crashing universes—

But after he had sat for several minutes with his eyes squeezed shut, a nauseated sweat soaking him, he realized that nothing had happened. Neither the boy nor the man had taken any notice of him. He relaxed his grip on the sweat-slick bar.

If a ghost proxy was outside causation, it should be just as easy to have two wandering around any given house as one, he realized. And anyway, the other ghost proxy wasn't anomalous; Grant remembered him from when he was twelve, getting on the bus and sitting in that very seat, remembered stealing looks at him as the boy was now doing. At twelve he hadn't been able to pin down what had drawn his attention. But watching them, Grant could see the resemblance that had triggered the feeling of recognition. He didn't remember his twelve-year-old self seeing a *second* copy of the man, but presumably that was because he hadn't turned around to look.

Grant let go of the bar and quietly took off his raincoat, then tilted his head as if reading, so that if anybody did look, they would see only the top of someone's head instead of an identical twin to the man in front.

After a dozen blocks, the man pulled the cord that ran above the bus windows, making an obsolete *bong*. The driver rumbled the bus slowly to a stop and opened the doors with a pneumatic hiss. The man had climbed down the steps before the boy suddenly stood and headed for the door too. It wasn't the boy's stop, Grant knew, remembering his apprehension at doing what his parents had told him never to do, but he had been unable to let the man just vanish. Already at twelve he had developed a craving for the numinal, though he could not have put it into words.

The high steps were awkward for the boy, and by the time he had gotten down them, Grant had passed through the two little rubber-edged doors of the rear exit. The man in the raincoat was already rounding the nearest street corner, walking briskly. Grant turned away in case he or the boy glanced back.

The bus roared away with a splash of big tires and a smell of diesel exhaust quickly blown away on the damp gusts. The twelve-year-old was following the man, walking so quickly, it was almost a parody of someone trying not to run. Grant headed down the sidewalk in the other direction. He knew what happened now: the other Grant was gone by the time the twelve-year-old got to the corner: the boy stood there for a minute and then walked slowly back to the bus stop, full of puzzlement and exultation. No need to crowd him; there was nothing that needed doing here. Grant had come only on a whim, following a memory. He had never expected to find another copy of his ghost proxy. His memory had been only of a large man with graying hair; he had, of course, never connected the man with his own grown-up self.

He sauntered to the end of the block, stood casually holding his raincoat over his arm. After a couple of minutes, as he had expected, the boy came back around the corner, his head tipped a little to one side, as if trying to hear a distant sound inside his own head. He walked slowly down in front of the darkened store windows and stood at the bus stop again. Grant sauntered away up the block, though he knew the boy didn't notice him, didn't notice anything but what he held inside himself, gingerly so as not to hurt or break it; a strange almost-comprehension, like the prelude to a secret knowledge.

Grant strolled with elaborate casualness up and down the sidewalk, ignored by the few passers-by hurrying before the next cloudburst, until another bus came roaring slowly along, the boy hauled himself up its steps, the door folded closed, and it lumbered away, leaving the street full only of the voice of the wind. He walked up the street to the corner around which the boy had followed the man in the raincoat.

He turned the corner and the man in the raincoat was leaning against the brick wall three feet from him.

Grant stopped violently in his tracks, knees half-buckling, staring, heart pounding as if he would faint, nostrils and pupils flaring.

After a minute, fascination got the better of fear, and he slowly straightened up. He stared at the man, stared into his face. The man had a wild look, a kind of ragged distractedness, like the look of a mentally unstable person. The look of someone who had lost his bearings.

He could feel the very same expression on his own face, as if he were looking in a mirror.

And suddenly he understood. The man was someone who had started with a goal but now wandered aimlessly, indulging himself in memories, preoccupations, fantasies; someone who had lost the thread of his story, and who for that reason was being stalked by the infinities, which were now close on his trail.

He put out his hand, but the man suddenly turned and walked away up the sidewalk, hands in the pockets of his overcoat. Grant let him go; he understood the message. He had no need to talk to him; and he couldn't have learned anything more from him anyway, because the locus he came from was only a few minutes ahead of this one.

Now the man seemed to be standing still with his back to him, but at the same time he was moving at a strolling pace up the sidewalk as before, as if the world in which he stood was undocking from this one; and then suddenly he shrank and disappeared abruptly in a distance that was somehow superimposed on the street and trees and buildings, as if he had never been in this world at all, but had been projected from a camera.

It was no wonder the ghost proxy had attracted his twelve-year-old self's attention, but Grant knew now that he had come for Grant the elder, Grant the other ghost proxy—himself. It had been the boy who had been the onlooker, who had sensed something but been excluded from it because it wasn't meant for him. So Grant's coming here out of curiosity about the numinal moment he remembered from his twelfth year had actually *caused* the numinal moment, which in turn had caused him to show up here to watch it, and to receive a message from himself. He started to let his mind boggle at this, but then realized he needn't bother: it was just a small pulled thread in the fabric of the worlds, a perfect little self-consistent loop, which those trapped inside time would see as something quite different from what it really was.

Standing on that empty, blustery street with the threat of rain in the low sky, he visualized the other ghost proxy's expression once again—distracted, strained, unbalanced—and once again felt it pulling at his own face, the perplexed expression of someone profoundly lost. He had realized his danger the moment he had seen it. He must start climbing again, focus again on the task he had undertaken. He had tried to follow his feelings toward the celestial worlds, and that had worked once or twice, but at some point his feelings had led him astray and he had begun chasing himself instead of the Source of Fate, too beguiled to ask whether his travels were really moving him to higher rungs, or just to loci where maybe he would have a chance to clear up his personal regrets, or sharpen them.

THIRTY

FLYING

Before anything else, he had to make sure that what had just happened happened. It took only a few minutes. He visualized himself standing at the stop where he had seen himself picked up, and the bus approaching on the gray, blustery morning, touched the universe ball in his solar plexus; the ball spun up alarmingly and one of its "pages" burst outward and blew over him—

—damp gusts stirring his hair and the skirts of his raincoat, and there came the bus, roaring and wallowing, diesel smoke pouring from its exhaust. He got on, avoiding the two sets of eyes he could feel on him, and sat at the very front, staring out the windshield. A few stops later he got off and walked quickly up to the street corner. Halfway up the block, a recessed doorway offered a hiding place, and in the window of a closed shop across the street he saw a distorted reflection of the boy's form appear at the corner, stand there for what seemed a long time, and disappear again. Then he simply came out of his hiding place, walked to within a few feet of the corner, and leaned on the wall, waiting. Perhaps ten minutes later a man came barreling around the corner, jumped into the air, and then looked as if he might have a heart attack. Grant's whole assignment was just to stare at him, which he did, trying not to laugh. Then he turned around and headed back up the sidewalk, touching the universe ball.

He needed help. Following your feelings was a trap, and even if it hadn't been, he realized now that traveling to the Source of Fate one locus at a time would take an unimaginably long time. But *someone* must know how to do it, because it had been done before—at least, they had told him it had.

Could he visualize a sage who knew everything about traveling, visit his locus, and ask him what to do? The problem was that traveling—at least the way Grant knew how to travel—could only take you places you had "seen" before, even if only in a dream or vision. Trying to visit a world you had conceived in the abstract just tossed you off in some more or less random direction. While all possible loci existed, memory was the stake in the ground that drew you to a specific one. So the question was, did he have a memory of such a sage?

On August evenings at the end of summer semester, West Campus had been nearly deserted, a few square miles of giant classroom buildings separated by vast tracts of lawn and brand-new sidewalks, resembling planned neighborhoods for sale in Florida, lines running off between imaginary houses in crabgrass flats. In the evenings, lacking a girlfriend or beer buddies, Grant had taken to walking out along these sidewalks, listening to the crickets in the grass and, whenever he passed one of the dark buildings, the hum of a vast air-conditioning system. Heat radiated from the immaculate sidewalks, and the cloudless sky would fade from melodramatic orange-pink to a cooling blue, followed by a deep violet-gray dusk that shaded gradually into night.

He had been lonely in those days, a young man without anything at all except the future stretching before him like the empty crossing sidewalks. But as he had walked night after night, he had imagined an Angel summoned by his yearning, the incarnation of a desire so strong, it seemed impossible it could be denied. In his daydreams he *saw* her walking across those endless lawns in a faint effulgence to answer him, to whisper her secrets to him. The fantasy had been so strong that the memory of it was as clear as any of the things that had really happened to him in his life, she coming toward him in jeans and T-shirt like a college girl seraph in her dangerously beautiful flesh, eyes reflecting the whole world in their emerald depths.

It was there Grant headed now, holding the image of the Angel coming across the grass as he touched the universe ball.

He found himself on a sidewalk at dusk, crickets trilling. There was a movement in the distance, and the Angel walked calmly toward him from her distant fields and woods, a faint light glimmering around her. He stood trembling as her light tread approached and she stopped in front of him. Her eyes were green, her skin alabaster. Rings of silent music surrounded her. The hand she held toward him was long and slender, like the hand of a Buddha.

He fought to concentrate, resist the pull of a powerful bliss that radiated from her, to resist especially its pull on the universe ball, which felt like it would tear out of his body if he didn't move toward her.

He took a step forward, fighting its gravity, struggling at the same time to formulate a coherent question, everything flashing through his mind at once, trying to fit itself into a question.

But she seemed to listen to his thoughts, a small exquisite ear cocked in his direction, her face serious.

He staggered another step toward her, fighting. He was barely a foot away now.

"I understand you, Traveler," she said quietly, seriously. "And I will help you.

"Don't fight. There's no need. Let yourself fall."

She touched his arm, and there was an explosion of white and gold. He let go and fell into her as if off a precipice, into her pearly light.

It was a fresh morning in August, the time of year just before thoughts of school start to press uncomfortably at the horizon of children's minds, a day poised at summer's zenith, when the empty, hot afternoons seem motionless, and you can even imagine that the yellow light of autumn will never creep in, that the smell of its early-morning chill will never come. Fairy-tale clouds floated close to the summit of the street that two small boys climbed.

David Grant had become so used to traveling as a ghost proxy that it took him a minute after his initial disorientation to stand still in astonishment and look down at his body, his pale, plump legs in short pants, his small hands. His friend—Kelly—who had been droning in his six-year-old voice about something, broke off and looked at him.

"Davey, did a bee sting you?" asked Kelly anxiously.

"No. I'm okay," said Davey in his own piping voice, and started walking again, slowly. Satisfied, the boy next to him resumed his monologue about the neat airplanes he and his dad had seen at the museum. But Davey's attention was aflame elsewhere: the Angel was a real Angel, and she had put him here. What was that heavy thing in his stomach? As he thought this, it began to hum and expand, and he jerked his attention away from it as if burned. He looked around again.

He was the little boy walking up the hill on the fairy-tale morning.

The morning when, as a man, he had killed the little boy.

He peered with sudden panic up the sidewalk, but no man stood at the top. He could remember clearly the sight of the boys coming up the hill, feel the gun heavy and cold in his hand. He fought the urge to run away. There was no man up there now. And the Angel had put him here. The Angel wouldn't let him get hurt, would she?

His six-year-old brain struggled with a memory stream it had a hard time processing. *He* was the real Davey—the rest of them were just robots! If somebody shot him—

He watched up the hill fearfully. He could fly away now to a different robot in a different world and be safe. He remembered how, stretching a thought toward the ball in his stomach and feeling it spin faster and faster.

But the Angel had put him here. He had asked her for help, and this was what she had done. His hands were trembling and his stomach was tied in knots. He stopped walking again and bent over, hugging his stomach, twisting his bare legs against each other.

"Do you have a tummy-ache?" the blond boy interrupted himself again to ask.

There was still no man at the top of the sidewalk. And suddenly David realized that they had nearly reached the candy store; it was just on their left. The man was not going to come!

He felt limp with relief. "I'm hungry," he said, the child's body interpreting his stress and relief. He unclinched himself.

"Come on," said Kelly, and headed toward the door, its weathered, hand-smudged gray paint chipped in places to show other layers from the past, white and black. Kelly pushed it open, and a little bell jingled. So David Grant, six years old, entered the candy store carrying in himself a sphere that was a doorway to all the universes, and the knowledge of how to escape death, and a long chain of memories that snaked through the worlds.

After the bright fresh air, the small shop seemed drab. The floor was linoleum in squares of white and gray. There was a display case with a sloping glass front that towered over the boys, and next to it a lower wooden counter with a cash register. Someone was behind the display case, placing candies carefully onto plates on the lighted glass shelves, arranging them in delicious-looking piles.

Kelly was already pressing against the glass, moving urgently from one pile to another, his lips moving as if repeating a memorized strategy. Davey joined him, mouth watering copiously, gloating over the candies, which were all his in a way because he had a nickel and he hadn't yet picked one out.

"They're all good," said Kelly. "They're all so good, good, good."

They were. Davey stared intensely at one beautiful pile after another: chocolate, marzipan, caramel, coconut, colored sugar, ignoring the small pale hand that was now making a pile of pink spheres, each in its own tiny pleated paper cup.

"I want that one," said Kelly, pointing downward at an angle and leaning against the glass with his other hand, his mouth misting it, nearly slobbering on it.

"This one?" said a girl's voice from behind the case, and now the small white hand moved uncertainly between piles as Kelly said, over and over: "No, *that* one. No, *that* one." Finally the white hand lighted on the right pile, and Kelly pushed himself away from the glass and fumbled in his pocket for his nickel. The girl—Mr. Wasliewski's granddaughter—came out from behind the display case holding the truffle. She was a little older than the two boys, blonde, and—Davey thought—astonishingly beautiful, with her hair in braids and round, rosy cheeks. Davey broke off his search to stare at her as she stood on a stool and proudly and with difficulty turned the crank on the cash register, let Kelly's nickel fall into its drawer with a professional-sounding clash, then slammed the drawer shut with her hip. It was the most erotic thing Davey had ever seen. An odd, sweet ache formed in his chest.

Kelly was already greedily eating his chocolate, holding it before his mouth awkwardly with his elbow in the air, chocolate spittle on his lips, chewing with intense, abstracted concentration.

"How about you, Davey?" said a deep, hoarse voice, and Davey turned his eyes with a guilty start from the girl to Mr. Wasliewski, who had come out from the obscure spaces behind the display case and was leaning on the top of it and peering down at Davey. Mr. Wasliewski was old and gray-haired and very tall, and had an accent. "You can't find something nice?" He smiled gently and vaguely, as if he had just come out of a daydream. His hair was a little messed up.

Davey mutely put both hands back on the glass front of the display case and leaned close, studying the candies, but now not able to concentrate because *she* was watching; yet he studied them gravely because he wanted to do what was expected in front of *her*. Mr. Wasliewski watched him—with amusement, Davey sensed, annoyed—craning his neck so he could see him studying the candies. "Nothing good for Davey? Not good enough? Wait; I have something."

He went away, and there was the sound of him doing something in the back, and then he reappeared behind the counter next to the girl. He held a pair of tongs and in them was a large, dark, round candy. "What about this?"

Mr. Wasliewski held the candy at Davey's face level, and its strange appearance drew him away from the display case; he leaned toward the candy so that his nose almost touched it, only the edge of the counter against his chest holding him back.

The sphere was dark blue with white streaks; it looked hard and sparkly, almost translucent, like hard candy, or some kind of candy gemstone, a thought that made him suddenly want to possess it.

"Is it an Easter egg?" he was able to ask finally.

"Let me show you," said Mr. Wasliewski, and leaned down over the counter, darkening the candy. *She* leaned closer too. Davey was already as close as he could get.

"You see, it's the world," said Mr. Wasliewski, pointing a finger about an inch away from it gingerly. "But not only this world."

As he spoke the candy seemed to flicker. David stared, enthralled. Then he saw that the candy was spinning, spinning very fast even though it was still held in Mr. Wasliewski's tongs, as if it was an invisible ball of glass inside of which a dark, dark blue thing with tiny streaks of white spun faster and faster, and as it spun glowed, giving off a sort of bluish-white radiance, as if the invisible glass surrounding the ball was really a transparent neon light.

"You see," Mr. Wasliewski's voice came from far away. Davey was mesmerized and couldn't turn away, but he was aware that in the corner of his vision two blue eyes reflected the bluish glow like seeing diamonds. And at that very same moment two other things came to him; the first was that Mr. Wasliewski had not meant to show him a candy at all, but a toy he had invented, with a spinning globe and a light; and second, that the universe ball in his stomach had started to spin too, as if it was the same as the spinning ball in front of his face; it spun very fast, faster and faster, monstrously fast, so that it seemed the gravity of its spinning must collapse the universe.

In panic he tried to pull away, but it was as though the candy had taken on the universe ball's gravity, pulling him even closer to it, so that it filled almost his entire range of vision, so that the only things he could see were it and the eyes.

The universe ball burst out of his chest with a violence that must have exploded his body, because he suddenly felt that he didn't have a body anymore. He was just eyes watching the infinitely big–infinitesimally small ball spin so that the humming gravity of its momentum filled space, sparks of boundlessly dense black and white fire spinning faster than thought, giving off the bluish-white light.

The Angel's voice came into his mind or his ears. "Let yourself fall. Don't be afraid. Let yourself fall."

Surprised, he tried to look up, thinking maybe the little girl was speaking. But there was no up anymore, or anything except the sphere.

He let go, and fell toward it.

Suddenly the sphere was slowing.

Or he was orbiting in the same direction as its spinning; he couldn't tell which; the peculiar thought flashed into his mind that he had lost his body and so had no inertia and could move as fast as light, as fast as the spinning of the ball. Soon his motion and the sphere's were nearly synchronized, and he finally saw what it looked like. He had only seen it spinning before, a blur of depths, but now it was hardly moving at all, and he looked down into a titanic whirlpool of light and *feeling,* like an exploding neuronal galaxy each tiny spark of which was music, the whole an all-encompassing hum so gigantic that it left him almost without any sense of himself at all, as if he was just an infinitesimal standing wave in all that sentience.

But in all that he recognized something—one of the houses

he had traveled to. He focused on it—and it blew over him like a moving wind of world, like suddenly pushing his head and then his body through a curtain into a room—the sleepy street where he had sat on the bench in the early 1960s; its comfortable sunlight, smell of lawns and car exhaust, quietness. Even standing on that sleepy street, though, the hum of the sphere in the very deepest marrow of his being kept part of him outside it; once he was done looking at it, his mind grasped the hum like a handle to pull himself out, and the world blew down his body like a wind and was gone. A short way around the sphere, seemingly a little deeper in toward the maw of the titanic whirlpool was another house he recognized: the litle town in Canada, still water reflecting darkly as he stood on the bridge, smell of the water and its occasional faint gurgle coming up to him in the quietness. That world blew over him too; the next one he recognized was nearby, but even a little deeper: the evening in the village with the lights of houses near and far in the still dusk, creaking of crickets, smell of grass faintly flower-perfumed—

Now step back from them, something said inside him. A thought? Was the old man talking to him? The little girl? His own soul, or the Angel?

Step back. See.

He pulled reluctantly out of the village into the enormous hum. The three worlds he had peeked into were like doors in the whirlpool, in which he also spun. The thought came to him that all the worlds could open at once and crush him.

Don't let them, the thought said. Pull back a little more but don't lose sight of the three doors, the thought said. Now look. Look!

With all his might, he did. Holding himself away, watching the three doors.

And he saw it.

There was a trajectory.

He had been right; the 1960s street, the Canadian town, and the celestial village had been rungs leading upward—or rather inward. They fell along a steep inward trajectory among the supernatural incinerating brilliance of worlds. The trajectory curved along lines of force leading toward the core, from which all the worlds grew.

The Source of Fate.

Let yourself fall, said the thought. Along the curve.

If he oriented himself just right and let go, he would fall along the trajectory he had stumbled across on his travels, which led inward.

With all his strength he focused into the vortex, sighted along the trajectory. The intense gravity of the core grabbed him. The three worlds that made up the three points defining the trajectory came roaring toward him around the vortex. He sighted along them, and then, slowly and gracefully, like a diver, left his height.

Golden-ivory halo of vibration in the perfumed gray thunder of the world—

Silken milk of fiery moonlight, haunting music in luminous darkness—

Gemstone cliffs overlooking deep gulfs of stories—

He was an abstract body, like the diagram of a diamond man falling into an incinerating Light that was also Music, yet for just a moment he could think, remember—

THIRTY-
ONE

THERE AND BACK AGAIN

She walked in the gardens every morning, wearing the robes of her order against the chilly October air. Her hair had been cut short, and her face without cosmetics was grave and drawn, like the face of some beautiful flesh-mortifying saint of the Middle Ages.

Her final recruit had been successful beyond the church's wildest expectations. The dramatic results had surprised her; she had grown indifferent to religion in the past few years, she realized now; it seemed as unreal to her as everything else. Yet there had been a run of good luck unprecedented in anyone's memory, almost like the miracles from the old stories: formerly indifferent business ventures had prospered and prosperous ones had brought forth wealth beyond rational expectation; there had been fortunate political developments, many beautiful children born, even near-miraculous recoveries of the sick. So almost overnight she had gone from a nun to a kind of church elder, especially in the narrow circle of those who knew what she had done; but word had trickled down to even the "progressive" majority that she had accomplished something mighty and crucial, though most thought it was some covert political or financial coup. So now everywhere people deferred to her, listened respectfully to the few words she spoke, tried to anticipate her desires, but no one dared approach her, not even, it seemed, Thotmoses or Hatshep, who might or might not be her real parents, she realized now. It was more like being a pagan high priestess than a Christian nun, she complained to herself.

She had worked all her life for this; it had been her only goal, her only reason to live, but she was scarcely surprised when it brought her no pleasure; she had known for a long time that something was wrong with her. Instead, once Grant's success had been confirmed, a terrible fatigue had welled up in her, a freezing emptiness. This last effort, her supreme labor, had broken her, as the work broke everyone sooner or later, sending them to "retirement" in special convents that were rumored to be little more than pious insane asylums. The adulation of the community was a matter of indifference to her, just as everything was a matter of indifference. She had been bred, trained, *created* to do this work; it had been her whole life, in a way that the cliché concealed rather than disclosed. Now that she could no longer work, the training and breeding were like a caged tiger which, deprived of meat, turns on its owner.

Perhaps someday she would become Hatshep's apprentice in running the family businesses, her judgments the better for being devoid of any shred of interest. But for now the state of being devoid was like a freezing fog that pressed around her, a physical pain like icicles through her heart. There were drugs, of course, and she was offered them, but the pain was at least a feeling, which she intuited was her last and only link with sanity. So she held tight to it, and walked in the gardens every day. The rhythm of walking soothed her, sometimes even gave her a slight appetite, so that eating her small meals wasn't such a chore. At other times she remained dead and indifferent, and to people who saw her she was like a cold, beautiful statue.

Then in late October, on a chilly day of watery sunlight and a pale blue sky, she rounded a corner of the garden path and saw someone walking toward her. He wore khaki pants, a blue polo shirt, and expensive casual shoes.

She stopped, staring. A twinge of feeling came into her throat, like someone at last moving a paralyzed limb.

She couldn't tell whether this was the causal proxy that his memory stream had rejoined, or a ghost proxy. But whichever it was, he had returned with the memory of the Source of Fate, of that she was certain. He was smiling at her as he approached; but at the same time it was as if he saw her from a great distance, as if most of him was absorbed somewhere far away, on some unimaginable abstract plane. Like her, she realized with another twinge: distant, unmoved.

She stood, her eyes on his as he stopped in front of her. It was a minute before she could think of anything to say. "You came back."

"Yes." He smiled again. "I had some things left to do."

Another twinge moved in her; a lifetime's curiosity. "What was it like?"

"Hm," he said, thoughtful and amused. Then he put his hands gently on her head.

An enormous sorrow went through her, and a rage that had long ago burned away her heart, and a hatred that knew no depths. He held her in an iron embrace as she screamed and screamed, and cried, struggling so she could break loose and kill him, kill them all, and kill herself.

"That's enough for now," he said, and let her go. Suddenly the sorrow and rage and hatred were gone. He caught her as she fell, held her as she drooped in his arms half-conscious, and then helped her balance on her feet. She was trembling violently. That's good, she realized suddenly. Trembling is good; it means feeling. She leaned against him, head turned sideways against his chest, as if to warm her cold body against him.

After a long time she pulled back a little, though she was still trembling. It was impossibly presumptuous, but she asked again: "What was it like?"

He gave no outward sign, but she sensed that he was struggling to frame an answer. He wouldn't answer anyone else, she knew. A small, precious comfort blossomed in her, almost a feeling of pleasure. She was so preoccupied with it that she almost forgot what she had asked when he said: "We small beings yearn for infinity; infinity yearns to be small, to have a story. So I thought, why go the long way around? I remembered as hard as I could, remembered details, small things, and—here I am." His eyes came back into focus on hers. "I would have come for you sometime, regardless. I owe everything to you."

He took her arm, and she leaned on him as they walked together in the pale sunlight.

"Seeing it tired me out," he said. "I need a rest. Among small things. A vacation somewhere quiet—"

She felt herself smiling.

In a suburban nursing home, a quadriplegic with severe trauma-related dementia lay in a drugged stupor and hallucinated that he was married to a rich, beautiful girl who belonged to an exotic human subspecies, and that he had been picked out among all the men in the world to fly up to God to save the girl and her race.

———

The house he shared with Jana was tucked away on a dead-end
street off a little court in a wooded neighborhood. She was barely
twenty; mistress to the ocean, she rode upon its back; goddesslike
in her innocence, she didn't believe she could ever be hurt. Every
afternoon he took a break from his book and went for a walk,
mulling over the character of his universe-hopping protagonist,
smelling the ocean a few miles away.

He sat in his large, handsome office, feet on the desk, gazing absently out the floor-to-ceiling windows at the river over the terrace of the first-floor restaurant, which gave the view a French
Riviera look, trees shading bright parasols over tables, waiters and
girls in sundresses and men in suits coming and going over the
tree-stained bricks. It was Friday morning, and the thought of
the impending weekend gave him a warm feeling. . . .